RSACS

0

D1127344

JUL   1986

Holy Mackerel!

Holy Mackerel!
The Amos 'n' Andy Story

by Bart Andrews & Ahrgus Juilliard

E. P. DUTTON / NEW YORK

Published in the United States by
E. P. Dutton, a division of New American Library,
2 Park Avenue, New York, N.Y. 10016.

Library of Congress Cataloging-in-Publication Data
Andrews, Bart.
Holy mackerel!
1. Amos 'n' Andy (Radio program) 2. Amos 'n' Andy
(Television program) I. Juilliard, Ahrgus. II. Title.
PN1991.77.A6A6 1986   791.47'72   85-20638
ISBN: 0-525-24354-2

Published simultaneously in Canada
by Fitzhenry & Whiteside Limited, Toronto

COBE

Designed by Nancy Etheredge

10 9 8 7 6 5 4 3 2 1

First Edition

To

the black performers

who paved the way

CONTENTS

ACKNOWLEDGMENTS
xi

PROLOGUE
xv

1.
THE CREATION
I

(vii)

2.

ON THE AIR

15

3.

DEPRESSION BLUES

32

4.

TV OR NOT TV

45

5.

A CAST OF CHARACTERS

60

6.

WHAT'S SO FUNNY?

85

7.

THE CONTROVERSY CONTINUES

99

8.

COLOR TV

119

9.

THE EIGHTIES ENIGMA

138

EPILOGUE

148

THE "AMOS 'N' ANDY" LOG
155

INDEX
182

Photograph section follows page 124.

ACKNOWLEDGMENTS

No book writes itself and this project presented unique challenges, not the least of which was the paucity of people who were willing to talk about the subject of "Amos 'n' Andy" for a book. The list of "no shows" is, unfortunately, longer than the acknowledgments.

Our most heartfelt appreciation goes to our editor, Bill Whitehead, who saw the merit in this project when few others did, and who "sold" the book to his comrades at E. P. Dutton. Working with Whitehead is one of those rare experiences in publishing when, as authors, you *know* it is all worth it even when the going gets awfully rough. Bill's belief in this book and his determination not to postpone its publication when deadlines got stretched to elastic proportions are not only to be commended, but also lauded.

There would be no book had it not been for the fertile imaginations of Freeman Fisher Gosden and Charles Correll, who created Amos, Andy, Kingfish, Sapphire, Calhoun, and Lightnin' more than fifty years ago, and the actors who brought them to life on television—Alvin Childress, Spencer Williams, Jr., Tim Moore, Ernestine Wade, Johnny Lee, and Nick Stewart, respectively.

While Stewart continues to be an active member of the Los Angeles black community—operating his thirty-five-year-old Ebony Showcase Theatre and providing positive roles for black performers—he chose not to be interviewed for this book. Despite his decision, we applaud him for the work he continues to do, erasing the damaging stereotypes for future generations.

We cannot possibly forget the kindness of Richard Correll and his wife, Patti, who opened their home and their hearts to us when few others felt so inclined. We also thank them for generously loaning us the photos that appear in this book, many of them rare enough to be included in Smithsonian exhibits.

Now that the writing of the book has been completed, we can appreciate the hard work that Michael Avery and Bob Greenberg did to produce their thoughtful documentary, " 'Amos 'n' Andy': Anatomy of a Controversy." We thank them for sending us an early version of their script and for inviting us to a screening of the finished product.

To the staffs of the UCLA Theatre Library, the USC Special Collections department, and the Margaret Herrick Library of the Academy of Motion Picture Arts and Sciences, thank you for your favors and your valuable resources.

Hats off to Lee Mishkin Animation for the time off

for research; Severn Darden for his hospitality; Robert Alvarez for introducing us to Rich Correll; and Thomas J. Watson for early research material.

Ahrgus Juilliard wishes to acknowledge Caine Carruthers, Dijon Carruthers, Mary Wilson, and Ben F. Carruthers for keeping the faith; and Bart Andrews wants to mention the contribution of his business partner Sherry Robb and associate Jim Pinkston for "holding down the fort" when the Indians started attacking, and Marc DeLeon for being there.

PROLOGUE

George Bernard Shaw once remarked that there were three things he'd never forget about America, "the Rocky Mountains, Niagara Falls and 'Amos 'n' Andy.' "

A creation of writer/performers Freeman Gosden and Charles Correll, "Amos 'n' Andy" was the longest-running act in the history of broadcasting—thirty-two years on radio; seventy-eight episodes on television. Jack Benny, who headlined vaudeville shows during the heyday of "Amos 'n' Andy" in the thirties, once said, "I can recall walking past motion picture theaters and seeing signs promising to stop the movie and turn on the radio when it came time for the show."

President Calvin Coolidge wished not to be disturbed when "Amos 'n' Andy" came on the air. Department stores open in the evening piped in the broadcasts so shoppers would not miss an episode. The program was frequently referred to in the *Congressional Record.* There was a sharp drop in telephone calls when the show went on the air.

The radio show once drew 2.4 million letters from listeners who wrote in to suggest names for Amos and Ruby's newborn daughter; and when Ruby became ill some years later, 65,000 fans wrote to express hopes for an early recovery. When her condition took a turn for the worse, 18,000 indignant listeners threatened to boycott Pepsodent toothpaste, the program's sponsor.

As with all the major radio hits, a television version was inevitable. "Amos 'n' Andy" hit the TV airwaves in 1951—an all-black cast playing all the regular roles. From the start the program proved to be a headache for all concerned: The NAACP lodged a twelve-point protest against the show, claiming it demeaned the entire Negro race with its characterizations of blacks as lazy and shiftless. CBS got nervous, especially when the show's sponsor, Blatz beer, pulled its support, and eventually canceled the TV show in 1953, when it was still doing well in the ratings. The cache of half-hour black-and-white episodes was quickly trotted out to pasture in syndication, where they ran repeatedly for the next thirteen years and earned a staggering sum of money for the network. Continued protests from the NAACP and other civil rights organizations apparently compelled CBS to pull the show from syndication in 1966, locking up the film in a vault, never to be seen again.

As *Esquire* magazine once reported, " 'Amos 'n' Andy' refuses to stay put in a coffin; it continues to rattle its loose, happy bones." When the *Los Angeles Herald-Examiner* polled its readers in 1980 to find out which oldies they would rather see on TV than reruns of current shows,

"Amos 'n' Andy" managed to place high on the list. But its chances of being broadcast again? Don't count on it.

Did Gosden and Correll maliciously set out to undermine and denigrate black America? The record shows that both men—one, Gosden, a Southerner—had "strong personal feelings for blacks," and were deeply hurt when accusations were made that the show had racist overtones.

Before his death in 1972, Charles Correll told a Chicago newspaper reporter, "I don't think blacks as a body resented the program. That certainly wasn't what we intended, nor did we ever feel it when we were on the air. The fact is, we were delighted to be working with them."

How could a show that was virtually embraced by an entire country be summarily loathed several decades later? The mere mention of this historic program today draws pockets of cheers and volumes of jeers. Was this complacent fantasy of black life, this demolition derby of bad English, truly beyond reason and good taste? Looking back, was the show a total embarrassment?

Critic James Wolcott claims that, contrary to popular notions, the Kingfish and Andy weren't intended to represent contemporary black men; they were deliberate anachronisms. There were lots of black characters on the show who were "fine-spoken and industrious—like the salesmen for the Superfine Brush Company, who cheerfully set out each morning to meet their quotas, singing the company jingle—or sternly professional, like the judge who disbarred Calhoun." While the rest of Harlem moves into high gear, "the Kingfish and Andy amble along at their own easy pace, letting the drones buzz by. The Kingfish, with his gold-chained vests and floppy hats and wide-tailed coats, has the courtly aplomb and boomy, rumbling eloquence of a retired southern gentleman. Leisure has become his life pursuit. He's so dedicated to loafing that he can't enjoy a nap in the park because the grass hasn't been trimmed and odd blades of grass keep tickling him in the ear: 'Aw, Andy, it was just awful.'

"Andy was a big, moody child, with hands as big as catcher's mitts; when the Kingfish welshes on his invitation to have Andy move in with him, Andy menacingly clenches his thick fist and growls, 'Kingfish, you promised to love and cherish me like I was your own son, and if you *doesn't* . . .'

"As in so much American comedy, marriage in 'Amos 'n' Andy' is a snare and a straitjacket—a cruel prank played upon men who'd rather be fishing, swapping lies, wiping beery foam from their lips in a cool, dark bar. Instead, they find that married life is one long chore; the honey-tempered angels they wooed in innocent youth have turned into witches, shrews. . . . When Andy announces his engagement to a twenty-one-year-old beauty queen, the Kingfish slaps him on the shoulder and chortles, 'Welcome to de ranks of de livin' dead.' Later, as the wedding day nears, the Kingfish admits to Andy, 'I never thought I'd see you walk de last mile.' "

The Kingfish's browbeating wife, Sapphire, and her meddling mother were a match for ten Kingfishes:

KINGFISH: Have some more peas, mother-in-law dear?

MAMA: When I want some, I'll help myself.

KINGFISH: Oh, well I just—

MAMA: Why, I get along all these years without yo' tellin' me what to eat.

KINGFISH: Well, if you don't want 'em, don't take 'em. That's all right wid me.

MAMA: Ah, you're begrudging me the food. Well, I eat little enough without yo' complaining all the time.

KINGFISH: Now, listen, Mama, can't we just . . .

MAMA: You mind yo' own business. I'm talkin' to my daughter.

SAPPHIRE: George, stop pickin' on Mama!

There is little recourse to the argument that the Kingfish, Sapphire, and Mama did not accurately reflect the so-called black experience. Thirty-five years after their depiction, this trio is still far removed from the reality of black life. Was the show *ever* an honest portrayal of blacks, even taking the comedy elements into consideration?

Amos and Andy were only black on the outside. Their birth, nurturing, and development—all of the inner "machinations"—were white. "Amos 'n' Andy" never really was a "black" show. There were no black scriptwriters, no black producers, no black directors. At the time "Amos 'n' Andy" went into production as a TV series, it would have been a miracle to have found any black people working behind-the-scenes. Blacks rarely had any symbiotic connection with what eventually became lucrative renditions of their own music and life-style. It was therefore inevitable that black representations were devoid of authenticity.

Such racial falsehoods are what ultimately drove "Amos 'n' Andy" off the air. However justified civil rights leaders' arguments were against the perpetuation of the show, there is no denying that the program influenced an entire nation. From its inception as a radio serial in 1928, the show became a hallowed part of American family life, invading white homes that ordinarily might never have had a black visitor.

1

THE CREATION

"Out of the library of American folklore, those treasured stories such as Huck Finn, Paul Bunyan, and Rip Van Winkle—which have brought us laughter and joy for generations—come the warm and lovable tales of Amos and Andy, created by Freeman Gosden and Charles Correll. Presented by Blatz Brewing Company of Milwaukee, Wisconsin, on behalf of Blatz dealers everywhere."

On Thursday, June 28, 1951, at 8:30 P.M. (EDT), an announcer read the promotional copy that introduced the first television episode of "The Amos 'n' Andy Show" to the American viewing public. No one—not the show's creators, or its stars, or the man who ran the CBS Television Network, William S. Paley—could have predicted the effect this legendary pair of fictional characters would have on society.

Who could have guessed that fifteen years later the program would be driven off the air because its portrayal of Negro life fed, rather than dispelled, racial bigotry?

It all began rather innocently on August 12, 1919, in Durham, North Carolina. A twenty-nine-year-old ex-bricklayer named Charles J. Correll, who had been hired the previous summer to stage-manage amateur theatrical shows for the Joe Bren Producing Company, found himself in the North Carolina city to direct a talent show for the Elks Club. There he met a recent newcomer to the Bren organization, a former tobacco salesman, Freeman Fisher Gosden, age twenty, who had come to Durham to ask advice of his new associate, Correll. They immediately became friends, and Gosden, a capable tap dancer, taught Correll's Elks a dance routine in return for Correll's production expertise. It was the beginning of one of the longest associations in show business history.

One of four children, Freeman Gosden was born on May 5, 1899, in Richmond, Virginia. His father, Walter, had entered the Confederate Army at the age of seventeen; he was one of the seventy-five Rebel raiders, under Confederate Army cavalry officer General John Singleton Mosby, who refused to surrender with Lee at the end of the Civil War. Educated in Richmond, with the exception of a year at military school in Atlanta, Georgia, Gosden left school to sell tobacco on the road.

Gosden's real interest throughout his youth was in a theatrical career. At the age of ten, the natural-born daredevil entered a diving contest in Annette Kellerman's swimming exhibition; at twelve, he was performing magic tricks and assisting the great magician Howard Thurston. As a youngster, Gosden enjoyed impersonating people, playing the ukulele, singing, and tap dancing, and he frequently performed in minstrel shows. During World War I, he served as a radio operator and electrician in the Navy, and, upon discharge, became an automobile salesman.

Of Scotch-Irish descent, Charles Correll was born on February 2, 1890, in Peoria, Illinois, where his relatives had moved after leaving the South during the Reconstruction period. (They were related to Jefferson Davis.) As a grade school student, Correll sold newspapers after school, and when the circus was in town, manned a lemonade stand. In high school he studied shorthand, using his newly acquired skill upon graduation in the office of the state superintendent of construction in Springfield, Illinois.

Soon after, he returned to Peoria to learn the craft of the stonemason from his father. While he spent his days as a construction worker, he spent his evenings practicing piano, and eventually was employed on a regular basis at a movie theatre, playing background music for silent films. He wanted desperately to be an actor, and did, indeed, win contests as a "hoofer," in addition to singing in quartets and in minstrel shows. When an opportunity in a local theatrical production presented itself, Correll jumped in with both feet, agreeing to play even bit parts at a moment's notice. A producer from the Joe Bren company, then in Peoria to stage one such performance with local talent, liked Correll's work and offered him a job managing rehearsals in another town.

The Joe Bren Producing Company was an organization that produced shows for fraternal and charitable groups throughout the country, the company furnishing scripts, music, costumes, scenery, and direction. Their motto was "Talent for Every Form of Entertainment." After Correll worked with Gosden on the occasion of the latter's first assignment for the company—the production of The Jollies of 1919 for the Durham Elks benefit fund—the pair parted. Each traveled about the country training amateur choruses to sing patter songs, teaching them simple dances, routing scenery and equipment, and supervising productions. The two occasionally crossed each other's path during the years that ensued. Then, in 1924, the Bren company added indoor circuses and carnivals to its repertory. Both Gosden and Correll were called to the company's Chicago home office, Gosden to be manager of the circus division, Correll to be manager of the show division.

Bachelors, the pair shared an apartment, where the neighbors told of hearing them sing harmony, with Correll at the piano and Gosden on the ukulele. After a friend heard their "song and chatter" routine (they billed themselves "The Life of the Party"), he suggested they perform on radio. A single engagement on WQGA in early 1925 was all that it took to encourage the pair, who subsequently auditioned for Bob Boneil, manager of radio station WEBH, a small station located in a tiny studio off the main dining room of the Edgewater Beach Hotel in Chicago. Boneil, who had no money to pay them, agreed to reward the performing duo with free dinners just prior to their late-night broadcasts, which debuted in March 1925. Their once-weekly show soon became so popular that it was broadcast every night but Monday, from 11:30 to midnight. The format consisted of Gosden on his ukulele, Correll at the piano, and the pair harmonizing such songs as "When the Red, Red Robin Comes Bob, Bob, Bobbin' Along" and "Yes, Sir, That's My Baby." After eight months of broadcasts from the Edgewater Beach Hotel and several out-of-town vaudeville appearances, Gosden and Correll decided to resign from the Bren organization and devote all of their energies to radio, for which they had been tendered an attractive offer.

In November 1925, executives of the radio station owned by the *Chicago Tribune*, WGN, offered Gosden and Correll full-time positions, having enjoyed their work on WEBH. Located in the classy Drake Hotel, the station guaranteed the pair a salary of $250 a week. Because they were on six nights a week, often for several hours a night, their limited repertoire began to wear thin. To expand the act, they began chatting between songs and impersonating a variety of characters within the framework of comic sketches. Just before he was fired by WGN, Henry Selinger, the station's manager, made it known that WGN was interested in developing a program similar to the comic strip *The Gumps,* which happened to be syndicated by the *Chicago Tribune.*

Gosden and Correll were amenable to dramatizing a comic strip, but they felt *The Gumps* was not appropriate. Instead they suggested a serial about two Southern blacks named Sam and Henry. On January 7, 1926, in the office of Ben McCanna, who was in charge of radio at the *Tribune,* Gosden and Correll worked out the contrasting voices and characters of "Sam 'n' Henry," forerunners of "Amos 'n' Andy." At first, the management wanted nothing to do with a series about two black people, although they finally relented and allowed the pair to try it out on the air. On extremely short notice—five days—Gosden and Correll put all the pieces together for what was to become radio's first serial, a continuing storyline with regular characters.

Targeted for broadcast six days a week, "Sam 'n' Henry" debuted on WGN Radio on January 12, 1926. The ten-minute effort was not only scripted by the former bricklayer and tobacco salesman, but also performed by the duo, right down to the voices of minor characters.

To understand what prompted the pair to decide on a show featuring two black characters instead of white, we have to go back to Gosden's and Correll's childhoods. Correll's ancestors were from the Deep South; his grandfather was confined to a Union prison camp during the Civil War, after which the family migrated to Peoria. Gosden hailed from Virginia, where his family had lived for three generations. As a boy, he was raised by a "mammy," and has said in interviews before his death in December 1982, that his exposure to black people was frequent and that he enjoyed hearing them speak. One such member of the Gosden household was a black youngster, Garrett Brown, who was raised by Gosden's parents until the boy was sixteen. He was an amusing kid who had developed a jargon all his own. Such expressions as "Ain't dat sumpin' " are said to have originated with Brown. Gosden and Brown were as close as brothers, and delighted in putting on skits for Freeman's sickly father. These impromptu theatricals were minstrel shows. Consequently, Freeman Gosden became interested in minstrel shows, in general, attending them whenever a traveling troupe of performers came to his hometown of Richmond.

Correll, too, was an aficionado of amateur minstrels, even before his employment with the Joe Bren company. He was fairly adept at telling jokes in a Negro dialect, and, later, with Gosden, wrote a Negro dialect song, "The Kinky Kids' Parade," for a 1925 musical revue staged in Chicago. Their expertise in this area of entertainment made them popular with Joe Bren customers, many of whom preferred minstrel-style entertainment for their smokers and fund-raisers. And while there was no doubt that minstrel shows generally were on the decline by the early 1920s, there were still many famous blackface comics traveling the vaudeville circuits of this country. Before his fame on Broadway, Al Jolson toiled with Dockstader's minstrels from 1907 to 1911. Even Eddie Cantor, appearing in Florenz Ziegfeld's revue *Midnight Frolics,* donned burnt cork.

The minstrel show, known in some circles as the "American National Opera," was an original form of entertainment that began in this country and literally swept the nation in the 1840s. During this period, minstrels, as the blackfaced white performers called themselves, were enjoying enormous popularity. This increase in interest began as part of the so-called common man's culture, dating back to the Revolutionary War. The "common man" character was developed from the most important new element to emerge in drama in the States since that time—the Yankee farm boy. The song "Yankee-Doodle" was sung by the British to ridicule Americans, reducing them to "illiterate country simpletons."

The "common man" character epitomized all that

was good, plain, and high-principled. More importantly, he represented the virtues of good, clean rustic living. Such a character was first introduced in 1787 in the play *The Contrast* as Jonathan. "Brother Jonathan" was treated as a country bumpkin, while the author extolled the virtues of farm life that contrasted to the shallow existence of "foppishness" preferred by the British. Soon this character became a comic fixture in American theatre. Because he hailed from the country, he was depicted as an odd dresser, and spoke with a "funny" dialect. His character was incorruptible; and though he worked as a servant, "no man was his master." This noble sentiment touched on the very core of American democracy. The "Brother Jonathan" character was the embodiment of what the average citizen believed himself to be. Another character to emerge at this time was the boasting frontiersman, a backwoodsman type similar to daring Davy Crockett.

By the 1830s new urban characters appeared: A riotous composite of a volunteer fireman, gutter bum, barroom brawler, and heroic defender of the downtrodden became known as "Mose the B'Howery B'Hoy." This legendary character was a fearless daredevil who also possessed a sympathetic and chivalrous side. He often boasted that he loved to fight "men and fires, but mostly men." He was a character that most people who had migrated from rural areas to urban environments could relate to. Consequently, the common folk's culture had taken root, and characters larger than life—or caricatured—were now firmly established as an integral part of American entertainment.

However, the "character" who was to weave himself insidiously into the fabric of American consciousness was the minstrel. The blackface skits and striking physical appearance made minstrels very much in demand in traveling circuses and even as entertainers between acts of a stage play. Just as the "Brother Jonathan" character claimed to be the personification of a true Yankee servant and Davy Crockett impersonators claimed a similar stance, the blackface "character" became the so-called epitome of the Negro. But unlike the heroic qualities of the others, the blackface minstrel was a total buffoon—the reverse of clown white—but entirely the same. Despite the minstrels' claims that they were presenting authentic Negro culture, there was no more resemblance to reality in their portrayal than was evidenced in the larger-than-life qualities of the other folk characters.

There is no denying that the minstrels' mimicry of the Negroes' rural jigs made their performances very appealing to many. And though the portrayals were usually grossly inaccurate, the minstrel's goal—as is often the case in show business—was to amuse his audience. Comic twists and a wild abuse of the English language—along with the ragtag clothes that made him appear beneath the "common man," and the clownish makeup—made the caricature unique, and by the late 1820s, nearly every stage show featured an Ethiopian delineator.

Blackface performer Thomas D. Rice had a shrewd eye for new material that would be a catchy addition to his minstrel act. One day he encountered a crippled Negro stableman doing a snappy song-and-dance as accompaniment to his stable chores. Recognizing a great new number for his repertoire, Rice literally bought the ragged shirt off the stableman's back, and also convinced the man to teach him the number.

Rice became an instant sensation with "his" new routine. He adopted the name "Jim Crow" Rice and was well received on the New York and London stages. The dances he performed became the rage of two continents. Nearly everyone was attempting the fancy twist and comical turns of the "Jim Crow" dance. Rice capitalized on this routine up until the 1850s, making a major name for himself in theatrical circles—all from the material he learned from the crippled stableman.

Thomas Rice's popularity gave rise to other minstrels who were relentlessly forced to pursue original material for their acts. There is no doubt that "Jump Jim Crow" became the foundation for most of the minstrel acts that followed. There are countless other stories about how Rice came to immortalize the plantation-style song-and-dance. Some say he simply saw a little slave boy doing it, and decided to blacken his face and wear tattered clothes. Whatever the truth, Dan Emmett and many other top entertainers of the day adopted the songs, mode of dress, and comic dialect as well, making thousands of dollars in the process.

No royalties or recognition, of course, were paid the Negroes from whom the material was taken. Blacks were barred from most theatres anyway, and those that did allow blacks to attend segregated their establishments. Originally, blacks were not able to perform in minstrel shows They were finally admitted into the elite cadre of entertainers in the late 1850s.

Critics of the day found that increasing numbers of Negroes performing in minstrel shows brought indigenous qualities and the genuine basic Afro-American rhythm. These troupes introduced new dances, music, and farce that had not yet been appropriated by white performers.

Many Negro stars came to the forefront from these touring shows, although there were a few individuals, like Andrew Allen and Picayune Butle, who had performed as soloists in the North. Performer James Bland went to England in blackface, attracted the attention of British royalty, and remained there as a star for many years—without the burnt-cork makeup—later composing such tunes as "Carry Me Back to Old Virginny."

In *The Black American Reference Book,* editor Mabel M. Smythe wrote, "The white minstrel performers developed so broad a burlesque of what the general public took to be 'Negro life' that their shows created a stereotyped concept of black Americans which is with us to this day. The sooty, burnt-cork makeup, the exaggerated wide lips, the gold teeth, the gaudy clothing, the broad jokes, the fantastic dialect, the watermelon and razor props, the dice that continued right down to *Porgy and Bess,* became so much a part of the commercial theatre in the United States that black performers themselves, in order to be successful, felt compelled to imitate these blackface whites. As a result, Bert Williams, in the *Ziegfeld Follies,* made himself twelve shades darker than he really was and spoke a dialect he had never heard except from white performers."

By the time Gosden and Correll had latched onto the idea of doing a "black-voice" radio show in 1926, minstrel shows were on the wane, although they were still an acceptable and popular form of entertainment. Such joke books as *Darky Jokes, Minstrel Jokes,* and *Coon Jokes* were available in most five-and-dime stores, and any group hoping to stage its own minstrel show only had to buy a copy of one of them, burn some cork, and sell tickets. It isn't surprising, therefore, that Gosden and Correll created the characters of Sam and Henry in an environment that had easily accepted the comic portrayal of blackface Negro stage stereotypes.

When "Sam 'n' Henry" premiered on Tuesday, January 12, 1926, Gosden, who played Sam, and Correll, who played Henry, had carefully structured their serial. When they created the characters, they decided to capitalize on the fact that many black Southerners had moved to cities in the North after World War I to look for work. So they made Sam Smith and Henry Johnson a pair of young men who were yearning for a better life than what was available in their hometown of Birmingham, Alabama. With all their savings, they purchased train tickets to Chicago, where they hoped to find work in the construction field. The first of the 586 "Sam 'n' Henry" episodes featured this dialogue as the two were riding aboard a mule-drawn wagon en route to the train station:

SAM: Henry, did you evah see a mule as slow as dis one?

HENRY: Oh, dis mule is fas' enough. We gonna git to de depot alright.

SAM: You know dat Chicago train don't wait fo' nobody—it jes' goes on—jes' stops and goes right on.

HENRY: Well, we ain't got but two mo' blocks to go—don't be so 'patient, don't be so 'patient.

SAM: I hope dey got fastah mules dan dis up in Chicago.

HENRY: You know some o' de boys said dey was goin' to be down dere to de depot to tell us go'bye and take dis mule back.

SAM: Not only some o' de boys—but Liza goin' to be down dere too—and she's gonna kiss me go'bye she said. You know, Henry, I kin'-a hate to leave dat dere gal.

HENRY: Dere you go—wimmen on de brain—how we gonna evah be millionaires in Chicago when you always talkin' 'bout wimmen?

Gosden and Correll were able to portray the real-life problems that blacks from the South were experiencing when they arrived in urban areas of the North. The problems that beset the pair were many, and because the show was a serial—a show with a continuing storyline—the dilemmas seemed almost real because they were not resolved within the confines of one ten-minute program, as is the case with most situation comedies. Early scripts found Sam and Henry unable to find work in their chosen field of construction. And when they were finally hired, they were fired because they were caught loafing on the job. With time on their hands, they started gambling and were promptly arrested for shooting craps.

The easily duped Sam was a constant victim; the classic "pigeon" for all manner of con men and hucksters. He purchased a fountain pen that didn't work, was conned by a fortune-teller, and bought a life-insurance policy from a man on the street. True, the humor inherent in the "Sam 'n' Henry" situations sprang from the characters' gullibility, naïveté, and—yes—ignorance. This infantile innocence fostered black stereotypes begun nearly a century before with the rise of the minstrel shows. The characters fell into two distinct categories: "sambos" and "dandies." The "sambos" were dumb; the "dandies" were slick. In both cases, the characters' ignorance or flamboyance was the source of amusement to an audience.

On the other hand, Gosden and Correll were careful not to depict their characters in a demeaning light. Sam might have been gullible, but, more importantly, he was honest, hardworking, and loyal. The humanness with which they imbued the characters made them palatable to audiences, a lot less offensive than their minstrel-show ancestors.

As Arthur Frank Wertheim wrote in the book *Radio Comedy*, "Any evaluation of 'Sam 'n' Henry' must consider both its positive and negative features. It perpetuated clichés about Negroes and reassured white listeners that their new neighbors from the South were less intelligent and less diligent than themselves. If the series gave whites a feeling of false superiority, it also mirrored the difficult life of rootless Southern blacks in a Northern metropolis."

What had begun as a humorous look at the "simple life of the darkies" in minstrel shows developed into a menacing brutality in *The Birth of a Nation,* famed filmmaker D. W. Griffith's classic adaptation of Thomas Dixon's *The Clansman.* The 1915 film was historic on several levels: It revolutionized the "art" of motion pictures, but its "genius" was roundly denounced by the five-year-old National Association for the Advancement of Colored People (NAACP) as an "outrage." As part of the public outcries, theatres where it was being shown were threatened with bombings.

The Birth of a Nation glorified the Ku Klux Klan and clearly depicted blacks as a threat to white society. With this depiction, no longer was the Negro just an ignorant, harmless, and childlike creature. He now had developed into a dangerous brute. Though the basic plot centered around two families torn apart by the Civil War, it was clearly established that the black was the negative force behind the familial conflict. Uncle Tom and Topsy, Mr. Bones and Mr. Tambo, Jim Crow and Old Zip Coon—all were tame compared to the depictions in *Nation,* and yet the film is still hailed as a masterpiece of cinema. Griffith vehemently denied that the film had any racial overtones. The astute critic James Agee supported Griffith's denial decades later, adding as well: "Among moving pictures it is alone . . . as the one great epic, tragic film."

Griffith responded to the early criticism by offering $10,000 to charity if Moorfield Storey, the white head of the Boston branch of the NAACP, could find a "single incident in the [movie] that was not historic." Storey refused Griffith's invitation to see the epic to prove a point was "historic."

"Sam 'n' Henry" was not a resounding hit at first. In fact, Gosden and Correll were so depressed by the show's early ratings they wanted to give up. The owners of station WGN had to convince the pair to continue doing the program. Within five weeks the show had picked up considerable speed, the continuing storyline being just the right audience bait. At the end of February 1926, the station owner, the *Chicago Tribune,* nailed the pair to a two-year contract for their exclusive services. Gosden and Correll, as Sam and Henry, became so popular in Chicago—the program's only market—that they started doing personal appearances . . . in blackface. One such live performance at the McVicker's Theatre netted them $250. (Two years later, as Amos and Andy, they would receive $5,000 for a similar in-person engagement.)

By 1927 Gosden and Correll had devised a brilliant

concept: They wanted to form "a chainless chain" of recorded shows that could be syndicated to stations throughout the country. Instead of just broadcasting live their "Sam 'n' Henry" shows in Chicago alone, they wanted to record them on disks and then rent those disks to other stations. Unfortunately, the *Chicago Tribune* refused to agree to the plan, claiming that they had full ownership to the title "Sam 'n' Henry" and, hence, the exclusive rights for WGN to air the program. This frustrated Gosden and Correll because they were under an exclusive agreement for $300 a week that still had almost a year to run. Trapped by the fine print in their contract, the pair earned extra money by making numerous public appearances as Sam and Henry in such towns as Rockford, Illinois, some eighty miles from downtown Chicago. During 1927, Gosden and Correll occupied themselves with personal business: Correll married Alice Janes in January, and Gosden wed Leta Marie Schreiber in June.

Naturally, the pair did not renew their contracts with WGN, giving the *Tribune* station notice that they would terminate with the live broadcast of December 18, 1927. An advertising executive acquaintance suggested the men approach rival station WMAQ, which was owned by the *Tribune*'s rival, the *Chicago Daily News*. The management of that station was interested in Gosden and Correll's concept of the "chainless chain" and agreed to hire the pair. But because the format title of "Sam 'n' Henry" was owned lock, stock, and blackface by WGN, the two writer/performers had to dream up a new show—with a new title—for their WMAQ assignment.

The new title was "Jim 'n' Charlie."

2

ON THE AIR

Legend has it that Amos Jones and Andy Brown were born
the night of March 19, 1928, on the elevator of radio station
WMAQ. Freeman Gosden and Charles Correll, on their
way up to the studio to begin their all-new radio show,
heard the elevator operator greet one of the incoming pas-
sengers with "Well, well, famous Amos" and another with
"Hello, handy Andy." Reportedly, Gosden and Correll
looked at each other, nodded, and exited the elevator with
a new title for their program. A great story, but, unfortunately, not a word of it is true.

Following the end of Gosden and Correll's stint on

"Sam 'n' Henry" (other actors took over their roles and WGN continued broadcasting the show), they spent the next three months making personal appearances, such as one at the Rialto Theatre in Louisville, Kentucky, and working on a format for their new endeavor. The first script they wrote introduced two Negroes named Jim and Charlie. Dissatisfied with the sound of these two monikers—and still stinging from the realization that they could not use "Sam" and "Henry"—they toyed with other possibilities, finally latching onto the notion of using names that were alliterative and euphonious. In the 1929 book authored by Gosden and Correll, *All About "Amos 'n' Andy,"* the writer/performers suggested that because the name "Amos" was a biblical one, it was the perfect label for a character described as "trusting, simple, unsophisticated." And Andy, they reasoned further, characterized a personality that was "lazy" and "domineering."

The one indisputable fact was that when "Amos 'n' Andy" premiered that Monday night in March at ten o'clock in the evening, it was an instantaneous hit. Fans of the old "Sam 'n' Henry" show followed Gosden and Correll to their new radio digs at WMAQ and were quick to adapt themselves—as were the creators themselves—to these new characters, Amos and Andy. Whereas Sam and Henry hailed from Birmingham, Alabama, Amos and Andy moved to Chicago from Atlanta, Georgia, where they had worked on a farm. They dreamed of going north, where they could strike it rich.

On the very first broadcast, Bill Hay, the announcer (who also moved with Gosden and Correll from WGN), introduced Amos as "a hardworking little fellow who tries to do everything he can to help others and to make himself progress." Andy, on the other hand, was described as "not especially fond of hard work." On that first broadcast, Amos reflected: "Sometime, Andy, I wish I was back down in Georgia workin' fo' Mr. Williams, yo' know it. We didn't have a worry in de world den."

It took until show number 23, broadcast on April 19, 1928, to introduce Andy's get-rich-quick scheme:

ANDY: De thing we gotta do is git in some kind o' bizness so we kin work fo' ourselves.

AMOS: Whut kind o' bizness is we goin' git in?

ANDY: I been tellin' yo—if we kin git a second hand automobile an' make a taxi-cab out of it, dat'd be de thing to do.

AMOS: De trouble is though is to find dat second hand car. Whut kind o' car would yo' buy?

ANDY: Well, lemme see . . .

AMOS: Yo' know-a—if you git a closed car, dey cost almost twice as much as a open car cost.

ANDY: You is right about dat, a'right.

AMOS: I was talkin' to Sylvester today an' he say dat he knows where we kin git a open car—but it ain't got no top on it.

ANDY: Ain't got no top on it, huh?

AMOS: He say dat it's in good shape—got tires on it an' everything.

ANDY: How much do de thing cost?

AMOS: He say it don't cost much an' we kin buy it on time.

ANDY: Well, dat sounds pretty good.

AMOS: He say we might be able to git it widout payin' anything down on it.

ANDY: But it ain't got no top on it, huh?

AMOS: No, he say it ain't got no top on it—dat's de trouble.

ANDY: Wait a minute—I got a idea.

AMOS: Whut is it, whut is it?—'splain to me.

ANDY: We kin start sumpin' new—be diff'ent dan anything else in de country—we kin clean up a fortune—make barrels o' money—be millionaires—have de biggest comp-ny in de world.

AMOS: Wait a minute—wait a minute—'splain dat to me—how we goin' do it?

ANDY: You say de car ain't got no top on it.

AMOS: Dat's de trouble wid it—it ain't got no top on it—but we kin git de car on time.

ANDY: We'll buy dat automobile an' start up a comp'ny called de Fresh Air Taxi Comp'ny.

AMOS: Boy, dat's a idea—um—um—de Fresh Air Company —um—um.

And so that's how the Fresh Air Taxi Company of America, Incorpulated, was born. The rundown convertible cost the impecunious pair the grand sum of twenty-five dollars, and it was a rare day that saw them taking in five dollars in receipts. Money problems were the major themes of the early "Amos 'n' Andy" scripts.

For Gosden and Correll, *their* money problems—if they had had any—were definitely on the wane. Within a short period of time, their idea of creating a "chainless chain" of recordings, which they could lease to various radio stations outside of the Chicago metropolitan area, was catching on. After fifteen months of airing on WMAQ, "Amos 'n' Andy" was being heard on forty other stations —known as a transcription network—as far flung as WBZ (Springfield, Mass.), WJZ (Newark, N.J.), KDKA (Pittsburgh, Pa.), WAAM (Rochester, N.Y.), KSTP (Minneapolis, Minn.), and WDAF (Kansas City, Mo.).

"Amos 'n' Andy" enjoyed the same dramatic rise in popularity as radio itself. By the end of the decade, there were 618 radio stations in operation. Sales of sets had grown from less than $2 million in 1920 to almost $843 million in 1929.

During the early months of 1929, Merlin H. Aylesworth, the first president of the National Broadcasting Company, told New York radio critic Ben Gross, who had never listened to an episode of "Amos 'n' Andy": "These boys are different from any other comedians you ever heard. They're great; but there's one thing odd about them: They don't have any jokes." Aylesworth, the longtime managing director of the National Electric Light Association who was brought in to head NBC in September 1926, was only familiar with the style of humor expounded by the blackface comedy team of Mack and Moran, which was punctuated generously with gags and wisecracks. He knew that Amos and Andy were funny, but he couldn't explain why. Gosden himself once explained that "we were after the creation of character, not gags. We believed that once you establish your characters, if they're likable, the public will become fond of them. All you have to do to them is put them into recognizable situations. You don't have to have a laugh in every line to be funny."

At about that time, Niles Trammel, the thirty-four-year-old radio executive who ran the Chicago office of NBC, and who had the reputation for being the hottest advertising salesman in the medium, talked Aylesworth into auditioning Gosden and Correll for network consideration. Despite his youth, Trammel was a seasoned broadcasting veteran who eventually rose through the ranks to become chairman of the board of NBC. He could, in the parlance of show business, smell a hit.

Unknown to NBC, an assistant manager of the giant Lord & Thomas advertising agency, William Benton, suggested to his boss, Albert Lasker, that their client of long standing—the financially troubled Pepsodent toothpaste company, plagued in recent years by dwindling sales—sponsor a network version of "Amos 'n' Andy." Agreeing that a good comedy vehicle might be just the ticket for the ailing Pepsodent, Lasker phoned a friend at NBC only to discover that the network was anxious to sign Gosden and Correll rather than have to compete against them. The three-year-old network, formed by General Electric, Westinghouse, and RCA, already had signed Eddie Cantor in 1926 and Al Jolson two years later, but it would be several years before either of them would be appearing regularly on radio. NBC's "Red Network"—a more prestigious chain

(19)

of stations than NBC's "Blue Network"—needed a "popular" hit show and "Amos 'n' Andy" looked like their own ticket out of oblivion.

On July 27, 1929, NBC signed Gosden and Correll to a contract that called for the pair to begin broadcasting on the network August 19. The fifty-two-week deal, which initially called for six fifteen-minute shows per week, cost sponsor Pepsodent $750,000. Reportedly, $200,000 to $250,000 of that found its way into the pockets of Gosden and Correll. Newspapers and national magazines wrote of the rise of the "happy darky boys" who specialized in "Afro-American witticisms."

The racial protests that would haunt Gosden and Correll to their dying days began about two weeks after the network premiere, although there is little evidence that the initial negativism was widespread. One newspaper, the *New York Telegram,* called the show the "Abie's Irish Rose of radio theatre," while the paper's competition said of Gosden and Correll, "These two men have studied darkies in all their environment and their program is a close portrayal of their love entanglements and their business and club affairs." Another New York City tabloid, evidently disappointed by the nature of the show's style of "character comedy," said, "Amos 'n' Andy are the biggest fiascos in radio. If they're funny, I have no sense of humor."

But, critics be damned, within three months, "Amos 'n' Andy" had become the most popular show on radio. Its appeal was widespread, capturing nearly 60 percent of all listeners. Such expressions as "I'se regusted," "Ow wah! Ow wah!" and "Check and double check" quickly became part of the American lexicon. As the country neared a depression, Americans clung to "Amos 'n' Andy" with even greater fervor, taking refuge in simpleminded homilies the pair had become known for. When NBC decided to change the show's broadcast time from 11:00 P.M. to 7:00 P.M. (ET), the *St. Paul News* wrote: "The stock market may crash and millionaires be made paupers, but these events pale away into trivial insignificance before the nationwide upheaval caused by the changes in time of the 'Amos 'n' Andy' broadcast." Other newspapers printed forms that fans were instructed to cut out and send to Harlow P. Roberts, president of Pepsodent in Chicago. Within two weeks, more than a hundred thousand letters and telegrams had arrived at the offices of NBC, WMAQ, and Pepsodent.

The time-slot change was initiated because fans on the East Coast were complaining that eleven o'clock was just too late and that the children were too tired to get up for school the next day. Those on the West Coast, of course, had other problems: Putting the show on at seven o'clock, Eastern time, meant that they would hear the program at four in the afternoon, when most people were still working at their jobs. Fans were so angered that they threatened to boycott Pepsodent toothpaste!

It was Gosden and Correll themselves who came up with a solution, although it meant more work for them. The pair agreed to do *two* live broadcasts every night: one at seven o'clock for the East Coast stations, and another three hours later for listeners in the West. This practice eventually became the norm for other live radio shows.

Radio historians have long felt that "Amos 'n' Andy" helped temporarily to mollify the tragic aspects of the Depression. One day after the stock market crash of October 29, 1929, this dialogue exchange took place on the show:

ANDY: Well, Lightnin', 'course I would like to give you a job but de bizness repression is on right now.
LIGHTNIN': Whut is dat you say, Mr. Andy?
ANDY: Is you been keepin' yo' eye on de stock market?
LIGHTNIN': Nosah, I ain't never seed it.
ANDY: Well, de stock market crashed.

LIGHTNIN': Anybody git hurt?

ANDY: Well, 'course, Lightnin', when de stock market crashes, it hurts bizness men. Dat's whut puts de repression on things. . . .

That same week, Gosden and Correll decided to spend a full fifteen minutes—one episode of "Amos 'n' Andy"—concentrating on the crash. The Kingfish—who had been introduced on May 25, 1928, when the show was beamed over WMAQ and the other stations that represented the informal transcription network—claimed that he had lost $800 as a result of the downfall of the stock market. "Dey wiped me out," Kingfish told a confused Andy. "Yo' see, a week ago Thursday, de big crash started. De bulls an' de bears was fightin' it out an' de bears chased de bulls." By reducing to such simple terms the tragedy of the crash, every listener could sympathize:

ANDY: Dem tips is hard to fit, ain't dey?

KINGFISH: Dey is hard to stay away from. Ev'ybody's got a tip.

ANDY: Good ones?

KINGFISH: Bad ones. Ev'ybody knows de inside on de stocks, yo' see—dat's whut dey tell yo', so den you buy it an' it just look like dey waitin' fo' you to buy it, 'cause de minute you buy it, it goes down.

ANDY: Down where?

KINGFISH: Well, if you buy a stock fo' so much money, de fust thing you know it gits cheaper, den you lose.

ANDY: Well, whut makes de stock go up?

KINGFISH: Well, some o' dese big mens down on Wall Street git in a pool, an' when dey git behind de stocks, dey say dat's whut make it go up.

Historians also reason that "Amos 'n' Andy" arrived at the right place at the right time. Writing in *Emmy* magazine, Jack Slater said, "The show became identified with the ensuing Great Depression largely because the nation could empathize with the jobless, scheming, money-hungry, victimized Harlem blacks that the show satirized. . . . For fifteen minutes every evening, down-and-out America forgot its own troubles by identifying with the adventures and the troubles of Amos and Andy and Kingfish and lawyer Calhoun and Lightnin' and Madame Queen, many of whom were, like their listeners, members of the vast unemployed or underemployed."

The Depression also served to divert the public's attention from the various negative racial aspects of "Amos 'n' Andy." Interestingly, the show itself was not the only source of concern. Gosden and Correll may have been the highest paid entertainers on radio, but they were the victims of a form of reverse discrimination. Late in 1929, the pair agreed to go to New York for some promotional activities. A representative of NBC called a New York City hotel to make reservations for the two men. "I'm very sorry, sir," the room clerk replied. "The boys may be very popular—I enjoy the program myself—but this hotel never accepts Negro guests."

Although Negroes found occasional employment in radio, most of the choice black roles were essayed by white performers. Obviously, this was possible because the radio audience did not see the person to whom they were listening. The networks of the twenties and thirties (and for almost three decades later) fostered discriminatory practices in that they preferred hiring white actors to play black roles. Beulah, the black maid who worked for the white Henderson family, was first portrayed by Marlin Hurt, a white *man*. When he died in 1947, Bob Corley, another white actor, inherited the role. Hattie McDaniel, the Academy Award–winning actress, was later hired for the part only because Corley's voice changed and he couldn't affect the high-pitched strains for which Beulah was famous. Having white actors play black characters was a perpetuation of the minstrel form of entertainment dating back almost a hundred years.

While Gosden and Correll were quick to defend their creations—the former once said, "We have a deep respect for the black man. We feel our show helps characterize Negroes as interesting and dignified human beings" —the heavy-handed dialect perpetuated the overall distortions of Negroes and Negro life. As lovable and funny as Amos and Andy were, they were considered objectionable by many because they represented the *only* depiction of black life on radio.

The three familiar black stereotypes, according to J. Fred MacDonald, radio historian and author of *Don't Touch That Dial!*, were "Coons, Toms, and Mammies." "Amos 'n' Andy" featured all three characterizations. MacDonald described the Coon as "above all, the clown . . . murdering the English language with malaprops, conniving to fleece a comrade out of money, bumblingly avoiding gainful employment, and wheezing out his words in ignorant accents unfamiliar to actual blacks."

In contrast to the "stupid" and "scheming" Coons, there were the Toms—good, gentle, religious, sober. The Tom was, as MacDonald described, the "good nigger whose existence gave reassurance to white audiences that there were forces of reason at work within the black community."

And then there was the Mammy, created strictly for laughs. She was the so-called personification of black womanhood. MacDonald described them as "a blend of quick temper, earthy wisdom and love for her wards. No one could bake like a Mammy, and no one could shriek like one, either. She . . . would take backtalk from no person."

"Amos 'n' Andy" had its share of Coons (Kingfish being the epitome), Toms (Amos), and Mammies (Sapphire, Kingfish's shrewish wife). But despite the presence of such stereotypically negative personae, the program enjoyed an enormous popularity among blacks. Years after the show dropped out of its coveted Number One position, it remained a top favorite in the South. Whether the audience was composed of white rascists or blacks is anybody's guess.

In the May 1933 issue of the magazine *Radio Stars,* writer Wildon Brown noted that at the same time black attorneys were seeking a court injunction to halt the broadcasts of "Amos 'n' Andy," a fund-raising group from Harlem was sending telegrams to Gosden and Correll "for being friends of the Negro race."

The NAACP, long an outspoken foe of the program, said, "The sooner they're off the air, the better it will be for the Negro. Radio points to one side of the Negro, the worst side, most frequently."

Skin color aside, the program sought to present moral lessons in the difference between right and wrong. The laziness portrayed by Andy and the Kingfish was always balanced by Amos's diligence. Ministers wrote sermons that borrowed heavily from the show's themes. Editorial writers made a point of complaining that the world needed more Amoses and fewer Andys.

By 1931 "Amos 'n' Andy" had become a full-scale national craze. More than 40 million listeners tuned in nightly—quite a number when you consider that the 1930 census gave the population of the entire country at 123 million! Along with Will Rogers, boxing great Gene Tunney, and Charles Lindbergh, Gosden and Correll were hailed as "public gods." They were on a first-name basis with President Herbert Hoover; their faces adorned candy bars; Hollywood called them to star in a movie.

The show business bible *Variety* summed up the phenomenon in a 1931 review, while at the same time suggesting ways the show could be better:

"Amos 'n' Andy" . . . have the greatest number of author-ized—and unauthorized—articles named after them, get the largest salary of any team broadcasting, share with Rudy Vallee the distinction of being the only radio attrac-tion to be starred in a talking picture.

They are being imitated nightly; female counter-parts have sprung up, mixed teams are numerous, whole family groups are gabbing, all inspired, directly or in-directly, by Amos and Andy.

Episodic conversation, 15 minutes a night, has been a recognized entertainment form of radio. Some programs start out well but quickly stale. Few have suffi-cient wind to stand the long night-after-night grind. Freshness is lost, real humor is replaced by straining effort. That is why the "Amos 'n' Andy" scripts, self-written and self-staged, are the classics of the industry.

At present their stride is slow and their wit dulled as if in exhaustion from the previous pace. They have lately been concerning themselves with an asinine routine about Andy, the shiftless member, writing his life story for a newspaper syndicate. Here [Gosden and Correll] have gotten out of contact with common sense and the every-day touch. The sooner they get back to the orbit of aver-age experience, the securer will be their position.

Even though the average "Amos 'n' Andy" episode required only 1,500 to 2,000 words, it was Gosden and Correll who wrote every word of every show until 1943, when the show was expanded to thirty minutes and a staff of writers was hired. Working in a small office in Chicago's Palmolive Building, the pair often wrote the scripts on the day of the broadcast. Rarely were they two or three days ahead. They liked the pressure only a deadline can offer and felt that the scripts written under that circumstance were better.

Richard Correll, son of the late Charles Correll and himself a comedy writer with a long list of enviable credits, says, "Freeman was the real brains behind the team. My father was more laid back. While Freeman paced back and forth in the office verbalizing much of the black dialect, my father would be taking it down in shorthand. His background as a court stenographer came in handy. He also typed every script, making an original and one carbon copy."

Every scriptwriting session was different. Sometimes, the chore was over in less than a half hour. Other times, the four-page script would require three or four hours of painstaking work. "Because they knew the characters so well," Richard Correll continues, "they didn't have to rehearse."

The actual studio was located in the Merchandise Mart. To this day, WMAQ is located in the same Chicago landmark. Unlike a typical radio studio, this room looked like somebody's living room. There was even a fireplace. During the live broadcast, the pair sat at a wooden table opposite each other. Using one microphone, they adjusted their seating positions according to which character they were voicing. To play Andy, Correll spoke in a very low voice close to the mike, whereas Gosden—impersonating the reverent Amos—would pull back about two feet from the mike and use a distinctive high-pitched voice. Gosden, the more talented dialectician, also portrayed Lightnin' and the irrepressible Kingfish. There were times when the two actors had a rough time keeping a straight face. Once, according to Gosden, he had to splash some cold water on his face to keep from laughing out loud.

Gosden and Correll originated the concept of the comedy serial. In fact, they are given credit for devising the serial, which today is recognized as the perenially popular soap opera. John F. Royal, who was NBC's vice-president in charge of programs during the halcyon days of "Amos 'n' Andy," recalled in an interview shortly before his death that Gosden and Correll "gave the audience very little in that fifteen minutes a night. You could relax listening to them. They didn't force a lot of humor on you. They never gave too much—just eased along. And this was their secret. They were real students of entertaining by radio, and they were conscientious. No one was allowed in their studio. They took the delineation of their characters most seriously —and they succeeded."

So well did they succeed, in fact, that President Calvin Coolidge often excused himself from state dinners in order to catch "Amos 'n' Andy." Department stores open in the evening piped in the broadcasts so shoppers wouldn't miss an episode, but, more importantly, wouldn't stop shopping. Movie theatres, fearful that no one would venture out of their homes until the broadcasts were over, carried the show on their public address systems. Factories altered their work shifts to accommodate employees who wanted to listen to "Amos 'n' Andy." The telephone company reported a decided decline in usage from seven to seven-fifteen on the six nights the show aired. The program was frequently referred to in the *Congressional Record*.

The show once drew 2.4 million letters from listeners who wrote to suggest names for Amos and his wife's, Ruby's, newborn daughter, Arbadella; and when Ruby fell ill some years later, 65,000 fans wrote to express hopes for an early recovery. When her condition took a turn for the worse, 18,000 indignant "Amos 'n' Andy" listeners threatened to brush their teeth with Colgate, not Pepsodent.

The United States ambassador to the Court of St. James, about to depart on his new assignment, told reporters his only regret in taking the plum appointment was that he'd miss "Amos 'n' Andy." A doctor in the Midwest took out a newspaper ad asking his patients not to disturb him during the show. Sanitary engineers finally figured out why the sewer pipes barely carried a flow between 7:00 and 7:15 P.M., then erupted with a roar immediately thereafter. No one wanted to miss even a minute of the show.

Gosden and Correll made dialogue records that the

Victor Talking Machine Company issued during the early 1930s. The pair launched a comic strip that was syndicated by the *Chicago Daily News* that featured captions from the daily script of "Amos 'n' Andy." The boys ventured to Hollywood to star in *Check and Double Check,* which was released in 1930 under the auspices of RKO. Labeled "a monument to mediocrity" by one critic, the comedy featured the pair in blackface makeup. The actual Fresh Air taxicab was no longer something in a listener's imagination. In 1933, they agreed to provide their minstrel-like voices for an animated cartoon. A book of "Amos 'n' Andy" dialogue titled *Here They Are—Amos 'n' Andy* made its appearance on bookstore shelves during the show's heyday.

The show had the critical effect of boosting Pepsodent's sales. This, in turn, helped convince other potential sponsors that radio was a viable advertising medium. With the help of "Amos 'n' Andy," NBC grossed more than $150 million during the year of the crash, 1929, mostly from advertising.

As kings, Amos and Andy had their subjects. Their 40 million devoted followers included men, women, and children, black and white. Every teenager in the country was repeating such catchphrases as "Buzz me, Miss Blue!" and "I'se regusted!" "Brother Crawford," "Madame Queen," "Lightnin'," and "George 'Kingfish' Stevens" became as well known as the most famous movie stars of the day.

The Kingfish, portrayed by Freeman Gosden, was an especially fertile character. First introduced on the broadcast of May 25, 1928 (a year prior to the show's switch to the NBC network), the Kingfish was at his scheming best on show number 52, when he cajoled Amos and Andy into joining his lodge, the Mystic Knights of the Sea:

KINGFISH: Well, gent'mens, I was talkin' to Brother Fred heah, yo' lan'lord, an' he was tellin' me dat you two boys ain't been in Chicago for long an' I thought it would be a nice thing to git you two boys in dat great fraternity known as de Mystic Knights of de Sea.

ANDY: Whut is de name o' dat thing again?

KINGFISH: De name of de fraternity, brothers, is de Mystic Knights of de Sea, of which I is de King-fish. . . . We all stick together so dat de Mystic Knights of de Sea is like one big family. Dey is all brothers.

AMOS: Dey is all brothers—um—um—ain't dat sumpin'.

ANDY: How many brothers is yo' got?

KINGFISH: Well, we is got over 200 brothers dat we call sardines—den we has de officers—we had de Whale, de Swordfish, de Catfish, an' de Shad.

ANDY: Ev'rybody's a fish, huh?

KINGFISH: Yes, every brother's a fish. We call de members sardines an' den each officer is a big fish. Now, de Whale, de Mackerel an' de Catfish swims around de three chairs. I swim around de head chair—de big chair.

AMOS: Where do yo' hold de meetin's—in a swimmin' pool?

ANDY: Don't pay no 'tention to him, Kingfish.

KINGFISH: No, we talks jus' like we was in de water. De secktary of de lodge is known as de Shad an' de brother dat guards de door is de Swordfish.

ANDY: Do dey have meetin's an' ev'ything?

KINGFISH: Oh brother—we has great meetin's. Whenever a sardine gits sick, de Jellyfish sees dat he gits plen'y to eat an' in case any of de sardines die dey is buried wid fishly honors.

AMOS: Certainly do sound good to me—how much it cost?

ANDY: Wait a minute, Amos—wait a minute.

KINGFISH: Well, brothers, I brought two application blanks wid me, an' if you brothers would like to come into de Mystic Knights of de Sea, just sign dese two application blanks an' gimme two dollars apiece down an' you kin pay de balance when you comes in fo' 'nitiation.

The colorful Chicago neighborhood teemed with wildly wonderful characters. One of them was Madame Queen, Andy's flouncy girl friend. Gosden and Correll knew how to grab an audience and hold them in the palms of their hands. Because the program had a continuing storyline, they could set up any premise and spend days—sometimes weeks—dramatizing it. One famous episode involved Andy and his Madame Queen in late 1931. She was suing him because he'd withdrawn his proposal of marriage. Gosden and Correll went to great lengths to make the resulting trial as realistic as possible, even consulting the vice president and general counsel of NBC, A. L. Ashby. Masters at holding the audience in suspense, Gosden and Correll planned it so that just as Andy was about to be convicted, Madame Queen fainted. Listeners had to wait until Monday night to find out what happened. That day they discovered that Madame Queen's long-lost husband, believed to have been lost at sea, had suddenly reappeared. The case was dismissed, to the collective relief of Andy Brown's millions of fans.

Earlier the same year, Amos was charged with murder and a full-scale trial ensued. Fan mail begging the judge not to convict Jones flooded the network. Gosden and Correll admitted that the ploy was a "dirty trick." They resolved the matter by revealing on October 22 that Amos had dreamed the entire incident. Such story devices, while a little on the deceptive side, did manage to shore up the show's ratings until the inevitable happened: By August 1933, "Amos 'n' Andy" 's listening audience had dropped to 55.5 percent from a high of 74 percent three years earlier.

DEPRESSION BLUES

Times like dese does a lot o' good cause when dis is over, which is bound to be, an' good times come back again, people's like us dat is livin' today is goin' learn a lesson an' dey goin' know whut a rainy day means. People is done always used de repression. I is savin' up fo' a rainy day, but dey didn't even know whut dey was talkin' 'bout. Now, when good times come back again people is gonna remember all dis an' know whut a rainy day is—so maybe after all, dis was a good thing to bring people back to day're senses an' sort a remind ev'ybody dat de sky ain't *de limit.*

Amos's morality lesson, part of the February 6, 1932, broadcast, set the tone for the show during the Great Depression of the 1930s, when unemployment ran as high as 25 percent. What he was saying was shared by a nation: With a little work and a little faith, the country would be back on the track soon.

Writing in the *Journal of Popular Culture,* Arthur Frank Wertheim saw radio comedy of the decade as having embodied the very principles that managed to relieve the strain America was bearing. Within the humor's pressure-release valve was "a reaffirmation of traditional American values." Radio brought people out of despairing isolation into a sense of common experience. Will Rogers, radio's court jester, spoke over the radio about the importance of industriousness, noting that it was the carefree spending of the Roaring Twenties that had led to the crash. The Depression was an era in which large-scale suffering brought about a renewed purpose, and radio comedy's role was significant.

And, despite the declining radio audience, "Amos 'n' Andy" was still the most popular radio show of the period, among whites and, according to polls, blacks. Criticism against the show's stereotypes was not widespread, but it was vocal. With the sanction of the NAACP the *Courier*, a black newspaper in Pittsburgh, tried earnestly to have the Federal Radio Commission censure the show for the following reasons: "exploitation of Negroes for profit, portrayal of demeaning characters, and making the Negroes' means of support suspect." The paper's campaign tried to gain momentum among the black community, but to no avail. A rival black newspaper, Chicago's *Defender*, blasted the *Courier*'s position, going so far as to invite Gosden and Correll to perform at a city picnic for thirty thousand black children during July 1931. The rally was a huge success and the *Courier* retreated, knowing full well that theirs was a minority opinion. It was clear to most everyone that, by and large, black people loved "Amos 'n' Andy," or, at least, were tolerating it because there were more vital problems of the day to be concerned with—like surviving.

When President Roosevelt closed the banks in 1933, Americans feared that what little savings they had in banks was suddenly in dire jeopardy. Even Roosevelt himself was soothed by this speech delivered by Amos to his pals, Andy, Lightnin', and the Kingfish:

> De President of de United States is fightin' fo' more dan just 'mergency bankin' relief—he is workin' out a plan to

have a system in de banks dat will not only he'p 'em now but will he'p 'em fo' all time to come, an' dis banker says dat dat's zackly whut's goin happen an' Mr. Roosevelt means bizness, an' he's gittin' action, so yo' see, dis bank holiday is really a great thing fo' de country.

"Amos 'n' Andy" was not the only example of "black radio." There were legitimate Negro bandleaders and singers who flourished during the decade, but few were given the exposure that white bandleaders like Paul Whiteman and B. A. Rolfe enjoyed. Black music was represented not only by Negro bands but also by white musicians who realized the commercial value of "race" music. As in the case of "Amos 'n' Andy," Afro-Americans were more often than not portrayed by white actors, who were called upon to furnish such stereotypical members of the race as butlers, maids, and ne'er-do-wells.

Blacks had been part of the musical heritage of radio from its early days, in the 1920s, appearing in jazz ensembles, large dance bands, choirs. Flournoy Miller, a popular vaudeville and film personality, and his partner, Aubrey Lyles, were broadcasting on radio as early as 1922. By the late 1920s such musical performers as Noble Sissle, Fess Williams, and the Pace Jubilee Negro Singers were heard on the air.

By the mid-1930s, radio audiences were enjoying Paul Robeson as a featured singer on programs sponsored by General Electric and Eastman Kodak. Ethel Waters had her own show, as did Duke Ellington, "Fats" Waller, and Art Tatum. A number of variety shows featured Negroes like the Mills Brothers, Nina Mae McKinney, the Four Southern Singers, the Four Sheiks of Harmony, the Babolene Boys, and Jules Bledsoe.

As pointed out by radio historian J. Fred MacDonald in *Don't Touch That Dial!*, a look at a radio log of 1932 revealed "broadcasts by such Afro-American musicians as

Chick Webb, Don Redman (four nights per week over two different stations), and Cab Calloway (seven nights per week over three different stations)." Gospel music was also a popular staple of black radio.

The few black comics who made it on radio simply filled the same stereotypical roles in broad comedy vehicles, similar in content to the minstrel shows of years past. Increasingly more offensive in the 1930s, such racial characterizations were about the only roles black actors were allowed to fill. Hattie McDaniel, for example, displayed her well-known Mammy act on the "Show Boat" variety series over NBC in 1932. Johnny Lee, who would later play the lawyer Calhoun on the TV version of "Amos 'n' Andy," was a radio performer as far back as 1932, when he appeared in the all-black comedy "Slick and Slim." That same year saw the emergence of the standard black maid character in Gardenia, played by Georgia Burke on the soap opera "Betty and Bob." A similar characterization would win Hattie McDaniel the coveted Oscar in 1939 for *Gone with the Wind.*

Black performers were forced to alter their normal speech patterns in order to affect the pseudo-Negro dialect developed in the late 1800s by minstrel performers. Lillian Randolph, who played Madame Queen, Andy Brown's girl friend in the TV version of "Amos 'n' Andy," spent three months studying with a white vocal coach before she could master the idiosyncrasies of the black dialect. Johnny Lee said that he "had to learn to talk as white people believed Negroes talked." If a black performer could not master the minstrel accent, he lost his job. This happened to comedian "Wonderful" Smith, who was bounced from his role on Red Skelton's NBC show in 1948 because "I had difficulty sounding as Negroid as they expected."

If it was tough for black comedians and those actors and actresses who specialized in comedy, it was nearly impossible for black dramatic actors to find a job in radio. No matter what their accent, they were cast only as blacks. Discouraged by the lack of work, several Negro performers created their own companies that would hire them to produce shows. A local drama called "A Harlem Family" premiered in New York in 1935. Produced by the city's board of education, the serial featured an all-black cast and was also written and directed by Negroes. The same station, WMCA, also broadcast Mercedes Gilbert, "the colored poetess." Unfortunately, none of the black dramatic series was successful. This was peculiar, since a 1935 poll revealed that blacks enjoyed dramas, mysteries, and gangster plots above musical and comedy vehicles, where their greatest success on radio lay.

It was white audiences, ignorant of the true black experience and harboring a lifetime of prejudices, who enjoyed blacks on radio only when they were performing in comedies and in musical shows. This bigotry was part of America's cultural past and it was not easy to change. By the mid-1930s, many black performers had their own shows. The Mills Brothers, the Ink Spots, Bob Howard, and Adelaide Hall were among the more popular hosts. In 1936, Duke Ellington started his own NBC show, and the following year, Louis Armstrong had a network series with Fleischmann's Yeast as sponsor.

Black performers also appeared as regular characters on a number of programs during the 1930s. In 1938, comedienne Hattie Noel was a popular feature of "The Eddie Cantor Show." The most beloved of all was Eddie "Rochester" Anderson, who played Jack Benny's valet on radio and later on TV. Although his dialogue would come under constant fire because of its stereotypical clichés, it somehow was more palatable than that of other black comedy performers.

As the 1940s began, a host of new black stereotypes emerged, most of them maids. Beulah, the quintessential domestic, started out on the "Show Boat" series on NBC in 1940, and later got her own series. Lillian Randolph portrayed Birdie on "The Great Gildersleeve"; Ruby Dandridge appeared as Geranium on "The Judy Canova Show"; and Lillian Randolph essayed the role of another maid, Daisy, on "The Billie Burke Show." Black maids soon began making regular appearances on soap operas, very often for comedy relief.

Other black performers like Mantan Moreland and Ben Carter were the resident "Coon" comics on the "Bob Burns Show" on CBS. Nick Stewart—working under the professional moniker "Nick-O-Demus"—was a regular on Rudy Vallee's variety show as early as 1941 (Stewart later played Lightnin' on TV's "Amos 'n' Andy"). Even Butterfly McQueen, six years after her association with *Gone with the Wind*, signed on as the addle-brained secretary on CBS's "Danny Kaye Show."

When "Amos 'n' Andy" 's Gosden and Correll were offered a better deal with CBS in late 1938, they decided to move their entire operation to Hollywood's Columbia Square, the West Coast headquarters of the Columbia Broadcasting System. The show's defection from NBC—where it had sat near the top of the ratings for a decade—was foreboding. Although the show didn't begin on CBS until April 3, 1939, it had already begun slipping severely in the ratings. In an effort to shore up the faltering standing, Gosden and Correll decided to expand the scope of the show, for the first time hiring other performers to play new parts. It had been estimated that Gosden and Correll together had performed some six hundred "Amos 'n' Andy" roles since the show's inception in 1928.

Among the newcomers hired were two black actresses: Ernestine Wade was tapped for the juicy role of Kingfish's "Battleax," Sapphire, and Amanda Randolph became her demanding mother.

SAPPHIRE: George Stevens, I done made up my mind that I'm gonna have a husband that dresses good, knows nice people, and is got a steady job.

KINGFISH: Sapphire, you mean to say that you is gonna leave me?

SAPPHIRE: George, I know why you're a no-good bum. It's on account of your association with Andy Brown. Why don't you try to meet a nicer class of men?

KINGFISH: Well, I ain't got da opportunity to meet em, they's all workin'.

SAPPHIRE: Well, that Andy Brown is the cause of it all. What has he ever accomplished?

KINGFISH: Well, yesterday, he had a run of thirteen balls in da side pocket without leanin' on da table.

SAPPHIRE: Now, that's exactly what I mean: Andy hangin' around a pool table all day. Why don't he go to a cultured place like a public library?

KINGFISH: They ain't got no pool table dere.

With a new sponsor as of January 1938, the Campbell Soup Company, "Amos 'n' Andy" went on entertaining a nation about to enter a second world war. At home, however, another war was stirring, the seeds of which had been planted ten years earlier when "Amos 'n' Andy" went on the air. Aside from public factions warring, even black performers differed in their opinions of black stereotyping. The eminent black actor Canada Lee later spoke out against what he called "giggling maids, Rochesters, Aunt Jemimas, and shiftless, lazy individuals" usually played by blacks: "A virtual Iron Curtain exists against the entire Negro people as far as radio is concerned. Where is the story of our lives in terms of the ghetto slums in which we must live? Where is the story in terms of jobs not available? Who would know us only by listening to Amos and Andy, Beulah, Rochester, and minstrel shows?"

Lee's counterparts included several steadily employed black artists, among them Ernestine Wade, who felt the stereotypes were no more harmful than such negative roles as misers and villains. Wade's radio cohort, Lillian

Randolph, felt the same way, adding that stereotypes "did not affect the past, present, or future of blacks." She argued further that persuading black performers to turn down such roles would allow white performers to take the jobs.

More vocal than the two women was Eddie Anderson, Rochester of "The Jack Benny Show," who said, "I haven't seen anything objectionable. I don't see why certain characters are called stereotypes. . . . The Negro characters being presented are not labeling the Negro race any more than 'Luigi' is labeling the Italian people as a whole. The same goes for 'Beulah,' who is not playing the part of thousands of Negroes, but only the part of one person, 'Beulah.' They're not saying here is the portrait of the Negro, but here is 'Beulah.' "

By the late 1930s the NAACP had become a powerfully vocal organization under the leadership of Walter White. Many blacks, however, were critical of his efforts, feeling that he overstressed the black image, often at the expense of jobs for black actors. White, however mistrusted by black actors and white studio chieftains alike, had an important ally in former presidential candidate Wendell Willkie, who was a staunch supporter of the NAACP and who was about to become chairman of the board of 20th Century-Fox. Willkie wrote White in January 1942, saying, "I ought to have a tiny bit of influence right now. Let's go out to Hollywood and talk with more intelligent people in the industry to see what can be done to change the situation."

The following month the pair arrived in Los Angeles for the annual convention of the NAACP. They successfully managed to meet with various studio heads and the result was written up in the Hollywood trade paper *Variety* under the headline BETTER BREAKS FOR NEGROES IN H'WOOD: "Negroes are to be given an increasingly prominent part in pictures, it was revealed here by Walter White who asserted that Darryl Zanuck and other production chiefs had promised a more honest portrayal of the Negro henceforth, using them not only as red-caps, porters, and in other menial roles, but in all the parts they play in the nation's everyday life."

Thus, during the war Hollywood—spurred on by increased pressure from the NAACP, the federal government, political organizations, and perhaps more importantly, filmgoers demanding more substance in motion pictures during those hard times—embarked on what many critics believe to be the most enlightened era of racial understanding.

Gosden and Correll, while deeply concerned about the reaction to their show by the NAACP, had other problems. In January 1943 the show dipped in the ratings, reaching a low of 9.4. With their contract coming up for renewal by both CBS and Campbell's Soup (their sponsor since January 1938), Gosden and Correll decided that the serial format that they started in 1926 with "Sam 'n' Henry" had become stale. The story device was now the mainstay of soap operas, not comedy shows. If they were going to compete with the likes of Jack Benny, Bob Hope, and Edgar Bergen, they would have to devise a new playing concept for "Amos 'n' Andy," one that did not depend on a continuous storyline. Biting the bullet, the pair took an eight-month vacation beginning after the broadcast of February 19, 1943, for the sole purpose of injecting new lifeblood into "Amos 'n' Andy."

When they returned to the air on October 8, 1943, they were back on NBC, the network that had originated the coast-to-coast broadcast of the series back in 1929. Gone were the continuing stories. Under the new sponsorship of Rinso detergent, "Amos 'n' Andy" was now a once-weekly (Tuesdays at 9:00 P.M., ET), half-hour situation comedy with guest stars, an orchestra, outside writers, and, for the very first time, a studio audience. While Gosden and Correll still played the major roles (the former essaying

Amos and the Kingfish and Correll playing Andy), they had written new parts that were filled by outside actors such as Lou Lubin as the stuttering Shorty, the barber.

The show had taken on a glitzy look. No more organ music; the Jeff Alexander Orchestra supplied the music. No more Bill Hay, the announcer; Harlow Wilcox was installed to give the commercials a larger-than-life sound. At times, the stories were secondary to the Hollywood stars who appeared each week as guests. By this time, Gosden and Correll were headquartered on an entire floor of a swank building on Wilshire Boulevard in Beverly Hills. Their team of writers included Bob Connelly, Bob Mosher, Bob Fisher, Bob Ross, Arthur Stander, Harvey Helm, and Shirley Illo. It now took an entire week to prepare one thirty-minute program and as Charles Correll once said, "Every line was carefully scrutinized for humor and sharpness." The rating of the new format nearly doubled to 17.1 by January 1944, but still the program was a faint recollection of its former glory.

By the end of World War II, nine out of ten American families owned radios. It was estimated that more than 56 million sets were in use, and that Americans were spending more time listening to radio than they spent doing anything else except working and sleeping. According to the Hooper rating service, the top fifteen programs and personalities of the 1945–56 season were "Fibber McGee and Molly"; Bob Hope; "Lux Radio Theatre"; Edgar Bergen and Charlie McCarthy; Red Skelton; Jack Benny; the "Screen Guild Players"; Fred Allen; "Mr. District Attorney"; Walter Winchell; "Great Gildersleeve"; Eddie Cantor; Abbott and Costello; Jack Haley and Eve Arden; and Burns and Allen. Twelve of the top fifteen shows were broadcast on NBC, only two—"Lux Radio Theatre" and "Screen Guild Players"—were aired on CBS.

William S. Paley, who ran CBS, knew that in order to succeed in programming, his network would have to broadcast stars, the backbone of the radio business. Paley believed that stars were the force for attracting audiences and advertisers. NBC's dominance over CBS was a thorn in Paley's side. It was no secret that when "Amos 'n' Andy" was radio's biggest hit in the early 1930s Paley tried everything to bring that show down. Although he never quite managed to overpower Gosden and Correll's creations, Paley did manage to create several radio superstars. He chose Bing Crosby, a member of Paul Whiteman's Rhythm Boys Trio, for a big publicity buildup that had moderate success. Bing's crooning did manage to put a sizable dent into "Amos 'n' Andy" 's considerable audience. After making Crosby a star in that 7:00 P.M. time-slot, Paley tried his luck with the Mills Brothers, then with an overweight singer with a big voice, Kate Smith. These performers were merely Paley's bait to lure listeners away from the "Amos 'n' Andy" show on NBC.

New income-tax rates established after the war did more to change the face of radio than anything else. After $70,000 in income, a taxpayer was forced to give the U.S. government ninety-one cents out of every dollar he earned. Jack Benny's tax attorneys had urged the NBC star to form a corporation (Amusement Enterprises) of which he controlled the majority of stock. Corporations were taxed at a lower rate than individuals. CBS decided to take the idea a step further by trying to lure away talent from NBC by offering sizable capital gains deals to the performers. Other "businesses" had been benefiting from capital gains sales for many years, but the arrangement had not been employed by show business personalities. It was CBS executive Howard Meighan who decided to test the idea by suggesting that radio stars form corporations that would, in turn, own their shows. If these programs—as "properties" —were sold, they would have to pay only 25 percent in taxes on the capital gains.

By the summer of 1948, Lew Wasserman, the formidable head of the largest talent agency in the country, Music Corporation of America (MCA), and his executive vice-president, Taft Schreiber, set up a meeting with William Paley. As agents for Freeman Gosden and Charles Correll, MCA proposed that CBS buy the newly formed Amos and Andy Corporation. The asking price was set at $2.5 million. The negotiations were long and intensive. As William S. Paley wrote in his 1979 autobiography, "We realized that there were tremendous advantages for both sides if we could make a deal. Gosden and Correll would build up an immediate estate for their families, MCA would collect its agent's commission, and CBS would score a positive coup in the broadcasting industry."

Despite the stiff price tag, Paley knew that if he could swing the deal and lure Gosden and Correll back to CBS, he might be able to lure the other heavyweights—Jack Benny, Red Skelton, Edgar Bergen, Burns and Allen.

By September 1948 the deal with Gosden and Correll had been concluded. For approximately $2.5 million, CBS received exclusive ownership rights to the program for the next twenty years. Gosden and Correll, aside from receiving more than $1 million each, were also paid hefty annual salaries by CBS to continue doing the show. On October 10, after an absence of more than four years, "Amos 'n' Andy" returned to the CBS network in the 7:30 P.M. Sunday-night time-slot. Within a few short months, CBS did manage to induce Jack Benny and the others to leave NBC for CBS's "greener" pastures (green was the color of cash).

No sooner did Gosden and Correll move back to CBS than they began toying with the idea of turning the wildly successful creation into a television show. By the autumn of 1948 Milton Berle had won the hearts of the few million Americans who owned a TV set. Ed Sullivan hit the air that year as the finger-pointing host of "Toast of the Town." Arthur Godfrey, an enormous success on CBS

Radio, introduced talent to the nation on his "Original Amateur Hour." Allen Funt's ABC series "Candid Mike" got the video treatment that year as well. On another level "The Lone Ranger" and "Hopalong Cassidy" rode into view. It would be another year until a situation comedy from radio, "The Goldbergs," made it to television.

Gosden and Correll knew there was a future for "Amos 'n' Andy" on the new medium, but they also knew that they couldn't play the parts, not in blackface. Eighteen years earlier, they had learned their lesson after watching their RKO film *Check and Double Check* at a screening. Never again, they promised, turning down a firm eleven-picture deal with the studio. If they were going to do a video version of their valuable property that CBS now owned, they would have to cast black actors and actresses. But this was easier said than done.

4

TV OR NOT TV

Although Gosden and Correll had performed in an experimental broadcast at an RCA television exhibit at the New York World's Fair on February 26, 1939—playing their beloved characters in blackface—it never entered their minds to play the key roles in their projected TV version of "Amos 'n' Andy." According to Richard Correll, son of the late Charles Correll, "Dad and Freeman, despite what certain television historians have said, had no interest in playing Amos and Andy on television. First of all, they each played several roles on radio. How could they essay all the television parts and still be believable? Also, their experience with *Check and Double Check* and later with the *Big Broadcast* movie in the late thirties proved to them that doing a blackface act in the late forties would not be acceptable."

The pair began talking about a television version in 1945 when the radio program was airing on NBC. At that time the medium was not even in its infancy—that embryonic stage would come three or four years later. As World War II came to a close, NBC was broadcasting TV shows like "The War As It Happens," "Gillette Cavalcade of Sports," "Wings of Democracy," "NBC Television Theater," and "The Children's Program" on a sporadic basis. Its chief rival, CBS, was less visible: "Missus Goes A Shopping," "There Ought to Be a Law," and boxing matches constituted the network's prime-time schedule. ABC was not broadcasting in 1945, but DuMont—a network that lasted until the mid-fifties—had such postwar series as "Magic Carpet" (a children's program), "Shopping with Martha Manning," "Thrills and Chills," "Author, Author," "Magazine of the Air," and "Thanks for Looking." So, despite these meager offerings to serve as examples, Gosden and Correll were able to envision "Amos 'n' Andy" as a television program.

The following year, they began planning in earnest. Having decided that black actors would have to be cast in all the roles, Gosden and Correll also realized that finding precisely the right actors for the various parts would not be easy. The general public, having enjoyed the "Amos 'n' Andy" show since 1929, had their own set of casting requirements, but who knew what they were? Was Andy, in our fertile imaginations, fat, or was he tall and angular? Was the Kingfish always dressed as a slob, or did he wear suits? Gosden and Correll—having played the parts for nearly twenty years—had a fair idea of how their creations were supposed to look, but the more they discussed the physical requirements, the more they came to believe that

(46)

the right actors would be more likely found in the larger talent pool of white actors. But that meant white men in blackface, and if civil rights activists had anything to do with it, the show would never get on the air. Some consideration was made to cast both white and black actors in the parts, if the search for an all-Negro cast was not fruitful.

To get a better idea what talent was available, the writer/performers sent Charles Vanda, a Hollywood producer (later vice-president of the CBS affiliate in Philadelphia, WCAU-TV), through the South to interview Negro actors in theatres, nightclubs, and other entertainment spots. Vanda carefully combed the area from Texas to Virginia without success. That summer (1947), Gosden and Correll happened to see the national road company of the Philip Yordan play *Anna Lucasta*. The play had its origins off Broadway under the auspices of the American Negro Theatre (at the 135th Street Library Theater) before moving to Broadway on August 30, 1944, with the all-Negro cast. It was about the Lucastas, an ordinary working-class family in a coal-mining town—an odd group of selfish, grasping people whose daughter Anna has left home to lead what most of them consider a "life of shame" in the city.

The performance that Gosden and Correll saw convinced them that *only* Negro actors should do their "Amos 'n' Andy" TV show. After discussing it further, the pair decided to see the play again and perhaps arrange auditions for some of the players (there were fourteen actors in the cast). Unfortunately, none of the performers quite fit the bill, and the formal pursuit for actors slowed until negotiations with CBS were completed in the fall of 1948.

At that time, a CBS staff producer, James Fonda, was assigned to the project. With Gosden and Correll busy with their radio show—now being broadcast on the Columbia Broadcasting System—Fonda supervised the stepped-up talent search. Again, the question of using Negro *or* white actors in blackface was thrashed about, and it was decided to continue to test black actors but to try out some white actors as well. With only the Hollywood talent pool from which to choose, Fonda did manage to line up several actors to audition for the parts of Amos, Andy, and the Kingfish.

In April 1949, at the CBS Television headquarters at Columbia Square in Hollywood, tests were made of some eight teams of actors. These screen tests—shot using standard television cameras on Stage A of the Sunset Boulevard broadcasting complex—featured some sets and props. Gosden and Correll experimented by dubbing their own voices but the results were unsatisfactory, so this proposed technique—along with the tested thespians—was abandoned.

Fonda was then dispatched to New York, where, it was hoped, a larger contingent of black performers was available. With the aid of Henry Wagstaff Gribble, director of the New York company of *Anna Lucasta,* Fonda continued his search. From their headquarters at 485 Madison Avenue, the CBS casting experts compiled a list of two hundred black actors, with a little help from the Negro Actors' Guild. All of them were tested within a few days. Among them was a forty-year-old actor from Meridian, Mississippi, with a college degree, Alvin Childress, who had portrayed the bartender in the Broadway production of Gribble's *Anna Lucasta.*

In anticipation of his audition, Childress spent two months listening to air checks of the radio programs and impersonating all the voices, but it was the Kingfish role that Childress was after. The third actor to be auditioned in New York, he was not signed for the role until later, although everyone—including CBS, Gosden and Correll, and Fonda—felt that he was probably right for the role of Amos Jones, owner of the Fresh Air Taxi Company.

That same year, 1949, a musical play called *Sugar*

(48)

Hill, with book and lyrics by Flournoy Miller, opened in Los Angeles. Miller, who had also written *Shuffle Along* and other black revues, was promptly hired as a talent scout at the suggestion of Gosden and Correll. With Miller in tow, Jim Fonda left immediately for Chicago, another known source of black talent. However, after talking with several agents and interviewing a number of performers, the pair moved on to Detroit, where they first heard the name Tim Moore. Everyone agreed that Moore would be perfect as the Kingfish, decidedly the most difficult role to cast. The only problem was that nobody knew of his whereabouts. They would later find out that he had retired in 1946.

It was Flournoy Miller who first suggested Spencer Williams for the role of Andrew H. Brown, better known as Andy. Miller hadn't seen Williams in nearly fifteen years and—worse—he had no idea where he was living. Through a network of inquiries, he and Fonda finally learned that he was living in Tulsa, Oklahoma. They immediately wired the CBS station in Tulsa, KTUL, to aid in their search. The station obligingly broadcast a request for Williams's whereabouts. He had moved to the town in 1946, having fallen in love with it during his days making movies on location. He formed a partnership with Amos T. Hall, a lawyer, in a school for veterans, where they taught six vocations, including photography and radio. A priest, for whose church Williams had put on plays, told the busy Williams about the announcement. Williams, then fifty-six, contacted the local station, posed for some photographs, and made several recordings that were flown to Hollywood. When Gosden and Correll saw the pictures and heard the recordings they reportedly said in unison, "That's Andy."

Williams was flown to Hollywood to undergo a formal screen test for the important role. This time, Flournoy Miller played Kingfish to Williams's Andy and Alvin Childress's Amos. (Miller was not being auditioned as the Kingfish, but simply took the part to help out in the test.)

The remainder of the roles were played by the black actors who were regulars on the "Amos 'n' Andy" radio program. Both Williams and Childress were found right for the parts and were hired on a standby basis. While Childress returned to his wife, Alice, and their daughter, Jean Rosa, in New York, to wait for his formal call, Spencer Williams remained in Hollywood.

It was now March 1950 and there was still no Kingfish. Williams, who had worked with many Negro actors while producing films in the South, was put on the staff to help find the missing link, George "Kingfish" Stevens. As a talent scout, he set out for Dallas, Fort Worth, Houston, New Orleans, Memphis, and Kansas City, visiting Negro colleges, nightclubs, and stock companies. With his talent as a cameraman, he photographed everyone who seemed at all possible for the part, but—alas—even this thorough search was fruitless. He next traveled to San Francisco to scout possible talent, but didn't find an actor suitable for the role there, either.

In May, when the radio program went off the air for the summer, Freeman Gosden went to New York en route to his hometown of Richmond, Virginia. While in Manhattan he conferred with CBS officials, including William S. Paley, and it was decided to test teams of Negro actors and teams of white actors. Jim Fonda was sent to Washington, D.C., to interview prospects, then on to Baltimore and Atlanta, before catching up with Gosden in Richmond, where the latter had already auditioned fifty Kingfish candidates. Many of them *looked* the part, but couldn't act.

While playing golf in New York that summer with his old friend, General Dwight D. Eisenhower, Gosden learned of a man who had worked on Ike's staff in Europe during the war, who might be just right for the Kingfish role. The man was tracked down in Chicago, but proved unsuitable. A month later, both Gosden and Correll were dining with President Harry S. Truman, a great fan of the "Amos 'n'

Andy" radio show, when the subject of their unsuccessful search for a Kingfish came up. Gosden related to the President that he had tried Tuskegee Institute in Alabama, but found that the students were too young for the parts. Truman then suggested Texas State University for Negroes, but a review of available talent there also proved hopeless.

Back in Hollywood, Jim Fonda was still making inquiries about the whereabouts of Tim Moore, the black actor who everyone agreed would make the perfect Kingfish. As a last-ditch effort, Fonda decided to send a telegram to the Apollo Theatre in New York's Harlem. Lo and behold, the manager of the famed vaudeville house wired back that, as far as he knew, Tim Moore was living back in Rock Island, Illinois, his birthplace. Having retired from a long career in show business that had begun at age twelve, the sixty-two-year-old was busy enjoying his passion, fishing. But once an actor, always an actor—so when he got the call Moore sent photos of himself to Jim Fonda in Hollywood. He was so right for the part that Fonda hardly dared hope his voice would be equally acceptable. To allay his fear, Fonda asked Moore to go to the CBS station in nearby Peoria to have recordings of his voice made. They turned out to be disappointing, so Tim Moore was put on the shelf, in the hope that a better actor for the pivotal role of the Kingfish could be found.

Fonda then decided to return to New York to follow up some leads. Among those he tested on that trip were Cab Calloway and "Mr. Five by Five," a singer in Count Basie's band.

In July 1950 Fonda, having returned to the West Coast empty-handed, decided to give Tim Moore a better test at WBBM in Chicago. The audition was set for July 4. The moment Moore walked through the door, Fonda suspected he had found his Kingfish at last. The test itself proved encouraging enough to send Moore to Hollywood for a screen test and to meet Gosden and Correll.

After interviewing Moore about his background as an actor, Gosden and Correll were hopeful that their search might finally come to an end. On July 10 the all-important film tests were made with Moore as Kingfish, Alvin Childress as Amos, and Spencer Williams as Andy. They were successful and the trio of actors was signed formally to contracts, with the hope that an audition film—known as a pilot—could be produced within several months for consideration by sponsors and the CBS Television Network.

In anticipation of locating the perfect actors to portray the lead roles, Gosden and Correll put their radio writers to work shaping potential scripts, among them Joe Connelly, Bob Mosher, Arthur Stander, Harvey Helm, Shirley Illo, and Bob Ross. It was the summer of 1950—the "Amos 'n' Andy" radio show was off the air for thirteen weeks—and everyone was involved in the new TV venture. A half-dozen pilot scripts were written and rewritten under the meticulous scrutiny of Gosden and Correll, who had already spent four years dreaming of the transition. By September 22, everyone agreed that the script titled "The Rare Coin" (a.k.a. "The Rare Nickel"), by Joe Connelly, Bob Mosher, and Bob Ross, would be the perfect episode to use as a sample film.

It had been decided several months before that the series would be filmed, not telecast live. This was a departure for CBS whose existing comedies—like "Burns and Allen," "The Ed Wynn Show," "The Alan Young Show," and "The Goldbergs"—were produced live from the CBS headquarters in New York or Hollywood. Only dramas were put on film for television.

Most of the film studios in Hollywood wanted nothing to do with television, which they viewed as the ultimate competition, so CBS had a difficult time finding a location to film "Amos 'n' Andy." The Hal Roach Studios in Culver City—known for two decades as the home of Laurel and Hardy and the Our Gang troupe, among others—agreed to take on the assignment since they were already in production on "Beulah," an ABC film sitcom about a black maid, a video version of the 1945 radio series.

Under the supervision of studio manager S. S. Van Keuren, Jim Fonda was installed as associate producer to oversee the production of the pilot, with Gosden and Correll as the official producers. To direct the thirty-minute audition film, Abby Berlin, a forty-three-year-old ex-vaudevillian from New York City, was hired. Berlin had come to Hollywood in 1934 to join Columbia Pictures as a film cutter, later moving on to the sound department. He got his first chance to direct in 1944, helming the majority of the *Blondie* pictures. With the imminent release of his *Father Is a Bachelor* with William Holden, Coleen Gray, and Stu Erwin, Berlin settled into an office on the Roach lot to begin pre-production on "Amos 'n' Andy."

Casting of the supporting roles was, compared to the search for the actors to play Amos, Andy, and the Kingfish, relatively easy. The most critical female role was Sapphire Stevens, the Kingfish's wife, whom he referred to as The Battle-ax. For this pivotal role, Gosden and Correll had to look no further that the ranks of their radio version. Playing such roles as Mrs. Henry Van Porter and Sarah "Needlenose" Fletcher since 1939 was a young actress from Jackson, Mississippi, Ernestine Wade (née Jones). For many years, Kingfish's wife was only referred to on the radio show, but never heard. When she was finally written into the script for a speaking part, Ernestine was chosen to portray the sharp-voiced and shrewish Sapphire, and she was an immediate hit with radio audiences. So, with ease and with none of the frustrating aspects of the search for the male leads, Ernestine Wade signed on as Sapphire.

For the role of Algonquin J. Calhoun, the lawyer, Gosden and Correll tapped Johnny Lee, the actor who had portrayed the role on radio since October 1949. He was originally recruited after Gosden and Correll caught him in

Sugar Hill, a production that originated at an experimental theatre in Chicago and later played Hollywood for thirteen weeks. On the strength of his comic performance as Punk, the producers signed him.

As the prissy, social-climbing insurance man, Henry Van Porter, forty-nine-year-old actor and graduate of the prestigious Juilliard School of Music, Jester Hairston joined the cast of the pilot. Hairston had been appearing on the radio version of "Amos 'n' Andy" as Leroy, Sapphire's shiftless brother. Van Porter's new part had been played by Charles Correll on the radio.

The month of September 1950 was spent designing and constructing both costumes and sets, under the watchful eye of Gosden and Correll. For more than twenty years, the pair had envisioned what the Mystic Knights of the Sea's lodge hall looked like; how the Kingfish dressed; the type of hat Andy sported; etc. Now it was their responsibility to translate these visions into reality with the help of costume designer Harry Black and set designer McClure Capps. Stage 6 of the Hal Roach Studios lot was transformed into Harlem with its exterior streets, including the front of the lodge hall; and fashioned into interior settings like the Mystic Knights lodge hall, Kingfish's living room, a neighborhood drug store, and a courtroom with its adjoining hallway.

On Friday, October 6, cast and crew convened at 8822 West Washington Boulevard in Culver City—site of the Hal Roach Studios—to begin shooting the pilot, "The Rare Coin."

In this audition script, a rewrite of an "Amos 'n' Andy" radio show, Andy is in possession of a valuable nickel, worth $250 to a rare-coin dealer. Kingfish gets wind of the offer before Andy does, so attempts to steal the coin from Andy and pocket the spoils.

KINGFISH: Holy Mack'rel! Andy is got a nickel dat's worth two hundred and fifty dollars!

SAPPHIRE: George Stevens, it was bad enough openin' Andy's letter. You ain't thinkin' of gyppin' him outa dat coin, is you?

KINGFISH: Who? Me? . . . Innocent Stevens? Hah, hah, hah. I'll say I is.

As in the majority of scripts that followed, Andy and the Kingfish had more or less supplanted Amos and Andy as the central characters of the sitcom. In the pilot, the character of Amos—played by Alvin Childress—had only two brief scenes: one in the lodge hall with Andy, and the other in the courtroom, when he appears as a character witness for taxicab company partner Andy and the Kingfish. The character of Lightnin' was not introduced in the pilot and, in fact, would not be cast until the show found a sponsor and was put on the CBS fall 1951 schedule.

With rewrites being accomplished up to and including the three shooting days—Friday, October 6; Saturday, October 7; and Monday, October 9—"The Rare Coin" 's twelve-member cast worked diligently in order to complete the 26½-minute sample film on schedule and within budget, no small feat considering the complexity of their goal. This was the culmination of four years of planning and, in a way, it was a considerable gamble for Freeman Gosden and Charles Correll. Tampering in any way with a successful property always has had its pitfalls. There is no predicting what the public will respond to. The entertainment graveyard is fairly littered with examples of "sure things" that went sour. Gosden and Correll had no fewer apprehensions just because their radio show was a classic.

The pilot film, shot by cinematographers Robert De-Grasse, Lucien Andriot, and Benjamin Kline, was edited by Daniel A. Nathan with an assist from Art Seid. A musical score was added within six weeks, including the theme "The Perfect Song," taken, ironically, from the score of the racist epic *The Birth of a Nation.*

A few months later, on January 31, 1951, CBS announced officially that the "Amos 'n' Andy" show "will make its debut as a half-hour weekly television show . . . under the sponsorship of the Blatz Brewery Division of Schenley Industries. Announcement of the premiere date and time of the series, to be produced on film under the supervision of CBS, will be made later. The new 'Amos 'n' Andy' television series will be a visual adaptation of the famed radio program, with a Negro cast playing the leading roles. Freeman Gosden and Charles Correll, originators of the radio show, will aid in the production of the telecast series."

Speaking for the new sponsor, Frank Verbest, president of the Blatz Brewing Company, said in a public statement, "The Blatz Brewery is honored to bring to the growing American television audience a dramatization which has become part of the American scene. We are confident that 'Amos 'n' Andy' on television will duplicate the historic success which the show has enjoyed on radio for more than two decades."

The deal, negotiated by Blatz's advertising agency, William H. Weintraub & Co., Inc., and J. L. Van Volkenburg, CBS vice-president in charge of network sales, called for the broadcast on the full CBS Television Network (which consisted of sixty-one stations), with initial programming set for fifty-two consecutive weeks. Each episode was budgeted at $32,000.

With several scripts in inventory—those that were not shot as the pilot—the show was set to go before the cameras starting Saturday, February 24, with the production schedule calling for one half-hour episode to be completed every ten days. The staff, headed by Gosden and Correll, included James Fonda as the associate producer. He would eventually become supervising producer of the series, since Gosden and Correll were busy performing the radio version of "Amos 'n' Andy," which aired every Sunday night at 7:30 for Rexall Drug.

The key member of the staff—the director—was not signed until five days before the cameras started rolling. Abby Berlin, who had done such a masterful job helming the pilot episode, was not available to take on the weekly chores of directing a television series (he would eventually accept such a position on a 1954 series starring William Bendix, "The Life of Riley"), but luckily Charles Barton, one of Hollywood's best known and most beloved directors, was. Barton was signed on February 19, eventually directing seventy-seven episodes of the series. The forty-eight-year-old Barton had just completed a seven-year stint at Universal Studios, where he directed ten of the famed Abbott and Costello movies, including *Buck Private Come Home, The Wistful Widow of Wagon Gap, Abbott and Costello Meet Frankenstein, Mexican Hayride,* and one of the Ma and Pa Kettle films. Barton was a wiry little man who had appeared in westerns with Bronco Billy Anderson at the age of thirteen. Starting in 1919 as an office boy at Paramount, he came up the hard way, toiling as a property man, assistant director, gag writer, screenwriter, and sometime actor. He became a full-fledged director in 1937 with the Gail Patrick–Randolph Scott film, *Wagon Wheels.* Other Paramount pictures he made included *Murder with Pictures* with Lew Ayres and *The Last Outpost* with Cary Grant and Claude Rains. During a three-year stint at Columbia, he directed Frank Sinatra in his first film, *Reveille at Beverly.*

By the end of March CBS had scheduled the premiere presentation of "Amos 'n' Andy" for Thursday, June 28, at eight-thirty. Subsequent episodes would air in the time-slot throughout the summer and fall. To make way for the all-black comedy, CBS moved "The Show Goes On," a variety outing starring Robert Q. Lewis, to Saturday nights. (During its entire two-year run, "Amos 'n' Andy" enjoyed the same Thursday-night time period.)

The last regular cast member to be signed was Horace "Nick" Stewart, who was assigned the role of Lightnin', the janitor at the Mystic Knights of the Sea lodge hall. Known professionally as Nick O'Demus, Stewart had compiled a long and impressive list of credits in motion pictures, on radio, and on the legitimate stage. The thirty-six-year-old had twenty years' experience in show business, including appearances in fifty films dating back to 1937, when Mae West herself tapped him for a role in *Go West, Young Man* after seeing his comedy-dance act at the Los Angeles Paramount Theatre in 1936. "Amos 'n' Andy" was his first TV show, although he had experience on radio in such shows as "Beulah," "Duffy's Tavern," and "The Alan Young Show."

During the days of filming leading up to the premiere, the producers realized that one of their cast members had become an unofficial production aide. Spencer Williams, who was playing the title role of Andy, had been an actor, producer, and director in Negro films during the late thirties and early forties. In fact, he was partly engaged in producing such films when he was discovered in Tulsa, Oklahoma, for the "Amos 'n' Andy" role. Williams brought the benefit of his long and varied experience to "Amos 'n' Andy" script conferences and rehearsals and to the shooting of the television series. As a CBS publicity release explained, "He is an expert in the fine shadings of dialect, mood and emotional reaction of his race."

At the network's request, Gosden and Correll amassed a studio audience at Columbia Square and allowed them to watch the pilot episode in order to record their laughter and applause for the sound track. In addition, the pair introduced the audience to the actors who would be playing the regular roles. A kinescope was made of these introductions and spliced into the sample film, and then shown to the sixty-one CBS affiliates around the country. It is interesting to note the narration that accompanied the beginning of the film: "The 'Amos 'n' Andy' television show, which follows, was made on film. It was shown to a

(58)

studio audience of 500 people representing all walks of life, both white and colored. Their reactions, as they watched the film, were recorded and dubbed back into the sound track exactly as they occurred. No attempt has been made to cut any of the spontaneous reaction even though at times it seems to cover some of the dialogue."

To match the efforts expended in the massive search for the right actors to play the key roles on the series, CBS pulled out all the stops in publicizing the premiere of "Amos 'n' Andy" set for June 28. The show's sponsor, Blatz Beer, invested an unprecedented $250,000 in advance advertising, including a double-page spread in the June 25, 1951, edition of *Life* magazine that read:

MEET A LEGEND FACE TO FACE. . . .
World premiere, week of June 24th
At last, you can *see* America's most heart-warming cast of comedians in the finest entertainment television has ever produced. See them all . . . Amos, Andy, Kingfish, Lightnin', and so many other beloved characters. Tune in . . . meet a legend face to face!

Proudly presented by
BLATZ BEER . . . MILWAUKEE'S FINEST
on behalf of its dealers everywhere. Blatz Brewing Company, Milwaukee, Wis.

5

A CAST OF CHARACTERS

It was less than a week before the 1951 Fourth of July celebration that would enthrall 150 million Americans. In 10 million homes, families were already enjoying the less-than-five-year-old medium of commercial television. On June 28, on CBS, people were tuning in to such shows as "Strike It Rich" (on the air less than two months), the Steve Allen and Garry Moore variety shows, and a soap opera titled "The First Hundred Years" during the day. The evening's TV fare started off with fifteen minutes of news featuring anchorman Douglas Edwards, at 7:30, followed by "The Stork Club," a variety show hosted by Sherman

Billingsley, live from his famed Manhattan nightspot. At eight o'clock, a half-hour dramatic anthology titled "Starlight Theatre" alternated biweekly with a live version of "The Burns and Allen Show."

At eight-thirty, a new program was about to premiere, replacing a comedy-variety outing titled "The Show Goes On" (it did—on Saturday nights, until 1952). "Amos 'n' Andy," the twenty-three-year-old brainchild of Freeman Gosden and Charles Correll, had finally made it to television, the culmination of years of planning and hard work. Its competition that summer night was made up of the second half of "Stop the Music," a two-year-old game show starring Bert Parks on ABC; "Broadway to Hollywood—Headline Clues," another game show on which Eddie Fisher reportedly made his television debut, on the Du-Mont network; and "Treasury Men in Action," an anthology/crime drama on NBC. CBS and Blatz Beer had spent so much money publicizing the premiere that a huge number of people tuned in that night to see what all the fuss was about. The fuss the publicity generated was nothing, however, compared to the furor that would begin just five days after the program's debut.

On Tuesday, July 3, 1951, the National Association for the Advancement of Colored People fired its first round of protest, denouncing the show as insulting to blacks. In fact, the powerful civil rights organization had already been in federal court urging an injunction to prohibit CBS from airing the first show. At its annual convention, held in Atlanta, Georgia, in early July, the NAACP passed a resolution condemning the new television series. The resolution stated, in part: "The new television show, 'Amos 'n' Andy,' depicts Negroes in a stereotyped and derogatory manner, and the practice of manufacturers, distributors, retailers, persons, or firms sponsoring or promoting this show, the 'Beulah' show, or others of this type is condemned."

In a formal suit against the Columbia Broadcasting

System, the forty-two-year-old organization specified its objections as follows:

1. It tends to strengthen the conclusion among uninformed and prejudiced people that Negroes are inferior, lazy, dumb, and dishonest.
2. Every character in this one and only show with an all-Negro cast is either a clown or a crook.
3. Negro doctors are shown as quacks and thieves.
4. Negro lawyers are shown as slippery cowards, ignorant of their profession, and without ethics.
5. Negro women are shown as cackling, screaming shrews, in big-mouth close-ups using street slang, just short of vulgarity.
6. All Negroes are shown as dodging work of any kind.
7. Millions of white Americans see this "Amos 'n' Andy" picture and think the entire race is the same.

From the start, however, the TV show did well in the ratings, eventually ranking number 13 in the Nielsen list for the 1951–52 season, not too many rating points behind "Your Show of Shows" and "The Jack Benny Show." As is the case with most forms of popular entertainment, the so-called jury of public opinion counted most, and the consensus was that "Amos 'n' Andy" was fun and worth watching.

John Crosby, the respected TV critic for the *New York Herald Tribune,* made an interesting observation just a week after the series' debut: "Back in 1946, I wrote that 'Amos 'n' Andy' was about a characteristic of the Negro race as Al Jolson singing 'Mammy,' that it was not a Negro world but a world of blackface—a fantasy world . . . like something out of Walt Disney. Naturally, when you have to show real Negroes, show a real Harlem, quite a lot of the tinsel rubs off."

Writing about the problems "Amos 'n' Andy" encountered during its brief but heralded run on television, CBS founder William S. Paley said in his autobiography, "Here was a difference between radio and television we had not foreseen. Gosden and Correll had created a warm and funny fantasy world in the listener's imagination on radio. When that world became visual, it also became concrete and literal. . . . We soon learned that creating television programs was a dynamic art with a life of its own. Producers had to find new forms or new variations on old forms. What worked on radio or on the stage or even in the movies did not necessarily work on the small screen."

TV historians agree that few radio shows made the transition to television with any degree of success, but clearly the problems the video version of "Amos 'n' Andy" encountered upon its debut were unique; there was a dearth of black talent on the tube in 1951.

As media historian J. Fred MacDonald said in his book *Blacks and White TV*, "Television . . . had the potential to reverse centuries of unjust ridicule and misinformation. In terms of utilization of black professional talent, and in the portrayal of Afro-American characters, TV as a new medium had the capability of ensuring a fair and equitable future. This possibility was well appreciated by a black critic [Alvin E. White] who suggested in the early 1950s that 'as a new industry, TV has a great opportunity to smash many un-American practices and set new standards. Will TV meet the challenge or will it miss the boat?'"

Aside from sports presentations, news programs, and game shows, early TV was dominated by variety shows. Hungry for talent during that embryonic stage, TV programmers frequently highlighted such Negro performers as dancers, musicians, comics, and singers on a regular basis. As Steve Allen once put it, "Talent is color blind."

So bright seemed the future of television for blacks that the June 1950 edition of *Ebony* magazine featured an article that reported how many Afro-Americans were being employed in TV. The outlook was encouraging enough that the magazine contended it was "a sure sign that television is free of racial barriers." The NAACP, though discouraged by the motion picture and radio industries' lack of positive action over the proceeding years, found the state of early television equally reassuring.

Ed Sullivan, host of the popular "Toast of the Town" variety hour that debuted on June 20, 1948, was instrumental in presenting blacks to his vast nationwide audience, among them opera star Marian Anderson, jazz singers Ella Fitzgerald and Sarah Vaughn, and the Will Mastin Trio featuring a young Sammy Davis, Jr. It should be noted that in 1950 Sullivan maintained that the medium was playing an important role in helping "the Negro in his fight to win what the Constitution of this country guarantees as his birthright." A year later—only a month before the premiere of "Amos 'n' Andy" on television—Sullivan was quoted in *Ebony* as claiming that the medium was at the forefront of the Negroes' continuing struggle for civil rights, bringing it "into the living rooms of America's homes where the public opinion is formed, and the Negro is winning."

Sullivan's statement may have been a bit premature, if not overly optimistic. Television historians agree that the first black performer to host or star in a network program was pianist-singer Bob Howard, billed as "TV's jive bomber." He debuted on the CBS network on August 2, 1948, in a fifteen-minute nightly musical series titled "The Bob Howard Show," which aired weeknights at seven o'clock. The program lasted sixteen months on the air, eventually replaced by local, affiliate programming.

The most ambitious all-black TV show of the late forties era was "Sugar Hill Times," on CBS. Debuting on Tuesday, September 13, 1949, at 8:00 P.M., the live weekly variety show had a rocky history. It had the unfortunate fate of being up against the wildly successful "Texaco Star

Theatre" starring "Mr. Television," Milton Berle, on NBC (TV's number-one show for the 1949–50 season, according to the Nielsen ratings). It aired three times as a one-hour show, then was finally broadcast as a thirty-minute offering on October 6 and October 20, the victim of poor ratings. Hosted by a popular New York radio personality, Willie Bryant, "Sugar Hill Times" may best be remembered as the launching pad for newcomer Harry Belafonte. The show's dismal history can perhaps be traced to a number of problems: time-slot (against powerhouse Berle), a low budget, and faulty programming.

How could an all-black variety show—featuring lesser-known talent—compete against Uncle Miltie's star-studded hour, which often featured such black mainstays as Bill "Bojangles" Robinson, Duke Ellington, and baseball great Jackie Robinson? The October 5, 1949, edition of *Variety* criticized the network's handling of the ground-breaking program. Historian J. Fred MacDonald claimed, "If big-name guests were strategic to the popularity of 'Toast of the Town,' 'Texaco Star Theatre,' and the like, was it unrealistic of CBS to launch a black variety program in 1949 with talented, but relatively unknown, personalities? Perhaps 'Sugar Hill Times' failed as much from the legacy of stultifying, segregated American entertainment as it did from feeble budgets and suicidal scheduling. Significantly, the all-black format never reemerged in network variety programming."

During the last few months of Bob Howard's CBS show, another black singer-pianist, Trinidad-born Hazel Scott, made her debut on the DuMont network. The summer show, which went on the air on July 3, 1950, and lasted thirteen weeks, was telecast three times a week for fifteen minutes. The first network program to be hosted by a black woman featured Scott, wife of New York Congressman Adam Clayton Powell, Jr., performing café favorites and show tunes.

Less than a week after Scott's limited series went off the air, radio's popular "Beulah" sitcom came to television. The first "dramatic" series with a black lead, "Beulah," which starred actress Ethel Waters, made its bow on October 3, 1950, on the ABC Television Network. While the show featured a black actress in the title role and other black performers in supporting parts, the series starred the white Henderson family, played during the first two seasons by William Post, Jr. (Harry Henderson), Ginger Jones (his wife, Alice), and Clifford Sales (their son, Donnie). Here was a series of landmark proportions—the first to star a black actress—but, as had been the usual fate of blacks in motion pictures and on radio, it featured the stereotypical Mammies, Uncle Toms, and Coons. Beulah's employers may have been more bumbling than she, but not by much. What little dignity Waters, and then Louise Beavers, brought to the role was diminished by the repetition of such catch phrases as "Love dat man," "Somebody bawl fo' Beulah?" and "On the con-positively-trairy!"

Just as the first season of "Beulah" was coming to a close in the spring of 1951, the television version of "Amos 'n' Andy" was about to make its debut. It was a TV first: the first dramatic program with an all-black cast. Expectations were naturally high. Success would mean steady employment for a large number of Negro actors and actresses, not to mention the positive aspects of having a show on a major television network that depicted blacks in everyday life situations.

But within a month of the show's premiere, the NAACP had put enough pressure on CBS and the three other networks (NBC, ABC, and DuMont) to force the broadcasters to alter their policies regarding the hiring of black performers. In the July 19, 1951, edition of Hollywood's *Daily Variety,* under the headline WEBS QUIETLY INCREASE JOBS FOR NEGROES IN TV, it was reported that a new code of standards had been adopted by NBC, ensuring that programs "will present with dignity and objectivity varying aspects of race, creed, color and national origin." Such professional associations as the Television Authority Committee on Employment Opportunities for Negroes met with officials from the four networks "to secure representation of Negroes on television programs," but, more importantly, to ensure that such representations reflected the Negroes' "role in everyday life." It was hoped that this altruistic session would result in producers hiring more black performers—singers, dancers, specialty acts, etc., as well as Negro actors—to fill parts in dramatic and comedic properties showing their normal daily routine.

By August, members of the "Amos 'n' Andy" cast were publicly defending their work. As reported in an issue of *Quick* magazine, "Growing crisis among Negro entertainers has been set off by CBS's 'Amos 'n' Andy' show. When the NAACP branded the program a continuance of a harmful stereotype of the Negro as shiftless and amoral, the Negro cast itself defended the show and pointed out that since the NAACP's pronouncement, other shows have shied away from Negro performers for fear of similar treatment. The result of this crisis has been the formation of a Coordination Council for Negro Performers. The committee hopes to pass on what Negro entertainers should or should not do. Its first action: endorsement of 'Amos 'n' Andy.' The 'Amos 'n' Andy' situation points up the two main difficulties Negro entertainers face: 1) finding work, and 2) finding roles that do not slur their people."

However, writing in the August 23, 1951, edition of the *California Eagle,* the black paper's entertainment editor denounced the all-black TV show. Recalling "the slow and steady poison of twenty years of 'Amos 'n' Andy' on the radio," he pointed out that many "middle class and sheltered whites" would get the impression that "the happy and smiling Negro is the good Negro—the stolid, unemotional Negro is the bad kind." In closing his critique, the editor said emphatically, "To my way of thinking, the 'Amos 'n' Andy' show is not controversial. It just doesn't belong on TV or anywhere else."

The black stage and film actor James Edwards (best known for his performance in *Home of the Brave*), an outspoken champion of dignified roles for black performers, vociferously lambasted his "Amos 'n' Andy" acting colleagues by stating that "for the sake of 142 jobs which Negroes hold down with the 'Amos 'n' Andy' show, 15 million more Negroes are being pushed back twenty-five years by perpetuating this stereotype on television. The money involved (and there's a great deal) can't hope to undo the harm the continuation of 'Amos 'n' Andy' will effect. We don't have to take it, not today."

On the other hand the *Pittsburgh Courier,* a respected black periodical, defended the show's actors, saying the program "provides for the first time lucrative and continuous employment for many talented troupers who have waited a long time for this kind of open-door opportunity into the great and rapidly expanding television industry." (Interestingly, this article appeared two days before the show went on the air.)

Ernestine Wade, the actress who played the no-nonsense wife of the Kingfish, Sapphire Stevens, told an interviewer in 1973 about her association with "Amos 'n' Andy": "It was a happy experience. I know there were those who felt offended by it, but I still have people stop me on the street to tell me how much they enjoyed it. And many of those people are black members of the NAACP."

A member of the radio cast since 1939, Wade owes her career as an actress to a lonely childhood. Without brothers, sisters, or playmates around her home in Jackson, Mississippi, young Ernestine spent many solitary hours talking to her dolls, pretending they were alive. "This made me a natural mimic," she once explained. "I talked to my dolls for hours, casting my voice into their characters to answer myself. Because of this childhood game, I learned to use many types of voices and speech."

When she joined the Gosden and Correll radio show in the late 1930s, she was cast as Valada Green, Andy Brown's "sweetie-pie." Before the days of studio audiences at the radio facilities, she sometimes essayed three roles simultaneously, like Mrs. Henry Van Porter, wife of the society man, and Sarah "Needlenose" Fletcher. The role with which she eventually became associated was that of the Battle-axe, Sapphire Stevens. A role once only talked about on the radio version of "Amos 'n' Andy," Sapphire was eventually written into one of the scripts for a speaking part. Wade, already on the CBS payroll, was tapped to portray the sharp-voiced harridan with the whiplashing tongue.

Wade's pliable voice had been her biggest asset since childhood. By the age of seven, she had developed her vocal cords to a point where she was in demand as a singer at musical recitals around Jackson, Mississippi. She continued performing publicly until the age of fifteen. In the meantime, beginning at thirteen, she studied music until she became an accomplished organist and played weekly at church affairs. As a result of her diligence, her singing carried her steadily toward the "big leagues." After a few years as a chapel soloist, she joined the famous Hall Johnson Choir.

She first went to Hollywood as a legal secretary, a career she pursued occasionally until the start of the "Amos 'n' Andy" television show. Her vocal skills soon brought her a number of voice-over roles in pictures, including that of a butterfly in the classic *Song of the South.*

As "Amos 'n' Andy" was about to premiere on the tube, Wade said about her employers, Freeman Gosden and Charles Correll, "It's always been enjoyable working with them because of our easy relationship on the [radio] show, and now it's a double honor to play Sapphire on television."

The part of Sapphire was, in many ways, an enigma. Here was an attractive woman—hardworking, devoted to her husband and mother, proud, and honest—married to a man, many years older than she, who never had any visible means of income, who lied to her continually, and who called her names for the sheer sake of having *something* to say to her. What could Sapphire have seen in the Kingfish? It was obvious from her deep-rooted sense of pride that she did everything in her power to keep her end of the "marital bargain." She kept an immaculate house for her husband, treated him with respect when he deserved it, and never cheated on him. Of all the characters on the series, she was the only one to refer to him as George, never the Kingfish.

Her dream of being a member of a respectable, middle-class family was constantly being tested by Kingfish's dubious shenanigans. She never tried to impress the neighbors by pretending to be someone or something she was not, although it was clearly evident that she yearned for the kind of security her husband was incapable of providing. Sapphire tried in vain to keep George on the "straight and narrow." She was wholly supportive at the slightest indication that he might be striving to elevate the quality of their lives. But she was equally shrewish when she believed he was faltering on the brink of crookedness, something at which he was a master.

The Kingfish, as portrayed on television by Tim (Harry R.) Moore, was the scoundrel of the group, a roguish resemblance of characters once played by W. C. Fields. He was described by his creator as someone with "a twinkle in his eye, a smile on his face, and the devil in his heart . . . a fella who was always looking out after his brothers, but, first and last, after himself." Despite these negative traits, the Kingfish was the most popular figure on the program, which could have been more aptly titled "The Adventures of the Kingfish." The farcical approach taken by actor Moore included broad facial expressions, ill-fitting clothes, and an artificial booming laugh. This character, imbued with a pompous air, could spout five-dollar words with aplomb and then massacre them by a turn of a syllable.

Kingfish had no job, implying that he earned "unreported" income. The terms "lazy," "shiftless," and "crooked" could all be applied to this ne'er-do-well, but completely lovable, persona. He used his close friends as foils, pawns, and suckers. Somehow, they rarely saw beneath his flamboyant exterior. Kingfish was the big fish in a very tiny pond.

The lodge provided the man with an outlet for his self-esteem, since he was viewed generally with little more than disgust on the homefront. Actual sympathy was often aroused for the Kingfish when he was the brunt of wrath from his wife and mother-in-law.

The classic, scheming Coon character of Kingfish was an integral part of the "Amos 'n' Andy" cast, and could only have been played by a master actor. Tim Moore was born in Rock Island, Illinois, in 1888, the fifth of thirteen children. He left school when he was eleven, having, as he once put it, "excelled in nothing but recess."

He started in show business a year later when he became part of an act billed as "Cora Miskel and Her Gold Dust Twins," and immediately took off, at age twelve, on a tour of continental Europe. Nine months later, he returned to the United States and became the star of Dr. Mick's medicine show, at $8 a week (the year was 1901). Two years after that, at age fifteen, he was lured away by the bigger money he could make as a jockey. Unfortunately, he acquired "the habit of eating too much," and soon was too heavy to fit into his silks.

Young Moore decided to go home to Rock Island and settle down to a steady, respectable job. He worked in —and was fired from—every factory in town, including the plow works, sawmills, sash company, oilcloth factory, butter tub works, and others. He said he "liked to wrestle the other fellows, and it slowed down the work." A job as a waiter at the Rock Island Club lasted only one day; he spilled soup on a member.

Having a keen interest in sports, he became a boxer at seventeen. Billed as "Young Klondike," he took on all "comers" within ten pounds of his weight and managed to win most of the time. After several years in and out of boxing—and in and out of show business, too—he finally decided that footlights were easier to face than a pair of boxing gloves on an opponent.

He started his vaudeville career in a musical entitled *Rarin' to Go,* but realized his true ambition to become a comic on Broadway when he landed an important role in Lou Leslie's *Blackbirds,* which played on the Great White Way for more than five hundred performances before opening at the Moulin Rouge in Paris. After a long run in France and another two-year stint in London, Moore returned to America and formed a vaudeville team with Vivian Harris, whom he eventually married. They toured as a featured comedy act with name bands, such as Charlie Barnett, Erskine Hawkins, Jimmy Lunceford, and Louis Prima.

In 1946, at the age of fifty-eight, Tim Moore retired from show business and indulged in his passion for fishing. He made a few appearances on Ed Sullivan's "Toast of the Town" during its first two years on the air, but basically had settled into a life of leisure when he received a telegram from CBS asking him to test for the role of Kingfish.

The Kingfish's chief foil was Andrew Hogg Brown, better known as Andy. A sympathetic character, Andy was vulnerable partly because of his innate ignorance and naïveté. Of course, he cannot be depicted as being entirely innocent when he becomes embroiled in the Kingfish's tricks: The old adage "You can't cheat an honest man" may very well be applicable. Andy was not completely different from the Kingfish. He was just as determined not to work as his roguish buddy. The main difference is that Andy simply is not as clever as the Kingfish.

The area in which Andy supposedly excelled was romance. Again, his gullibility and slow-wittedness made him the perfect "fool in love." Was it black stereotyping that made the creators of the show portray this large man with the tiny derby as a smooth-talking lover? Although a seasoned skirt-chaser, Andy was a confirmed bachelor, balking loudly anytime he neared the altar.

Andy's broad facial expressions and tongue-twisting abuse of the language further made him an object of ridicule to a large segment of the viewing audience, but what most people do not know was that the actor who brought Andy to life, Spencer Williams, Jr., was about as far removed from the role he played in the seventy-eight episodes of "Amos 'n' Andy" as could be.

Born in 1893 in Vidalia, Louisiana, Williams attended Wards Academy in Natchez, Mississippi, and then enrolled at the University of Minnesota, where he studied for two years before joining the Army in 1914. His military career took him all over the world, from Fort Slocum, New York, to Honolulu, Corregidor, Japan, Russia, and back to San Francisco, and later Cheyenne, Wyoming. He was with General Pershing in Mexico for ten months, first as a bugler and later as camp sergeant major. Williams went back overseas in 1917 as an intelligence sergeant in France. After World War I, he was assigned to Columbus, New Mexico, working with a mapping party.

Discharged from the Army in 1923, Spencer came to Hollywood in a move that eventually resulted in the beginning of his long theatrical career. He started by writing continuity for two film comedies titled *The Melancholy Dame* and *Oft in the Silly Night* at the old Christie Studios. This lot stood on the same Sunset Boulevard block as CBS's West Coast headquarters, Columbia Square, where, more than two decades later, Williams uttered his first "Amos 'n' Andy" lines for the pilot.

In 1929 he turned producer on a picture called *Hot Biscuits,* which was made as a silent the same year that talkies were introduced. "I didn't make any money on it because everybody wanted to see talkies," Williams once commented. He traveled with the road show of *Hot Biscuits* and another comedy, *The Metal That Won,* a story about a golf ball (a piece of metal in the golf ball made it roll crazily, as a comedy device).

Williams began producing all-Negro cowboy pictures in 1938. These included *Bronze Buckaroo, Harlem Rides the Range, Harlem on the Prairie, Two-Gun Man from Harlem,* and *Son of Ingagi.* By 1940 he had decided to take a 16-mm projector through the South, showing his own movies. On this tour, he met William H. Kier, who was also working with motion picture equipment, and the two formed a partnership to produce all-Negro films. Together they made *Marching On,* which was shot on an Army location site in Arizona; *Of One Blood; Beale Street Mama;* a training film for the Army Air Force at San Antonio; and a film in Technicolor for the Catholic church in Tulsa. Williams was particularly proud of a movie that he made almost entirely alone in Dallas at a cost of only $6,400. It was titled *The Blood of Jesus,* and Williams wrote, directed, set the sound, and still managed to star in it.

While making movies on the road, Spencer found Tulsa to his liking and went back there in 1946, where he formed a partnership with an attorney. Together they formed a school for veterans, teaching such vocations as photography and radio. Spencer was busy with his work at the school when the CBS affiliate in Tulsa broadcast a call designed to locate Williams for the network so that he might try out for the part of Andy Brown.

Andy's business partner and friend, Amos Jones, was also a member of the Mystic Knights of the Sea, although audiences saw little of the man, presumably because he was busy earning money for the Fresh Air Taxi Company (Incorpulated) as the firm's only full-time driver. To beef up the role, the show's creators tapped actor Alvin Childress as the program's narrator. Storylines rarely were built around Amos; usually his role in an episode was to save his partner Andy from disasters instigated by the Kingfish.

Although Amos did speak in black dialect, it was not nearly as offensive as Andy, Kingfish, or lawyer Calhoun's speech patterns. Clearly, Amos was depicted as the most stable of the lodge members—with a wife and young daughter—and the smartest.

Alvin Childress, who played Amos, was born in Meridian, Mississippi. The youngest of three children, he spent a quiet and uneventful childhood with his parents—a schoolteacher and a dentist—and his two older sisters. He decided to become a doctor at an early age, so the theatre was far from his thoughts when he enrolled at Rust College in Holly Springs, Mississippi, in 1927, as a premedical student with a heavy schedule of science courses. But during the next four years, his extracurricular activities centered around campus dramatics, and when he graduated in 1931 with a B.A. and went to New York, he took with him an introductory letter to the producer of a Broadway play titled *Savage Rhythm*. His drama coach had done a pre-selling job to John Golden, the producer, and Childress got a role.

The play folded after a short run, and since no other roles were immediately forthcoming, Childress took a job with the Service Bureau for Education in Human Relations, a WPA project at Columbia University. His activities within this unit included the writing of twenty-six playlets for use in schools, each playlet being an exposition of the contribution of one of its many racial groups to the culture of the United States.

In 1935 he became associated with the Federal Theatre Project in New York as a drama coach, then became an actor himself in such productions as *Sweet Land* and *The Case of Philip Lawrence*. In 1936 he was tapped for an important role in George Abbott's *Brown Sugar* on Broadway, and two years later, he returned to the Federal Theatre to appear in a production of *Haiti*.

Between 1932 and 1938 Childress acted in five motion pictures in New York: *The Crimson Fog, Dixie Love, Harlem Is Heaven, Hell's Alley,* and *Keep Punching,* all with Negro backgrounds and players. In 1940 he appeared on Broadway again in Elmer Rice's *Two on an Island*.

Meanwhile, Childress had become associated with the American Negro Theatre, a stock company that became famous for its original production of *Anna Lucasta*. The show moved from Harlem to Broadway for two years, followed by a one-year road tour. Childress later directed a Chicago stock production of *Anna Lucasta*.

Between stage and film roles, Childress was a regular performer on radio, heard on most of the nation's most popular broadcasts. He did appear on the "Amos 'n' Andy" radio program, but when he heard about the casting of the television version in 1949, he sought out the producers and auditioned. Childress brought to the role of Amos Jones a large helping of class, although apparently he was not as "black" as the producers had envisioned for the character. Consequently, the makeup artists were instructed to darken up Childress. Keen observers of the series have been able to see clearly the line of demarcation at Childress's throat.

One of the most offensive characters on the show was lawyer Calhoun, played by actor Johnny Lee. A caricature, Calhoun came under heavy fire from black Americans who took offense at this depiction of a professional man, the only such regular in the series. Still, Calhoun was one of the most memorable characters on the show. He was a "high energy" counselor of the old school who believed his sermonizing gestures were enough to convince any jury of his client's innocence. Calhoun would resort to stretching the truth, fabricating information, and even telling outright lies when necessary. These tactics degraded him, making the character nothing more than a common shyster. In Calhoun, we had the posturing of a street-smart black man with ill-fitting clothes and a little hat whose brim was always turned upward. There was none of the refinement that one associated with those in the field of law. His fast-paced strut indicated that he loved being in the center arena, perhaps one of the reasons he chose the courtroom as his stage.

Johnny Lee, who had played the Calhoun role on radio beginning in September 1949 and also in the seventy-eight TV films, was born in Springfield, Missouri, to school-teacher parents. His itinerant father eventually settled in the town of Pueblo, Colorado, where Johnny was raised and where his show business wanderlust blossomed. A series of amateur shows proved to the young man that he liked "singin' and dancin'," and he soon joined the Nashville Students, a minstrel show that toured the West Coast for a couple of years and in which he was billed as the "child wonder/comedian."

When the road show closed, he went back to Pueblo for a short visit, but his "dancin' feet" soon carried him to Kansas City and St. Louis. He toured Midwest vaudeville circuits for three years as half of the team Lee and Perry—Lee being the funny man, Perry doing the straight lines. When Lee returned to Kansas City, he went immediately into Billy King's *Moonshines*.

Lee and a vaudeville company later opened the Lincoln Theatre in Los Angeles and played there for six months. During this period, the production drew show business figures to impromptu midnight shows. Bing Crosby, then a member of the Rhythm Boys, was a regular at these extracurricular sessions, always ready to sing at the drop of a hat. Then Lee signed for a Bessie Smith vaudeville unit, when he met a comedian named Bootsie Swan. The team of Swan and Lee became well known and for ten years the pair worked the vaudeville circuits and nightclubs. Simultaneously, Lee played his first motion-picture role in a film titled *St. Louis Blues.* He got rave notices for his performance as a bartender.

Lee's first Broadway show was a musical, *Ginger Snaps.* He appeared in Bill Robinson's *Going to Town* and was Koko in *The Hot Mikado.* He teamed with Eddie "Rochester" Anderson for a comedy takeoff on Caesar and Marc Antony. He went to Hollywood for a featured role in the film *Stormy Weather,* and later provided the voice of Br'er Rabbit in Disney's *Song of the South.*

During the war, Lee was attached to a USO unit which toured the European Theatre of Operations in a musical titled *Shuffle Along.* When he returned to the States, he worked up a production of *Sugar Hill* at an experimental theatre in Chicago and took it to Hollywood, where it ran for thirteen weeks. During this run, Freeman Gosden and Charles Correll saw him in the role of Punk and signed him for the radio role of lawyer Calhoun, which eventually led to his association with the television series.

One of Johnny Lee's associates on both the radio and TV versions of "Amos 'n' Andy" was Amanda Randolph, the actress who played the Kingfish's mother-in-law. Amanda, whose sister Lillian was also featured in the series, got her start in show business in Cincinnati when Noble Sissle came through with his stage company, *Shuffle Along,* and engaged her as a general utility hand. Prior to that, she had supported her mother and sister by playing piano in movie houses.

(78)

For Sissle, she served as secretary, top soprano, understudy for several actresses, and as orchestra leader, all for $75 a week. She left Sissle for Lucky Sambo, a burlesque troupe, with which she traveled from New York to a string of Western cities. After the tour, she became the leading lady of Harlem's Alhambra stock company.

Amanda then joined a comedy act called Scott and Whaley, which went abroad, playing London for nine months. Upon her return to the United States, she became a single for the first time, booked onto the Loew's circuit in a song-and-comedy routine. Shifting to nightclubs, she ran the Exclusive Club in Harlem with her husband for a couple of years and later did her act in the Black Cat Club.

Broadway caught her comedy routine and moved her into *The Male Animal,* in which she played Cleota, the maid. When the show left New York, she stayed on to do radio. For two-and-a-half years, she played the title role in "Aunt Jemima" and for two seasons she was Lillie in "Abie's Irish Rose." She made her TV debut on "The Laytons," portraying Martha, the cook. After a year in her own show, "The Amanda Show," she moved to Hollywood where she appeared in the 20th Century-Fox film *No Way Out* (Sidney Poitier's film debut). At this time she made her first contact with Gosden and Correll, who were casting about for both the radio and TV versions of their classic brainchild. She was immediately cast as Mama, Sapphire Steven's mother, a role that soon became synonymous with stereotypical older black women.

Mama was the Kingfish's number-one detractor. She was a no-nonsense woman who believed her lovely daughter had made a mistake by marrying the worthless Kingfish, and she took every opportunity to remind Sapphire of her blunder.

Mama occasionally lived with her daughter and son-in-law, so we could assume that she was widowed with some sort of pension. Her savings, which seemed to be meager, were stashed away, far from the ever sticky fingers of the Kingfish. In an effort to protect her daughter's interest, she was always ready to do battle with her shiftless son-in-law, and seemed to show little gratitude for his hospitality, no matter how ingenuous. When push came to shove, Sapphire's loyalty was to her "mama," not her husband. Mama was not portrayed as the classic Mammy, but she did possess all the qualities that made black women appear to be difficult to deal with. Even the Kingfish sometimes referred to her as "Old Ironsides."

Nick Stewart was born in New York City, although he went to live with his grandparents in Barbados, British West Indies, when he was only two years of age, returning to Manhattan when he was eight. After attending Public Schools 139 and 5, he got his show business start by dancing in the streets, in the days when the Charleston was the nation's biggest dance craze. He used to hang around the Hoofers' Club and watch Bill Robinson and Buck and Bubbles do their acts when he was just fourteen.

Two years later, he landed his first professional job as a chorus boy at the Lincoln Theatre. Later, in the chorus of the Cotton Club, he started experimenting with his own style of specialty dancing. "But chorus boys were supposed to be handsome," he once claimed. "I didn't fit those qualifications, so when they were picking choruses they began to include me out. They said I was a comedy dancer and should work alone. So I took the tip and concentrated on comedy specialties."

He toured the United States, doing his act with Cab Calloway, Duke Ellington, and the Mills Blue Ribbon Band, and did vaudeville with the likes of Milton Berle. He first went to Hollywood in 1933 with a Fanchon and Marco unit, and again in 1936 with Calloway, when he played the Los Angeles Paramount Theatre.

Mae West caught his act and asked him to appear

with her in *Go West, Young Man.* This was Stewart's first motion picture. Since that film was released fifty years ago, he has appeared in more than fifty films, including *Colonel Effingham's Raid, Meanest Man in the World, Heavenly Body, Cabin in the Sky, Dakota, Night Train to Memphis, Gildersleeve's Ghost, I Love a Bandleader, Down to Earth, Perfect Marriage, Follow the Boys,* and *It's a Mad, Mad, Mad, Mad World.* And like a few of his "Amos 'n' Andy" colleagues, he did one of the voices for Disney's *Song of the South,* the voice of Br'er Bear.

Stewart was in the Broadway production of *Louisiana Purchase,* reaping an enviable collection of rave notices. He landed the comedy lead in *Carmen Jones,* which played at Hollywood's Greek Theatre in the forties, and performed in the Keenan Wynn production of *Twentieth Century* at Hollywood's El Patio.

But most of Stewart's early work consisted of, in his own words, "doing the same thing on stage that Stepin Fetchit did on film. That was the only means of exposure we had."

When 1951 rolled around and Stewart was hired by Freeman Gosden and Charles Correll to play the role of Lightnin' on a new CBS television version of "Amos 'n' Andy," he was deeply involved in Los Angeles theatre. The year before, he began building Ebony Showcase Theatre, now a block-long complex at 4720 West Washington Boulevard. Starting out with only ninety-nine seats, Stewart's theatre has helped launch the careers of several major black actors, including John Amos ("Good Times"), Isabel Sanford ("The Jeffersons"), Abby Lincoln, Al Freeman, Jr., and Greg Morris ("Mission: Impossible").

"When I took the part of Lightnin', I had the Ebony Showcase," Stewart recalled in a 1984 article in the *Los Angeles Times.* "In the daytime, I played the janitor and at night I built the theatre, presenting blacks in positive roles. I was trying to erase some of that [stereotyping] then.

"I knew something had to be done. The whole black community was in the same bag. We were programmed to think of ourselves as maids and butlers. You walked into a courtroom in those days talking correctly and you lost the case. That was the way it was. . . . When I started my theatre, all you saw were the Mammies."

Television shows of the early fifties rarely depicted *real* blacks. Like any actor in the precarious business of entertainment, Stewart took the stereotypical role of Lightnin' to survive, to keep on working. "Producers never showed blacks in any other parts but the Mammies, the Lightnin's, the Nicodemuses, the servants," Stewart continues. "The only roles that we could play were these roles. At one time, a black man could not get on the stage in America in his natural face. He had to wear blackface. The black humor influence was not our concept; it was started by white minstrels. In order for us to work we had to imitate them. It was buffoonery, an image created by the white man.

"This didn't only happen in the black community. It happened in the Irish and the Jewish communities. It fits in with the whole concept of black art. One would have to understand what that is all about. The theater and the arts have been used to vilify any person and any group that it wants to destroy. For some reason, there's been fear of black people, that's why the stereotyping developed."

Today, Stewart has no real regrets. "All of my comedy has been clean," he says. "Lightnin' the character won a lot of friends. A lot of people liked him and they liked me." Stewart adds that his experience on "Amos 'n' Andy" was "not painful. Talking bad about 'Amos 'n' Andy' is like kicking your mother. I had an understanding of what I was doing. I did that in order to build the Ebony Showcase Theatre."

Each of the series' leading actors has to be credited with elevating his portrayal to the highest level possible.

That most of them were required to attend sessions conducted by white vocal coaches to learn to speak like whites-imitating-blacks—the basis on which the show originally was established—is, in itself, a phenomenon.

These performers—Alvin Childress, Spencer Williams, Jr., Tim Moore, Ernestine Wade, Amanda Randolph, Johnny Lee, and Nick Stewart—accepted roles that did, perhaps, discredit their race, but they were actors and they wanted to act. When TV's "Amos 'n' Andy" came along for them, they were happy to take the few acting assignments available. As the Academy Award–winning actress Hattie McDaniel once said, "Either I can play a maid in a movie for $700 a week, or I can be a maid for $7 a week!"

Most of the nonregular roles on "Amos 'n' Andy" were usually portrayed as middle-class blacks. They were professionals, representing the black community at its best. The pharmacists, waitresses, judges, policemen, mailmen, and secretaries did not resort to the offensive antics of the majority of the show's leading characters. The white characters were also professionals, and perhaps it was for this reason that they did not fraternize with the scruffy likes of Andy, the Kingfish, and Calhoun. Interestingly, there was never a reference to the color difference, so, on the one hand, the series may have denigrated much of the so-called black experience, but it also subtly reflected an intermingling of the two races, something that was long overdue.

Many of the characters' traits could have been incorrectly labeled as white characteristics. Kingfish, for example, mentioned the *Wall Street Journal* in one episode as if it were a part of his daily reading requirement. Sapphire, like most women of her day, always found the time to shop for a new hat. Mama coddled and defended her shiftless son, Leroy. Andy thought of himself as a "dandy." Calhoun was self-confident in his role as barrister. Henry Van Porter, ever the cultured one, always referred to his never seen wife as Mrs. Van Porter. Amos, of course, was the epitome of a hardworking middle-class American.

Nick Stewart took the Lightnin' role because "I saw it as an opportunity. I couldn't have learned without an opportunity to play these roles, but I saw how this was poisoning the black community. . . . People used to say to my children, 'Hey, let me see you talk like your daddy.' People related you to the images they'd seen on the screen."

6

WHAT'S SO FUNNY?

Several years ago, top TV comedian Flip Wilson was asked about "Amos 'n' Andy." Did he watch it? Did he like it, or did he object to it? His response: "I watched [it] when I was a child and I thought it was funny—and I didn't object to the dialect." His colleague, Redd Foxx, was asked the same question, to which he responded, "I thought it was a funny show. Tim Moore was a funny dude, the whole cast. It was a situation comedy that depicted black people. It was funny, and that's what it's all about. You're not hurting anyone."

These responses are, by no means, typical. An army of black performers—including Richard Pryor (an "outrage") and Bill Cosby ("not at all funny")—has publicly denounced "Amos 'n' Andy." Even one of the series stars, Nick Stewart, has said, "Comedy about black people is designed for us to hate ourselves and for others to hate us. Just about every time we as blacks laugh at blacks doing comedy on television, we're hating ourselves. Most of the time those actors are doing something we should hate. Laughing at black comedy is like eating rat poison and not realizing it's killing us."

Whether or not the humor of "Amos 'n' Andy" was valid is a topic for lively discussion. The seventy-eight premises presented on television could have worked just as well for any sitcom of that early fifties era, "The Life of Riley," "The Trouble with Father," "My Little Margie," even "I Love Lucy." Ethel Mertz could have found that "rare coin" that Lucy wanted to appropriate for herself, just as easily as Andy and the Kingfish. A careful study of the scripts confirms that "Amos 'n' Andy" would have been lackluster without the abominable butchering of the English language perpetrated by the Kingfish, Andy, and Calhoun.

The following is a brief exchange of dialogue from the series pilot episode, "The Rare Coin." None of the bombastic phrasing or dialect—for which the series became known—remains. See if you think it's funny:

KINGFISH: Excuse me, Andy, can't you see that I'm busy taking a blood count? One, two, three, add four, subtract two. That's the most anemic blood I've ever seen.

ANDY: Kingfish, you mean to say you're an actual doctor?

KINGFISH: Well, I haven't told anyone, but I've been taking a correspondence course in doctoring from that big medical school in Baltimore—John Mansville.

ANDY: Yeah, I've heard about that place.

Unless you are equipped with an overactive funny bone, the above exchanges are not likely to move you to convulsive laughter. The point is that without the heavy-handed phrasing and equally overdone dialect, there was very little genuine, knee-slapping humor in these scenes. The scene itself may have been funny or at least humorous, but the dialogue was weak.

However, "Amos 'n' Andy" scripts were accused of not only butchering the English language, but also of depicting incidents and characters in a demeaning manner, of stereotyping an entire race of people. In a 1952 episode titled "The Broken Clock," there were numerous scenes that would have been offensive to most sensitive black Americans. The story itself was harmless enough: While attempting to return a defective clock, the Kingfish and Andy are mistaken for government mechanics sent to a manufacturing plant to test a super-secret electronic altimeter being developed. Thinking the altimeter is the replacement timepiece, the two depart. When the FBI is called in to locate the valuable altimeter, it takes the ever sage Amos to extricate the two from a charge of espionage.

This premise was typical sitcom, and could have worked well on other half-hour comedies of the decade. But, in fact, there were far from subtle undertones that made "Amos 'n' Andy" unlike any other sitcom on television. According to civil rights organizations, various aspects of "Amos 'n' Andy" episodes bordered on racism. In viewing "The Broken Clock" segment from that standpoint, the complaints appear justifiable.

The episode opens with the Kingfish being honored by his lodge brothers at a testimonial dinner to celebrate twenty years of service to the Mystic Knights of the Sea. Lawyer Calhoun is the toastmaster about to present Kingfish with a clock as a token of the members' esteem. The lodge hall is appropriately decorated, and seated around a banquet table are the brothers, including Lightnin', dressed respectably in business suits.

As Calhoun rises out of his seat to make a perfunctory speech it is obvious that his presentation will be all buffoonery. The fact that he is a lawyer—a professional man—is all but ignored. He begins his postulating, then suddenly terminates it when he realizes that the words are part of a eulogy once delivered over the body of a departed lodge brother. Fumbling, he extracts a second scrap of paper from his coat pocket, but it turns out to be part of a stag-party monologue.

Finally, with no written speech to rely on, he says he will speak from the heart as he launches into a painfully honest description of the Kingfish. The presentation takes on the air of a sermon, with Calhoun's delivery reminiscent of a stereotypical black preacher who's threatening his congregation with hellfire and brimstone.

Were Calhoun's preachy overtones an affront to religious blacks? Or, more importantly, was the fact that Calhoun is an attorney—a profession that blacks have had to work harder than others to achieve—more insulting to struggling blacks who believe the profession demands respect?

The following day, Kingfish shows the clock to Sapphire and her mother. He laments that his lodge brothers honor him, whereas the only two women in his life ridicule and insult him. Trying to ignore the barbs, he plugs in the clock only to find that it is broken. Mama lambasts him: "That's two things around here that don't work!"

Mothers-in-law have been the long-suffering targets of jibes by comedians and comedy writers for many years. The antagonism between the Kingfish and Mama was no different. Was it because Mama had no respect for the man in whose household she sometimes resided? Was this lack of respect, coupled with her meddling in her daughter's marital affairs, part of the perpetuating myth that blacks have a matriarchal society? If it were a white household, would the relationship between the two antagonists be written exactly the same?

In the next scene, we encounter Kingfish eyeing

Andy as he tries to repair the clock. Andy's cigar is perched in the corner of his mouth, his jacket is off, and his shirt-sleeves are rolled up, almost denoting he knows what he is doing. The Kingfish is obviously pleased, until Andy acknowledges, "There were too many little wheels inside the clock." The camera pulls back to reveal the clock parts strewn all over the desk. Was Andy's ignorance amusing to the average black person who knows that the repair of timepieces should be left to experts?

The Kingfish then decides to register a complaint with the shop where the gift was purchased. When given the proverbial runaround experienced by many people who try to take advantage of a warranty, he decides to go directly to the plant responsible for the clock's manufacture in the hopes of exchanging the bad clock for one in good condition. He further suggests that Lightnin' drive Andy and him in Lightnin's car.

There is nothing really unusual about the above scene, except that Lightnin', the show's classic Stepin Fetchit character, owns his own car. And a stylish convertible, at that. Is this typical of a character who has been characterized in previous shows as lazy, inept, and, maybe, even slightly retarded? Can this inconsistency be attributed to the writers, who had little regard for logic or continuity? It borders on the bizarre that neither the Kingfish nor Andy had an automobile, yet the lowly janitor did.

Many of the "Amos 'n' Andy" shows featured white characters. The actors usually were given the roles of professionals who possessed the most outstanding characteristics. Their dialect was "straight" and their dialogue intelligent. There was nary a buffoon in the bunch. As an example of another story inconsistency, the white plant foreman whom Andy and the Kingfish encounter readily accepts the two lodge brothers as government experts sent to test a top-secret altimeter, and, yet, neither the Kingfish nor Andy's demeanor or rhetoric has changed. A black soldier, charged with guarding the installation, initially doubted their legitimate status, yet the plant foreman hardly blinked an eye.

After an exchange of dialogue, the foreman dresses Andy and the Kingfish in Eskimo-type parkas so the clock can be tested at a temperature of sixty degrees below zero. The Kingfish makes a remark about how difficult it is to get a company to live up to its "lifetime" guarantee, but he and Andy follow instructions and remain in the freezer—no questions asked—for almost a half hour.

After this credibility-stretching ordeal, the two brothers leave with the valuable altimeter, thinking it is the replacement clock. How can it be that two adult men —who obviously know how to tell time—are not able to differentiate between the two instruments? Is this an honest mistake that the average white American could make, or does it go beyond that to become a slur on the ignorance of blacks?

When Andy and the Kingfish throw the worthless "clock" in the trash the following day, Lightnin' retrieves it, thinking it is a speedometer. Were the writers aware of the inconsistency? Or were they simply concerned with moving the story along expeditiously? Like Lightnin', we have to scratch our heads and wonder.

Shortly thereafter, two government men approach the janitor outside the lodge hall and inquire as to the whereabouts of Andy and the Kingfish. Lightnin' immediately falls into his "dumb Coon" status and directs them inside. It is interesting to note that one of the government agents, presumably with the FBI, is black. Tall, well-dressed, and fair-skinned, he could be mistaken for a white man. His race was confirmed the moment the white agent ordered him to check the trash cans for the missing altimeter. Why couldn't the black agent ask the white agent to do the checking?

When lawyer Calhoun arrives, a relieved Kingfish

asks that he help get them out of the mess. Calhoun doesn't hesitate in giving a histrionic character reference, but remembers moments later to ask what charge has been brought against his two clients. The agents tell him it is "espionage," whereupon Calhoun counters with "These two fellows ain't never started a fire in their life!" Here again, a lawyer who doesn't know the difference between arson and espionage? Calhoun adds insult to injury when he walks out on his friends in desperation. There is no loyalty nor sense of friendship displayed.

Now at the agents' mercy, Kingfish loses all sense of propriety and begs not to be arrested. He explains that he doesn't want Sapphire and his mother-in-law to find out about his latest predicament. The agents react quickly, assuming the two women are accomplices to the crime.

The next scene depicts everyone being arrested. During this encounter, Mama takes every opportunity to berate the Kingfish, even threatening to do him bodily harm. Mama's attire is typically flamboyant and tasteless—another sad cliché.

In the end, a sensible Amos saves the day when he innocently asks Lightnin' for a ride and finds the altimeter in the car. It is always Amos, the compliant Uncle Tom persona, who intervenes and saves his ignorant buddies from impending disaster. Of all the regular roles, this one easily could be substituted for a white. In fact, Amos, in the person of actor Alvin Childress, had the fairest skin of the leads. Even his dialect was toned down, and much less offensive than the minstrel-like tones of the Kingfish and Andy.

As another episode, "Kingfish Gets Drafted," opens, we discover three distinguished-looking black men discussing the fact that they must "find George Stevens" in order to meet their "quota." Examining a phone book, they find a listing for a George Stevens, care of the Mystic Knights of the Sea lodge hall. Once these men are satisfied that they have located the elusive Stevens, we learn that they are members of the local Selective Service board.

In the meantime, the viewers know that the George Stevens they really want is actually an ambitious nineteen-year-old who is employed as a clerk. Mistakenly, the Selective Service sends the draft notice to the Kingfish.

Andy and the Kingfish are engrossed in a game of chess when Lightnin' brings in the morning mail. As Andy turns to acknowledge Lightnin', the Kingfish naturally uses the opportunity to cheat Andy by making several dishonest moves across the board.

Lightnin' comments that there are little "windows" on some of the envelopes, a statement which is in keeping with his Coon character. This incident only heightens the inconsistency related to Lightnin's character: Would a man who owns and drives a nice car not recognize a business letter?

The Kingfish trashes the letters one by one, since most of them appear to be overdue notices from creditors. Stopping for a moment to ponder, he retrieves from the wastepaper basket the envelope from the federal government. Even though he has a "funny feeling" about the letter before reading its contents, he refuses to actually read it in the normal sense. Instead, he lays it upside down on the table and peeks at it. When he has successfully interpreted the word "Greetings," he assumes it is a mistake. At best, the Army could want him only as an air warden. No, the letter confirms, he must report for active duty in a few days.

Disheartened and confused, he breaks the news to Sapphire, but as fate would have it, she is elated and proud of her husband, the "hero." Kingfish's patriotism actually moves her to tears, so he accepts the fact that he will have to join the service.

The following day when he calls to find out where he should report, he is told of the error. Now the Kingfish does not want to face Sapphire and Mama with the news, so he begs the Army to take him, but they refuse.

After Sapphire throws a surprise going-away party for him—with Calhoun and the foppish Henry Van Porter in attendance—Kingfish beefs up his efforts to join some branch of the military, only to be refused by each. One doctor cannot find a pulse, and another cannot elicit a jerk response, no matter how hard he pounds on a Kingfish knee.

In desperation, Kingfish confides in Andy, who suggests that he pretend he is going away to Fort Bragg, North Carolina, but instead move into the basement at the lodge hall. All goes well until a teary Sapphire shows up at the Mystic Knights headquarters a week later, complaining that she hasn't heard from her husband and is so concerned that she is going to North Carolina to find him.

Andy alerts the Kingfish, and the two decide that Kingfish must make an appearance in order to convince Sapphire not to make the trip south, and, worst of all, learn the truth.

Part of the Kingfish's inherent charm is his ability to be unaware of his foolish appearance. True to form, the writers attire Kingfish in a World War I outfit, saddling him with rifles, swords, and various survival equipment, and he arrives home just in time to waylay Sapphire and Mama. He admits that he returned to save them from making the long trip. Mama is immediately suspicious, looking at her gullible daughter with pity. Not wanting to make waves (although this is a little out of character), she says nothing, even when Sapphire wonders aloud how the Kingfish knew they were on their way to visit him. Sapphire dismisses her doubts, caught up in the joy of seeing her ever loving husband.

While enjoying a splendid dinner, wife and mother-in-law hang on every word their soldier-boy Kingfish has to say. The storytelling is interrupted briefly when the telephone rings. Kingfish continues to hold his mother-in-law's attention, as Sapphire takes the call in the bedroom. When Sapphire learns the sad truth from an Army official, she first calls in her mother to tell her. The two women grab vases as weapons and then call in the unsuspecting Kingfish. He enters, shutting the door behind him, and the next sound we hear is the crash of glass, presumably over Kingfish's head.

The episode typifies the matriarchal shrew wife stereotypes long associated with black women. Even domestic violence, another cliché, was introduced here—an aspect mostly missing in domestic comedies featuring white actors. It was confirmed in this and nearly every other episode of the series that Sapphire was the classic fishwife.

A further point needs to be addressed about the costuming. Mama's "taste" in clothing, especially hats, was reflective of a long-standing myth about black women who put on a "false front." Mama wore a ratty fur wrap, no matter what season, and plopped hats on her head like ersatz crowns. Was this truly indicative of her need for "upward mobility," or was it just part of the race's alleged ignorance of tastefulness?

At the Kingfish's going-away party, lawyer Calhoun did his characteristic posturing. The disbarred barrister character would have been perfect for a minstrel show. Were the writers constantly maintaining that black professionals were just as unqualified as the "Coons"? Then there is the matter of Henry Van Porter, the foppish, effeminate "rich" man. By today's standards, he would have been labeled as gay. The fact that he had a wife, although she never appeared on the TV program, made no difference one way or the other. Although his character was not stigmatized by an outrageous dialect, Van Porter made a mockery of blacks who even attempted to practice social graces. How many young people watching "Amos 'n' Andy" would want to emulate Van Porter, despite his appearance of affluence? With all his money, his choice of clothing was poor, and his pince-nez ostentatious. This prissy character, despite the apparent financial security, could gain little respect from viewing audiences, especially impressionable young blacks.

On the positive side, the Stevenses' home was presented in a responsible light. The Harlem apartment was clean and cheery, a departure from the ghetto life sometimes portrayed on today's sitcoms. Was this "wishful thinking" on the part of the writers? Or was it ignorance of the true black experience? Or was it, in fact, really the way some blacks lived in the fifties?

In one of the last episodes produced in 1953, "The Invisible Glass," Kingfish is told by a respectable black businessman that stock he purchased at $5 a share has increased in value to $100 per share, and that he represents a client who wants to buy out the stockholders in order to effect a takeover of the company.

The anxious Kingfish says he will be in touch once he picks up the stock certificates, knowing full well he once sold the five shares to Andy for $20 per unit. With a potential of $500 looming in front of him, Kingfish devises a scheme to dupe Andy out of the stock without paying a cent for them. He tells his gullible friend that the police are arresting all the stockholders and, in order to avoid trouble, he should give the certificates back to the Kingfish. Andy immediately agrees, hoping to avoid problems with the law. Just as he is about to make the transaction, his partner, Amos, enters the picture. Sensing that the Kingfish is up to something, Amos asks Andy to explain the circumstances. It doesn't take long for the sage Amos to figure out that the scheme is a ruse to get the stock out of Andy. Though he is never truthful about the reason for wanting the stock, the Kingfish is forced to offer cash for the five shares, although Amos doesn't believe the amount is fair. When Amos forces him to refund Andy's original purchase price of $100, Kingfish turns on his heels, calling the insightful cab driver a "troublemaker."

Pondering his predicament, Kingfish arrives home only to overhear his mother-in-law tell Sapphire about her savings account. Brightening at the prospect of getting his hands on the needed funds to buy out Andy, Kingfish enters the apartment and makes a phony phone call during which it is described that the very same bank is going bankrupt, and that all depositors should withdraw their funds at once. Mama is too smart, however, to fall for any of Kingfish's schemes, leaving him with no other alternative than to hatch another scheme to get the stocks from his pal Andy.

With the aid of the nefarious Calhoun, Kingfish sets up a fake research lab in the lodge hall. When Andy arrives, he is convinced by the Kingfish that he has invented a formula for invisible glass, a surefire moneymaker. He offers to sell shares in this new venture to his faithful lodge brother, who immediately jumps at the chance to invest.

When Andy returns to the Fresh Air Taxi Company office, holding a piece of the "glass," Amos convinces him that the Kingfish is up to his old tricks. When an irate Andy returns to the lodge hall, coward Calhoun deserts his co-conspirator Kingfish, once again making the point that blacks possess little sense of loyalty.

As the seasons progressed, the shows became less leaden with stereotypical situations and characterizations. "The Invisible Glass" segment, for example, was much less offensive to black viewers than the earlier shows produced in 1951 and 1952.

"The Christmas Story," an episode that aired originally on December 25, 1952, had all the makings of a classic. The storyline itself was basic, and could have been utilized on any other sitcom of the day: Low on cash to buy a decent Christmas present for his goddaughter, Arbadella (Amos's young offspring), Andy takes a one-day job at a local department store, playing Santa Claus, to earn enough money to buy the child the gift she dreamed about —a beautiful doll. The thirty-minute episode was as touching as it was tasteful, culminating in Amos's reading of and interpretation of the Lord's Prayer, against the musical background of Malotte's "The Lord's Prayer." This was the first time that the Lord's Prayer scene was televised, having been a yearly tradition on the "Amos 'n' Andy" radio show since December 24, 1930.

The following conversation took place between Amos and his daughter Arbadella in the youngster's bedroom on Christmas Eve:

ARBADELLA: I've been saying the Lord's Prayer with Mommie. What does the Lord's Prayer mean, Daddy?

AMOS: The Lord's Prayer? Well, darlin', I'll 'splain it to you. It means an awful lot, and with the world like it is today, it seems to have a bigger meaning than ever before.

ARBADELLA: But what does the Lord's Prayer really mean, Daddy?

AMOS: Now, you lay down, and you listen. The first line of the Lord's Prayer is this: "Our Father which art in Heaven"—that means Father of all that is good— where no wrong can dwell. Then it says—"Hallow'd be Thy name"—that means, darlin', that we should love an' respect all that is good. Then it says—"Thy kingdom come, Thy will be done, on earth as it is in Heaven"—that means, darlin', as we clean our hearts with love, the good, the true, and the beautiful, then Earth where we are now will be like Heaven.

ARBADELLA: That would be wonderful, Daddy.

AMOS: Then it says—"Give us this day our daily bread"— that means to feed our hearts an' minds with kindness, with love an' courage, which will make us strong for our daily task. Then after that, the line of the Lord's Prayer is—"An' forgive us our debts as we forgive our debtors"—you 'member the Golden Rule?

ARBADELLA: Yes, Daddy.

AMOS: Well, that means we mus' keep the Golden Rule and do unto others as we would want them to do unto us. And then it says—"and lead us not into temptation, but deliver us from evil"—that means, my darlin', to ask God to help us do, an' see, an' think right, so that we will neither be led nor tempted by anything that is bad. "For thine is the Kingdom, the Power, and the Glory forever. Amen." That means, darlin', that all the world an' everything that's in it, belongs to God's kingdom—everything—Mommie, your Daddy, your little brother and sister, your gran'ma—you an' everybody—and, as we *know* that, an' act as if we know it, *that,* my darlin' daughter, is the real spirit of Christmas.

By the time this episode had aired in late 1952, and despite an Emmy nomination for Best Situation Comedy for the 1952 season (it lost to "I Love Lucy"), enough strong protests had been waged by important black leaders and by civil rights organizations such as the NAACP that CBS began to realize that keeping the show in production for a third season (1953–54) would be foolhardy. So the giant broadcasting network quietly commenced plans to cancel one of its first hits.

7

THE CONTROVERSY CONTINUES

After finishing in the number 13 spot on the Nielsen ratings list for the 1951–52 season, "Amos 'n' Andy" returned to the air for the fall season on October 2, 1952, with new episodes. Contrary to popular belief, it was not "I Love Lucy" that began the practice of rerunning episodes. As early as the summer of 1952, repeats of "Amos 'n' Andy" episodes were airing on CBS, much to the collective consternation of ten network affiliates like WTMJ–TV in Milwaukee, home of the series' sponsor, Blatz beer. The station threatened to pull "Amos 'n' Andy" off the air entirely, unless new episodes were made available by the sponsor.

Acceding to pressure, Blatz dropped the "experiment" and began airing only new filmed episodes by August.

Since the original contract for the series called for fifty-two consecutive weeks of shows beginning June 28, 1951, some twenty-six hours of "Amos 'n' Andy" adventures already had been unreeled in the first twelve months. With little backlog of segments as the second season began, CBS decided to alter the schedule for the sitcom by alternating it—on Thursdays at eight o'clock—with a new half-hour anthology program titled "Four Star Playhouse." So, when "Amos 'n' Andy" "returned" for the fall (although it really hadn't gone away during the summer months), it was on every other Thursday night.

Its first fall outing, which aired October 2, was titled "Arabia"; the next episode, telecast October 16, was "Kingfish Sells a Lot"; and the month's output of "Amos 'n' Andy" ended on the thirtieth with "The Race Horse," all of them filmed during the summer at the Hal Roach Studios in Culver City, California. The alternating-weeks schedule continued for the duration of the 1952–53 season with "Four Star Playhouse" (starring Dick Powell, Charles Boyer, David Niven, and Ida Lupino) sharing the time-slot.

There was a decided drop in the popularity of the show by October. NBC had a foothold on Thursday night audiences, leading off with Dinah Shore's fifteen-minute songfest and the popular "Camel News Caravan"—both lead-ins for Groucho Marx's super hit "You Bet Your Life" at eight o'clock. The half-hour "Treasury Men in Action" on NBC—which was the direct competition of "Amos 'n' Andy"—built up even further the audience captured earlier in the evening, until "Dragnet," Jack Webb's top-rated police drama, came on the air at nine and literally destroyed the competition on CBS, ABC, and DuMont.

Perhaps the public—which had taken to its bosom the Amos and Andy characters since 1928, almost a quarter of a century—was finally growing tired of their antics. The radio version, once a daily mainstay, was still on the CBS radio network, but only in a once-weekly format, every Sunday night at seven-thirty. Even that audience was beginning to dwindle, as was the general audience for *all* radio shows now that television had taken over as the new entertainment medium. It wouldn't be too long before the Gosden and Correll creation would become "The Amos 'n' Andy Music Hall," featuring the pair as disc jockeys, spinning popular records and performing in short comedy sketches, supposedly emanating from the mythical Grand Ballroom of the Mystic Knights of the Sea lodge. A far cry from the show's early years, when Gosden and Correll delighted audiences with their down-home character comedy every evening at seven o'clock.

A far-reaching campaign launched by the NAACP from the show's inception on television encouraged viewers and other sympathetic citizens to stop buying Blatz beer, a product of the show's Milwaukee-based sponsor. The effort paid off: By April 1953, Blatz had withdrawn its sponsorship of the sitcom, leaving CBS with a convenient reason for dropping the show. The network's Continuity Acceptance Board made a public statement that said simply, "The network has bowed to the change in national thinking."

The April 17 edition of *TV Guide* carried the following item, "No replacement set by CBS for 'Amos 'n' Andy' which vacates the network in June. 'Four Star Playhouse,' now alternating each week with 'Amos 'n' Andy,' goes weekly in September."

During the spring, such episodes as "Seeing Is Believing" (which introduced the rotund Gribble Sisters), "Andy Falls in Love with an Actress," "Kingfish at the Ball Game," and "Sapphire's Sister" aired—some shot just a month or so before air date, others the previous summer.

Although the final CBS ax had fallen, "Amos 'n' Andy" was far from being dead. With sixty-five episodes already in the can—a few of which would air up to June 11, 1953, the series' last network broadcast date—CBS Films, Inc., the syndication arm of the William Paley–operated broadcasting web (now known as Viacom), decided to order thirteen additional half hours (at a cost of $35,000 per episode) to add to the "Amos 'n' Andy" syndication package, making a total of seventy-eight segments that would be made available immediately to stations across the country. In fact, by August, all of the episodes were completed and licensed to various stations to begin airing in the fall. Even some CBS affiliates—disappointed with the network's decision to program the three-year-old "Gene Autry Show" in the eight o'clock spot on Tuesday nights opposite NBC's powerhouse variety show with Milton Berle and Du-Mont's "Life Is Worth Living," starring Bishop Fulton J. Sheen—opted instead to run "Amos 'n' Andy" repeats for their audiences.

Although CBS never revealed the reason for cancelling the show, the NAACP had waged a strong-willed campaign for better depiction of blacks in radio, motion pictures and, later, television. Its longtime chairman, Walter White, had been instrumental in toning down racially objectionable scenes in countless films. He also, however, made many enemies among Hollywood's black acting community by not lending his and the NAACP's support to such black films as *Stormy Weather, Hallelujah!,* and others in which blacks justifiably took pride, but all of which White considered segregationist.

It is well known that he infuriated a large segment of blacks in Hollywood for his part (putting pressure on Blatz, Inc.) in forcing "Amos 'n' Andy" off the air. As *Variety* once reported in an article about the Negroes' struggle for equality in films, "Black actors wanted the jobs the show provided, but White objected to the stereotyping—a classic example of the east coast/west coast schism within the NAACP over the relative importance of jobs or images."

When the NAACP was stepping up its efforts to get CBS to cancel "Amos 'n' Andy" by putting pressure on the Federal Communications Commission to enforce its recent (1952) edicts, Gosden and Correll were reportedly disappointed and hurt by the protests. Until his death at the age of eighty-three in 1982, Freeman Gosden refused to talk publicly about the show and its fate. One "Amos 'n' Andy" fan from California, who was privileged to interview Gosden on several occasions, says, "It bothered him the rest of his life that 'Amos 'n' Andy' fell from public esteem."

When the television program first came under fire only a week after its premiere in 1951, Gosden defined his brainchild by saying, "Both Charlie [Correll] and I have deep respect for black men. We felt our show helped characterize Negroes as interesting and dignified human beings."

In the year of his death, 1972, Charles Correll was asked by a Chicago newspaper reporter whether the program poked fun at black people. "We weren't kidding race," Correll explained. "We were kidding people—human nature—things that happened to anybody and everybody. The show was clean. It had no violence. Our characters tried to depict cross sections of life. Everybody knew a wheeler-dealer like Kingfish, living off his wits; a blustering Andy, who never learned from experience. I knew a lot of people like that—they were relatives of mine."

Interestingly, when "Amos 'n' Andy" departed network television in 1953, it was followed closely by the demise of "Beulah," another sitcom that had come under fire by civil rights groups from the time it went on the air in the fall of 1950. With both shows gone, television was left with few shows that featured black actors. There was a handful of series that depicted black characters—but only in supporting roles—like "The Jack Benny Show," featuring Eddie "Rochester" Anderson; "My Little Margie," with

Willie Best as the elevator operator Charlie; and "The Stu Erwin Show," also with Best, this time playing handyman Willie. As the fall of 1953 got under way, a new passel of programs premiered, but only one introduced a black character of any note. To play the part of Louise, the maid on Danny Thomas's new ABC sitcom, "Make Room for Daddy," producers cast Amanda Randolph, who had just come off a two-year stint playing Mama on "Amos 'n' Andy." But these four shows, employing three actors, represented only minor employment for the Negro.

Major black entertainers like Sammy Davis, Jr., Mahalia Jackson, Louis Armstrong, Lena Horne, and Harry Belafonte continued to be highlighted on variety shows such as "Toast of the Town," the daytime "Garry Moore Show," "The Jackie Gleason Show," "Texaco Star Theatre," and "Arthur Godfrey and His Friends," which regularly featured an integrated male quartet known as The Mariners. But these appearances were not a departure; they had been ongoing since 1948.

The television anthology—which gave TV in the fifties the label "The Golden Age"—was a broadcasting staple by 1955, with no fewer than twenty thirty-minute and one-hour dramatic programs on the air. These shows ("General Electric Theater," "Goodyear Television Playhouse," "Alcoa Hour," "Studio One," and "Fireside Theatre") provided needed employment for hundreds of actors and technicians. Negro performers like Sidney Poitier and Ossie Davis cut their teeth on such TV offerings as "The Man Is Ten Feet Tall" and "The Emperor Jones," respectively. Unfortunately, fewer than fifty blacks received these acting assignments over the course of half a decade.

The true breakthrough—after the cancellation of the all-black "Amos 'n' Andy" show in 1953—came on Monday, November 5, 1956, when the National Broadcasting Company premiered "The Nat King Cole Show," starring the well-known vocalist who had four number-one (according to *Billboard* magazine) hits—"Too Young," "Nature Boy," "For Sentimental Reasons," and "Mona Lisa." Cole held a unique position in the entertainment world—his appeal crossed racial lines. Whenever he appeared on the television variety shows of the era, like "Toast of the Town" and "The Jackie Gleason Show," he was warmly received. If there was ever a black performer who was going to succeed as the star of his own variety show, then it was certain to be Nat King Cole.

When the show went on the air and for the next eight months, it was telecast for only fifteen minutes once weekly, just preceding NBC's nightly news broadcast headed by the new team of Chet Huntley and David Brinkley. (On the remaining week nights, Jonathan Winters, Dinah Shore, and Eddie Fisher warmed up in the TV bullpen.) Cole's competition was "Bold Journey," a program that featured "home movies" of far-off expeditions on ABC, and "The Adventures of Robin Hood," starring Richard Greene on CBS. Most weeks, Nat King Cole rarely attracted more than 12 percent of the potential audience, losing consistently to the Merry Men of Sherwood Forest. On the average, Cole captured only 19 percent of the viewing audience, compared to "Bold Journey"'s 21 percent and "Robin Hood"'s whopping 50 percent.

It wasn't long before the show's alternating sponsors, Rise shaving cream and Arrid deodorant, decided to bail out, leaving NBC with two choices: cancel the groundbreaking program or air the show on a "sustaining" basis, that is, pay for the air-time themselves. The network decided to stick to their "experiment," even expanding the show in July 1957 to a full half hour. But when the program resurfaced on Tuesday, July 2, at ten o'clock, it was up against another CBS hit, "The $64,000 Question," then the fourth most popular show in the land. If the going was rough against "Robin Hood," it was downright impossible against the Revlon-sponsored, big-money game show.

To shore up the sagging status of his show, Cole's show business friends magnanimously offered to appear on future shows for minimum talent fees, often the least amount the union would agree to. For approximately $250, nearly every black musical artist showed up at one time or another, including Count Basie, the Mills Brothers, Cab Calloway, Harry Belafonte, Pearl Bailey, Mahalia Jackson, Billy Eckstine, and Sammy Davis, Jr. Nat's white "show biz" cronies offered to help, too: Mel Torme, Tony Martin, Tony Bennett, Frankie Laine, Julius LaRosa, Peggy Lee, Robert Mitchum, Stan Kenton, to name a few. Ratings did improve. The August 6 stanza of the show, featuring calypso-exponent Harry Belafonte, landed the show within three ratings points (according to Trendex) of "The $64,000 Question."

But ratings weren't Cole's only concern; still no sponsor could be attracted to underwrite the cost of the show and its NBC air-time. When an advertiser came forward willing to buy the time-slot, NBC was forced to schedule a new western, "The Californians," for premiere September 24, 1957.

Never-say-die, NBC rescheduled "The Nat King Cole Show," for a half hour on Tuesdays at 7:30 P.M., hoping to sell the show on a barter basis to individual sponsors in various cities. For example, in Los Angeles, Gallo wine and Colgate toothpaste underwrote the show; in San Francisco its underwriter was Italian Swiss Colony wine; and in New Orleans, Regal beer paid the bills. Unfortunately, the cooperative advertising scheme was not profitable; only twenty-five sponsors were signed in the seventy-six cities in which the show was carried. After fifty-nine consecutive weeks, "The Nat King Cole Show" was dropped, the last telecast dated December 17, 1957.

In the February 1958 issue of *Ebony* magazine, Cole responded to questions about NBC's decision: "They wanted me on the network; they wanted to keep me. But they had to shift me around because I didn't have a network sponsor, and shows with single, network sponsors get preferential treatment." Cole had fewer kind words about the advertising community, which he felt did not try to sell the show to major accounts. "Madison Avenue, the center of the advertising industry, and their big clients didn't want their products associated with Negroes. . . . Madison Avenue said I couldn't be sold, that no national advertiser would take a chance on offending Southerners."

In the final analysis, Cole refused to blame the cancellation of his shows on Southerners. "After all, Madison Avenue is in the North. . . . I think sometimes the South is used as a football to take some of the stain off us in the North."

As for the impeachable "Amos 'n' Andy," in its fourth year of domestic syndication, business was excellent. CBS Films, Inc., reported that the vintage series' ratings had not suffered as a result of the cancellation by CBS Television in 1953; that in their fifth, sixth, and seventh runs in certain cities, the programs were continuing to draw huge audiences, larger than those during the series' second season (1952–53).

While the NAACP may have been successful in putting pressure on the program's original sponsor, Blatz, Inc., and on CBS, finally getting the show cancelled, there was little effort after 1955 to continue the public-relations campaign. It was in that year that Roy Wilkins took over as president of the NAACP, putting racial discrimination in Hollywood on the back burner while focusing the civil rights organization's attention on the explosion of black causes elsewhere in the country.

On February 22, 1956, a critic in *Variety* wrote a scathing review of the "Amos 'n' Andy" reruns, attacking it as a daily reminder of "discarded and dated" minstrelsy, "invented by white plantation owners to make them feel benevolent toward their picturesquely slaphappy, indolent, craps-shooting, lovable, no-account field hands who wouldn't be able to make a living but for the white man."

The relentless campaign against such black series as "Beulah" and "Amos 'n' Andy" waged by the NAACP and other civil rights organizations since 1950 may have unintentionally done more harm than good. A survey in *Variety* showed that in 1959 job opportunities for blacks had hit rock bottom. Concentrating on nonacting employment, the hard-hitting article reported that of the 1,100 members of the Screen Directors Guild, none was black; of the 182 members of the Screen Producers Guild, none was black; of the 1,414 members of the Motion Picture Film Editors, none was black; of the 130 members of the Script Supervisors Guild, none was black; of the estimated 250 members of the Radio and Television Directors Guild, only one was black; of the 16,500 members of the International Alliance of Theatrical Stage Employees, less than a dozen were black; and that of the 1,100 members of Hollywood's National Association of Broadcast Employees and Technicians, only 6, at most, were black.

A similar bleak picture was painted for black actors, for whom opportunities had fallen off dramatically. The same *Variety* article reported that SAG (Screen Actors Guild, the talent union that, in those days, governed both movies and television) board member William Walker "pointed out that while in 1945 there were more than 500 Negroes in SAG and Screen Extras Guild, the number had fallen, by January 1 of last year [1958], to an estimated 25 in SAG and 125 in SEG, a total of 150, or only 30% of the former membership. This during the concurrent rise of overall membership since the advent of TV."

The election of John F. Kennedy in 1960 proved to be the impetus that propelled the NAACP to reassert its activist position. On November 17, 1961, representatives of the civil rights organization met with Hollywood industry leaders to discuss increased participation by blacks in the film and television industries. Following these "lively discussions," the NAACP issued a statement saying that the "general understanding was enunciated in which the industry committed itself to a policy of consciously striving to present the Negro as he appears in American life."

The industry, however, appeared to be short on memory, and the NAACP short on patience. Less than two weeks after the meeting, the local president of the NAACP, Edward Warren, threatened to picket theatres and TV studios if discriminatory hiring practices were not ended "in the very near future. The unions blame the producers for not wanting to hire Negroes and the producers blame the unions." Vowing to investigate the problem, Warren assured the industry, in an article in *Variety,* that the NAACP had run out of patience with "broken promises" and that "we are no longer interested in what they promise in the future. We want action now."

No pickets were posted until five months later when a small band of black activists, carrying signs saying GIVE THE NEGROES IN HOLLYWOOD A BREAK, picketed the Academy Award ceremonies at the Santa Monica Civic Auditorium.

Later that year, a Congressional investigation, spearheaded by black Representative Adam Clayton Powell (New York), was convened to probe the "color line" in Hollywood. Sidney Poitier, appearing as a witness before the committee, said, "I'm probably the only Negro actor who makes a living in the motion picture industry which employs thirteen thousand performers. . . . It's no joy being a symbol."

Poitier's compatriot, satirist Dick Gregory, told the committee that "the only TV show that hires Negroes regularly is Saturday Night Boxing." Top echelon executives from the three TV networks testified that they were nondiscriminatory in hiring and that they were working to improve the images of blacks that they broadcast.

Image was still an important element of the struggle. Similar concerns were voiced in 1962 by the Italian Antidefamation League, which took offense at the depiction of Italian-Americans on the ABC police drama "The Untouchables." The group claimed that the program, produced by Desilu, fostered the false image that all Italians were members of the Mafia. Privately, Al Capone's son, Sonny, fired off a letter to his old Miami school chum, Desi Arnaz, demanding that the studio ease up on its depiction of Italians—most notably his own father, who had served a term in prison for tax evasion. The use of violence on "The Untouchables" was challenged also by other concerned groups, so by the time the program returned for its fourth season on ABC, it was a watered-down version of its former hit self.

At the same time as the Congressional investigation, the New York State Division for Human Rights raised, with TV executives and producers, the problem of a dearth of blacks on television. The television faction promised to "take the matter under advisement," but it would be two years before a black appeared in a national commercial and three years before a Negro starred in a major TV series. The black American was surely the "invisible man" on television. Consider an incident that happened in Harlem in 1963. A civil rights organization offered neighborhood children one silver dollar for each black face they could spot on TV (no baseball players included). Over a period of six Saturday afternoons, the organization paid out only $15.

Back in Hollywood, a front-page story in the March 18, 1963, edition of *Daily Variety* reported that the Screen Actors Guild had asked producers for "rigid guarantees against discrimination in the hiring of actors" because of race, creed, color, or national origin in the opening rounds of contract negotiations with producers. SAG also asked for enforcement of such guarantees by an arbitration board empowered to assess damages, the first time it had sought such contractual guarantees. Six weeks later, an agreement "in principle" had been reached on SAG's proposals.

In May the federal government got into the act when Attorney General Robert Kennedy called in executives from forty theatre chains and organizations to urge them to integrate theatres in the South.

By June the struggle in Hollywood had heated up to a fevered pitch. James Tolbert, president of the NAACP Hollywood branch (formed the year before), called the previous year's meeting with studio heads unsuccessful, noting that "the many promises made to us at that time have not been kept." Before the month was over, Herbert Hill, the organization's national labor secretary, was dispatched to Hollywood to "get tough." NAACP ULTIMATUM TO HOLLY-WOOD read the front-page headline in the June 26 *Daily Variety*.

Hill, who would play a key role in the struggle in Hollywood for years to come, said at the time that twenty-five years of film industry negotiations had been an "exercise in futility" for the NAACP and had resulted in "no tangible gains." Hill delivered a strong, two-part ultimatum to the industry, threatening to instigate decertification proceedings against Hollywood's unions with the National Labor Relations Board unless corrective measures were taken to integrate the unions, and threatening to launch a wave of protest demonstrations against the film and TV studios if progress was not made "within a reasonable time."

Charging that the image of blacks on film and television continued to be that of a "menial" and of an "outgrown stereotype," and that, in most cases, blacks were "simply not there [on film] at all," Hill cited a recent survey that revealed that less than one percent of the membership of Hollywood's behind-the-scenes unions were black, and that many of the locals were "lily white."

Discrimination in the entertainment industry peaked on July 12, 1963, when, in a speech to the American Civil Liberties Union in Beverly Hills, actor Marlon Brando said that "actors should stand together and pledge not to support production companies which uphold principles of segregation. There is a lot of muscle represented by stars, if only because of the money involved, and if every star gets together and says 'that's it,' that would be the end of discrimination in our industry."

The following month, more than fifty Hollywood notables flew to Washington, D.C., to take part in the civil rights march on the Capitol and to hear Dr. Martin Luther King deliver his impassioned "I have a dream" speech on the steps of the Lincoln Memorial. Those in attendance included Gregory Peck, Paul Newman, Sidney Poitier, James Garner, Joanne Woodward, Diahann Carroll, Charlton Heston, Tony Curtis, Sammy Davis, Jr., Harry Belafonte, Rita Moreno, Robert Ryan, and Anthony Quinn.

Ironically, *TV Guide* would call the 1963–64 television season "The Year of the Negro," even though racial strides had been minuscule. In its July 3, 1964, edition, Richard Gehman wrote: "Despite the fact . . . that more Negroes worked in the medium in acting jobs as well as variety bits than ever before in history, Negroes still are not convinced that enough progress toward integration is being made." A search of broadcast schedules for that season turned up only one new series that featured a black performer, "East Side/West Side" with George C. Scott and Cicely Tyson. The few others that featured blacks in supporting roles were longtime hits like the Jack Benny and Danny Thomas programs.

Large numbers of black actors could be watched on a daily basis on no fewer than 218 television stations in the

United States in 1964 that carried reruns of "Amos 'n' Andy," which the NAACP now, more than ever, wanted off the air. Another civil rights organization, the National Urban League, issued the following statement that year: "The show depicts the Negro as a foot-shuffling handkerchief-head. The station owners who run it are going to catch hell, and the sponsors of the show will not sell to the Negro market."

Thirteen years after "Amos 'n' Andy" premiered on the CBS Television Network, the embattled series entered its thirteenth rerun cycle on Chicago station WBBM. This broadcasting milestone was reported in the pages of the June 3, 1964, edition of *Variety,* hinting that, during these racially tenuous times, the old programs only served to stir the cauldron of trouble, "promoting the old foot-shuffling, ignorant and lazy stereotypes."

In response to the article and protests from community leaders, the TV station management issued the following statement: "[We're] going to run the show despite the protest. . . . Trying to keep the program off the air is comparable to book-burning in Nazi Germany."

On Thursday, June 4, the *Chicago Defender,* a prominent black newspaper, announced, "Tonight inaugurates the long, hot summer," referring to the return of "Amos 'n' Andy" to Chicago television. While responsible civil rights leaders deplored the show's resurrection, there seemed to be little indignation voiced among the black community itself.

Defender editor, Chuck Stone, confirmed that "there hasn't been an uproar in the Negro community. Most Negroes are just going to watch and enjoy it."

Years later, the respected black leader Reverend Jesse Jackson would say, "I remember growing up as a kid watching Stepin Fetchit, and watching 'Amos 'n' Andy' with Tim Moore. You know, black people had enough sense to appreciate them as funny people playing out roles. Their [opportunities] were so limited, we laughed at them and laughed at their roles."

As Reverend Jackson correctly confirmed, opportunities *were* limited—severely limited—when, on July 7, 1964, at its annual convention in Chicago, the NAACP adopted a resolution calling for mass protest demonstrations against discrimination in motion pictures, TV, and radio should industry talks scheduled for July 18 not prove fruitful. The two thousand conventioneers confirmed that they were ready to put pickets into place, on three hours' notice, around theatres in forty-two cities to protest "targeted" films.

Following the industry confab, the NAACP's Herbert Hill reported that he had demanded the use of blacks in "virtually every television and motion picture production."

That year, the NAACP organized a boycott of Lever Brothers products in a test market, St. Louis, because the company was not using blacks in its commercials. Housewives distributed leaflets outside supermarkets, asking customers not to buy the company's products, which were listed. The boycott lasted eight long weeks, and resulted in virtually the first integrated television commercials. The civil rights group next threatened a *nationwide* boycott of Ford, sponsor of the all-white "Hazel" series, a production of Columbia Pictures' television arm, Screen Gems. As a result of the threat, "Hazel" was integrated.

As the NAACP continued to lobby with TV executives and program producers, hoping that the tide would turn, the network brain-trust explained to the New York State Division for Human Rights that blacks were absent from television because TV was not willing to pervert the truth about American life by depicting black governors or business executives, or blacks at the 21 Club or in Beverly Hills swimming pools. Michael Dann, CBS vice-president in charge of programming, said CBS scriptwriters "try to avoid artificial situations." This might have seemed like an adequate explanation—if you believe that "The Beverly Hillbillies," "Wagon Train," and "Mr. Ed" were examples of American realism.

In the summer of 1964, amid all the hubbub of civil rights protests against the media, Sammy Davis, Jr., was asked why his appearances on television were so sporadic. He responded thoughtfully, "I haven't had a series of my own, and I wish I did, but although I haven't the faintest idea of why I don't, I don't get sore about it. Things are getting better. I've had hate mail in the past—three years ago it was like seventy percent, now it's about one percent.

"A whole lot of people are working who never worked before. You ask me—the industry's healthier than it was. Maybe the whole country's healthier. Maybe we're growing up," Davis offered.

Asked what blacks *really* wanted, the thirty-eight-year-old superstar answered, "I'm no spokesman for Negroes, but I'll tell you what *I* want. . . . I'm so damned tired of apologizing because I'm Negro. Just give me the same chance as anybody else—that's all I want. Let me prove what I can do. I want to walk in and see a producer without apologizing for being colored. I want him to be able to hire me without apologizing for me to somebody else. . . . I want to be a human being and not have to apologize for it."

Davis, who finally got his own network variety show two years later, recalled a 1964 incident that illustrates how many major strides were taken within that two-year period: "A couple of my agents had an idea for a network show for me, 'The Swinging World of Sammy Davis, Jr.' All the guys —Sinatra, Dean Martin, Peter Lawford, a whole lot of others—said they would go on with me. Practically for nothing. Just to get something started.

"A couple of advertising agencies were interested in

it. Months went by. They finally said to us, 'We just can't sell it.' Sponsors are afraid of what the public reaction would be—they're afraid nobody'll buy their stuff if a Negro's selling it," Davis concluded.

A large number of other well-known black entertainers had similar experiences in the mid-sixties. Harry Belafonte, who starred in two well-received specials during the 1958–59 season, was once considered for a series of his own in 1962. "The sponsors said they 'personally harbored no prejudice,'" Belafonte said in *TV Guide*, "but then in later discussions they talked about interracial matters. Was I going to have black and white people together on the show? At that point, I had nothing further to discuss."

Davis's and Belafonte's peers were gratified that some effort had been made to integrate television by 1964, particularly in the area of national commercials. Lever Brothers, conceivably on the strength of the St. Louis boycott, produced fourteen commercials with blacks, while its chief competitor, Procter and Gamble, came up with eight. This arguably could have been considered "tokenism," but it *was* a step in the right direction.

"It's just not enough to put Negroes in a few commercials or bit parts just because pressure's been brought to bear," Belafonte commented in 1964. Pearl Bailey agreed: "When they just stick in a Negro here and there, it's as bad as putting a fourteenth person in *The Last Supper*. It's like taking a Rembrandt and painting in an electric lamp to make it modern."

Greater visibility on television was only one objective of the civil rights groups; equally important was the quality of roles assigned to black actors. The stereotypes present on "Amos 'n' Andy" and "Beulah" were verboten. If there were going to be black maids and porters, then there would have to be black secretaries and lawyers. It was easier to get networks and production companies to use black performers than to use them in positive roles.

The late Godfrey Cambridge recalled an incident in 1964 that illustrates the plight of the black artist during that era: "I was called to a TV station to play the part of a slave. My mother was being played by a white actress, which I didn't mind because I do a lot of different voices and accents myself. While we were rehearsing I mentioned that to the director, and I did some of my voices for him. He said he liked them. But later he said, 'We'll call you if we have any strictly Negro parts.' What he meant was that he would call me if he had parts for me as a slave, or mess sergeant, or porter, or anything like that. He wouldn't think of me as a doctor, a lawyer, or anything dignified. And you know what? This was a show about discrimination."

As pressure continued to be applied to the television industry more acting assignments opened up. There were more in 1963 than there had been in 1962, more in 1964 than in 1963, and so on. The progress was steady, but snail-paced. On numerous occasions, civil rights groups and official state agencies, like the New York State Commission for Human Rights under Governor Nelson Rockefeller, would encounter program suppliers who did not agree with this new policy of hiring blacks. George Norford, a member of the New York commission and the first black to be hired by a network as a writer (in 1951), recalled a series of meetings with the producers of westerns, a popular programming staple of the late fifties and early sixties: "They said, 'What'll we do? We produce shows set in 1870, 1880; it would be unrealistic to put Negroes in those scenes.' I said, it would not. When emancipation rolled around in 1863, Negroes were the first to get the hell out of the South. Where did they go? They went to the towns of the West—not in great numbers, but enough of them so it wouldn't be incompatible with reality to show them working as blacksmiths, wheelwrights, carpenters, and so on."

Westerns were not the only genre of shows from which black artists were conspicuously absent. While not as hopeless as in the case of westerns, detective series, also popular in the early sixties, did not feature blacks in significant numbers. Most of these programs were set in urban areas where the majority of blacks lived. Only occasionally did a viewer encounter a black face. Actors Diahann Carroll, Rex Ingram, Juano Hernandez, James Edwards, Cicely Tyson, and Dorothy Dandridge appeared in such shows as "Peter Gunn," "The Law and Mr. Jones," "Naked City," and "Cain's 100." Again, the roles were specifically written for black actors.

By the time 1965 had rolled around, CBS had all but completed plans to remove "Amos 'n' Andy" from both domestic and overseas sale, effective in 1966. (The show had become surprisingly popular in Kenya and Western Nigeria, where it played with English subtitles.) Five years earlier, CBS had canceled the radio version of "Amos 'n' Andy." When the network made the official announcement, it denied the reason for the cancellation was protests from black organizations.

Whether the powerful broadcasting network simply decided that it wasn't worth it—responding to the constant cries by the show's detractors—or truly felt that the show's portrayal of black life fed, rather than dispelled, racial bigotry is anybody's guess. The legal department of CBS answers all queries about "Amos 'n' Andy" the same way: "No comment."

COLOR TV

The heat from Los Angeles' sweltering summer of 1965 was felt throughout the country. On August 9 the nation's press was focused not on the glamourous side of the entertainment capital, but on Watts, its ghetto.

Racial tensions sparked flames throughout many big-city slums. The peaceful marches of Dr. Martin Luther King's civil rights movement were not accomplishing enough, fast enough, for many of the nation's frustrated blacks. They felt that a militant, and sometimes violent, stance had to be taken to achieve results. Their rage was as uncontrollable as the fires ignited, in a desperate effort to end economic and social oppression.

Much publicized, the symbolic protests were acceptable to the average white citizenry, but when the protests took on the proportions of guerrilla warfare and struck the homes and businesses of neighbors, the American people were forced to listen. It was obvious that the flames would continue to smoulder—and possibly explode—if the people's complaints were not taken seriously.

"Burn, baby, burn!" became the slogan of the day, and these threats were carried out in many of the big cities' black ghettos. Faced with this intimidation, the public was glad, at last, to listen to the voices of civil rights organizations like the NAACP.

The average white American was not even aware of the seriousness of the grievances of his black counterpart. When the brutality of the underprivileged's life-style was brought to light, they did not know how to respond. None too soon, the premiere of a prime-time adventure/espionage series took place on the NBC network September 15, 1965. Just one month after the destructive Watts riots, Robert Culp and Bill Cosby debuted in "I Spy."

It was purely coincidental that the most positive image of blacks ever to be seen on TV up until that time followed right on the heels of one of the most disruptive summers of racial unrest in history. "I Spy" was not conceived hurriedly to counteract the negativity of Watts. The ground-breaking series had completed its pilot episode some nine months before.

"I Spy" rarely focused on racial issues, in part because the role Bill Cosby played was not designed for a black. There was nothing in the original 1964 pilot script that referred to black and white. *TV Guide* asked the program's executive producer, former actor Sheldon Leonard, in 1965 why he signed a black for the part of a CIA undercover agent. His response: "There was no motivation. The part was conceived for a white man—but a whole man, a man of humor, physical fitness, and competence. I had signed Robert Culp and I looked around for his counter-part. Then I saw Cosby on a variety show and a bulb lit up —I was sure he was the man I wanted.

"I make an intensive underground investigation before choosing a person for a long-range project of this sort. From every source, I learned Bill Cosby was a tireless worker, a man striving to do his best. I called Grant Tinker of NBC and told him I had found a young comedian who had every quality we were looking for. 'In one way he is different,' I said. 'He is colored.'

" 'That's great,' Tinker said. 'I think I speak for everyone at NBC when I say that.'

"Cosby comes on as an engaging, warmhearted, intelligent man. If anyone takes exception to this man because of his color, it will have to be some nut."

The series, for which Cosby won a trio of Emmy statuettes during its three-year run, was mostly fun and games, in the James Bond tradition. Television was already playing host to such devil-may-care shows as "Burke's Law," "The Wild, Wild West," and "The Man from U.N.C.L.E.," but a black secret agent was revolutionary. The viewing public seldom saw a black in a position of power, equal to his white counterpart, which was revolutionary. Alexander Scott, Cosby's character, was obviously intelligent and skilled—a rarity for black roles up until that time. On the personal side, Scott almost never got the girl on "I Spy." Stanley Robertson, a black NBC program manager in 1968, remarked then, "I'm sure that if Sheldon Leonard were doing 'I Spy' now, he'd do it differently. . . . But you know, for its time. . . ."

It was progress. And it was no wonder that within eight months of the Cosby-Culp teaming, CBS removed "Amos 'n' Andy" from the airwaves for good. The glaring differences between Alexander Scott and the Kingfish, Andy, Lightnin', and even the level-headed Amos were painfully obvious. Scott was a realistically conceived character, while Kingfish and company were pale caricatures, better left silenced.

During the third and final season of "I Spy," Cosby addressed the issue of the limited number of blacks on television, taking the position that blacks rarely got the opportunity to portray human beings on the tube. "Writers and producers think you need a special reason for a role to be played by a Negro—that he has to pounce on someone or be pounced upon. Because of this, Hollywood has helped to promote a negative image of the black man. When a Negro comes on the screen, the audience immediately tenses up. They know they are about to witness some violence, whether physical, verbal, or emotional. If someone were to make a film about a Negro who didn't have any great conflict because of his color, who loved and was loved by a black girl and raised a black family, the audience would come back to see it again, looking for some hidden meaning."

One major black role model on TV was not enough to satisfy the quench of 22 million blacks who lived in the United States in 1965. Within the next three years six more Negro actors were tapped for featured or supporting roles in TV shows. By 1968, the home screens were fairly bursting with "color." "Black is beautiful" became the catch phrase of the decade; Cal Wilson, a graduate of the Watts Writers Workshop, said in an interview in *Look* magazine, "Black people are hot! You could almost go roller skating in the street and they'd put you on television!" The 1968–69 season boasted twenty-one prime-time series with at least one black regular.

Three series that premiered the season after Cosby began spying, and which featured blacks in important, positive roles, were "Daktari," "Star Trek," and "Mission: Impossible"—the latter two out of the Desilu stable. "Star Trek," which debuted September 8, 1966, and soon became a cult obsession, was the creation of Gene Roddenberry, an innovative writer/producer. He decided to staff his starship *Enterprise* with a black communications officer who answered to the name Uhura (feminine in Swahili for "freedom"). Played by former vocalist (with the Count Basie and Duke Ellington bands) Nichelle Nichols, Uhura was both intelligent and sexy, a career officer who was as capable and reliable as any lieutenant aboard Captain Kirk's spaceship.

The role of Uhura as an equal—and very sensual—member of the crew showed a great deal of progress from the days when only menial roles were doled out to black actresses. Sapphire Stevens seemed as far removed from Uhura as she was from the twenty-third century.

Before "Star Trek," the only other dramatic TV series that had boasted a black female in a recurring role was "East Side/West Side" starring George C. Scott. Cast as his secretary/assistant Jane Foster, actress Cicely Tyson was hailed for imbuing her role with dignity and class.

"Mission: Impossible" featured accomplished actor Greg Morris as Barney Collier. Using his wits to assist in some of the government's most complex plans to foil its enemies, Collier established the black man as more than an underling, in the same vein as Bill Cosby on "I Spy." Collier was an electronics expert, not a bumbler or an ignoramus, totally unlike most of the "authoritative" roles featured on "Amos 'n' Andy." America was waking up to the fact that black Americans had something of value to contribute to society.

The third role to be introduced in 1966 was featured on "Daktari," CBS's "jungle drama." Set in Africa, the show co-starred Hari Rhodes as Mike, a native assistant in an animal study center. Rhodes was not relegated to loincloths and native gear, but sported the latest safari wear straight from Abercrombie & Fitch. Many black viewers were heartened to see a native African who spoke in an educated manner and who was not cast in a "primitive" light. This "native" character was far more sophisticated than his New York City brothers of "Amos 'n' Andy" fame.

In 1967 only 2.3 percent of all commercials used blacks, Orientals, Puerto Ricans, or Indians. Only 24 percent of all TV entertainment shows used any members of those minorities, and only 18 percent of all dramatic episodes used any of those minorities. Almost half of those who did appear were extras and bit players. More than 150 Negro performers made almost 400 appearances on NBC network programs during the thirteen months from January 1967 to February 1968, but only 88 were on nighttime dramatic shows—and 44 of those were on "Tarzan"; "Ironside" had 8; "I Spy" 6; "Dragnet" 3; "The Man from U.N.C.L.E." one. The other 312 performances were spread over everything from "The Tonight Show" to the televised Macy's Thanksgiving Day Parade.

"Ironside," which debuted in September of that year, was a police drama set in San Francisco and starred Raymond Burr, late of "Perry Mason." Featured as his assistant was Don Mitchell in the role of Mark Sanger. A reformed delinquent, Sanger was more than an aide, he also served as bodyguard for the paralyzed police consultant Ironside. The program remained on the air until 1975, with Mitchell's character studying at, and eventually graduating from, law school.

Many viewers believe that before "I Spy," there were no black law enforcement officers of note on television. The few blacks seen were relegated to playing uniformed cops. Shows like "Dragnet," "The Naked City," and "The Lineup" were conspicuously devoid of black personnel, even though they were set in, respectively, Los Angeles, New York, and San Francisco—the nation's most cosmopolitan areas with large black populations. The exception was "Amos 'n' Andy," which, as early as 1951, included black detectives, black plainclothesmen, and sometimes even black federal agents in evidence.

In 1968 actor Don Mitchell admitted, "I wanted to

(PREVIOUS PAGE) Freeman Gosden and Charles Correll in blackface as Amos and Andy. (*Correll Family Collection*)

(RIGHT) Movie studios started raiding the air waves beginning in 1930, when Gosden and Correll were signed to a lucrative film deal by RKO Pictures. The movie they made, *Check and Double Check*, in which they appeared in blackface as Amos and Andy, was the studio's highest-grossing film until *King Kong* was released in 1933. (*Correll Family Collection*)

(BELOW, LEFT) Gosden and Correll poring over their fan mail. In July 1929, when NBC changed the time slot of "Amos 'n' Andy," 100,000 letters came gushing in. When Amos and Ruby were about to become parents, more than a million fans wrote in suggesting names. (*Correll Family Collection*)

(BELOW, RIGHT) Charles Correll, Freeman Gosden, and Bill Hay (seated), their announcer since 1926, prepare to broadcast an episode of "Amos 'n' Andy" from the Merchandise Mart in Chicago, home of radio station WMAQ. (*Correll Family Collection*)

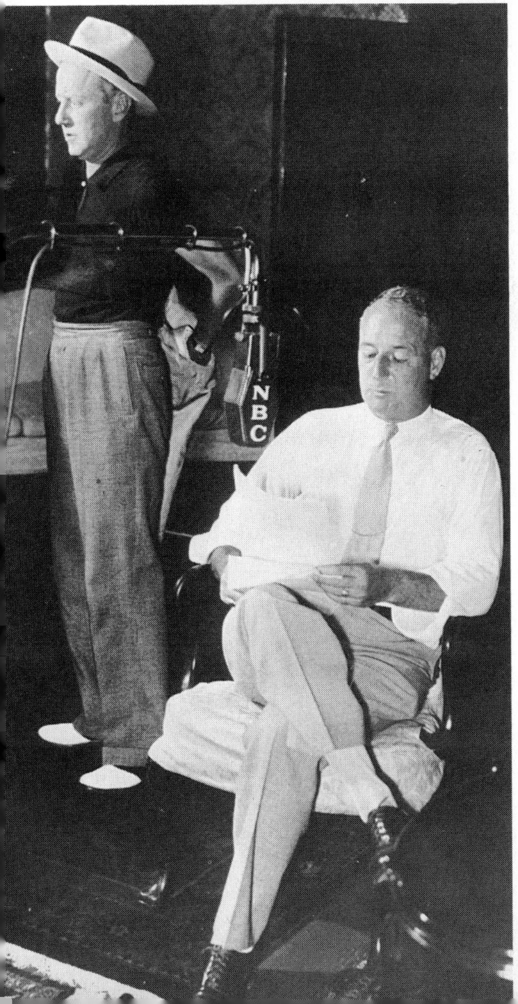

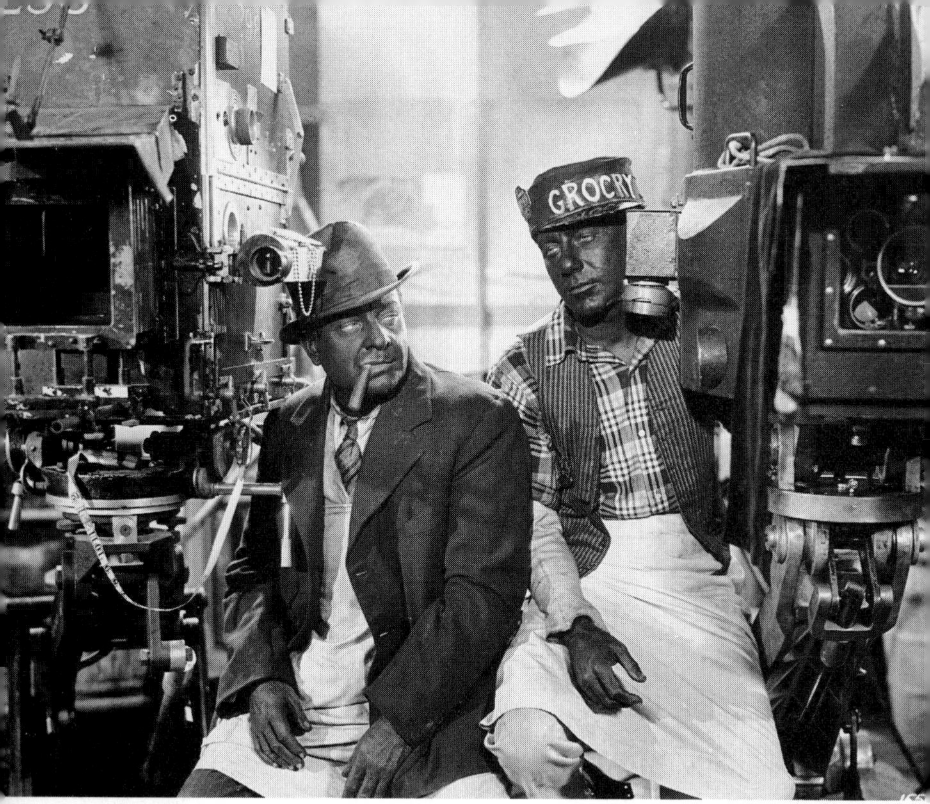
GROCRY

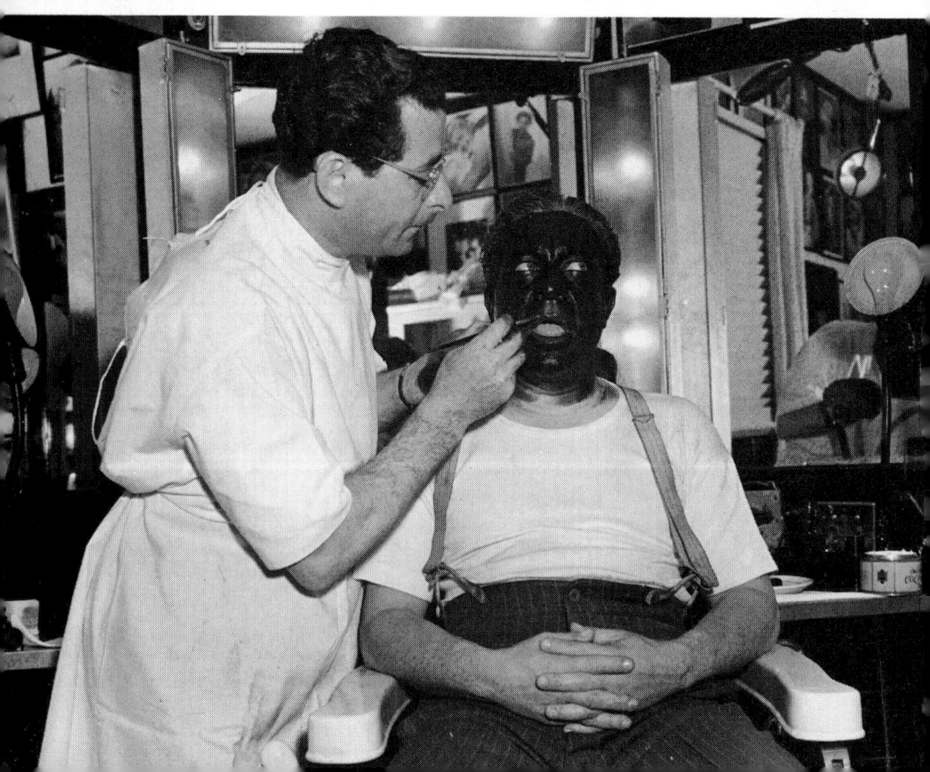

(OPPOSITE, TOP) In 1935, Paramount released *The Big Broadcast of 1936*, featuring George Burns, Gracie Allen, Ethel Merman, Charlie Ruggles, Bill "Bojangles" Robinson, and Gosden and Correll as Amos and Andy. In this ninety-seven-minute comedy, Amos and Andy ran a grocery store, not a taxicab business. (*Correll Family Collection*)

(OPPOSITE, BOTTOM) A Paramount Pictures makeup artist applies the necessary touches to transform white Charles Correll into black Andrew H. Brown for *The Big Broadcast of 1936*. (*Correll Family Collection*)

(BELOW) "The Perfect Song," the "Amos 'n' Andy" theme song for four decades, was also the "Love Theme" from *Birth of a Nation*. (*Correll Family Collection*)

(OPPOSITE, TOP) On tour in Freeman Gosden's hometown of Richmond, Virginia, the pair stops off at a children's hospital to spread cheer in 1933. (*Correll Family Collection*)

(BELOW) In their offices on Wilshire Boulevard in Beverly Hills, Freeman Gosden and Charles Correll sit down to write a script for "Amos 'n' Andy." Correll, once a stenographer, always did the typing. (*Correll Family Collection*)

(ABOVE) Correll and Gosden before the CBS microphone in 1941. They would return to the NBC Radio Network in 1944. (*Correll Family Collection*)

(OPPOSITE, BOTTOM) At their offices in Beverly Hills, the pair reviews fan mail with their secretary, Louise Suma, who stayed with Amos and Andy for thirty years. The map on the wall denotes the CBS affiliate stations that carried "Amos 'n' Andy." (*Correll Family Collection*)

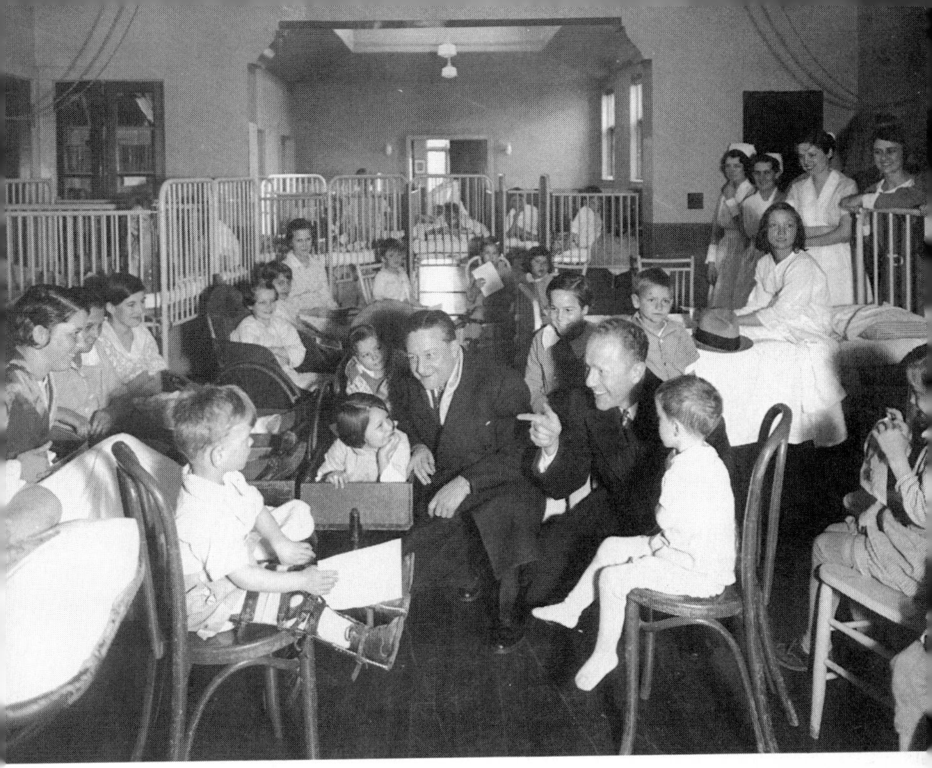

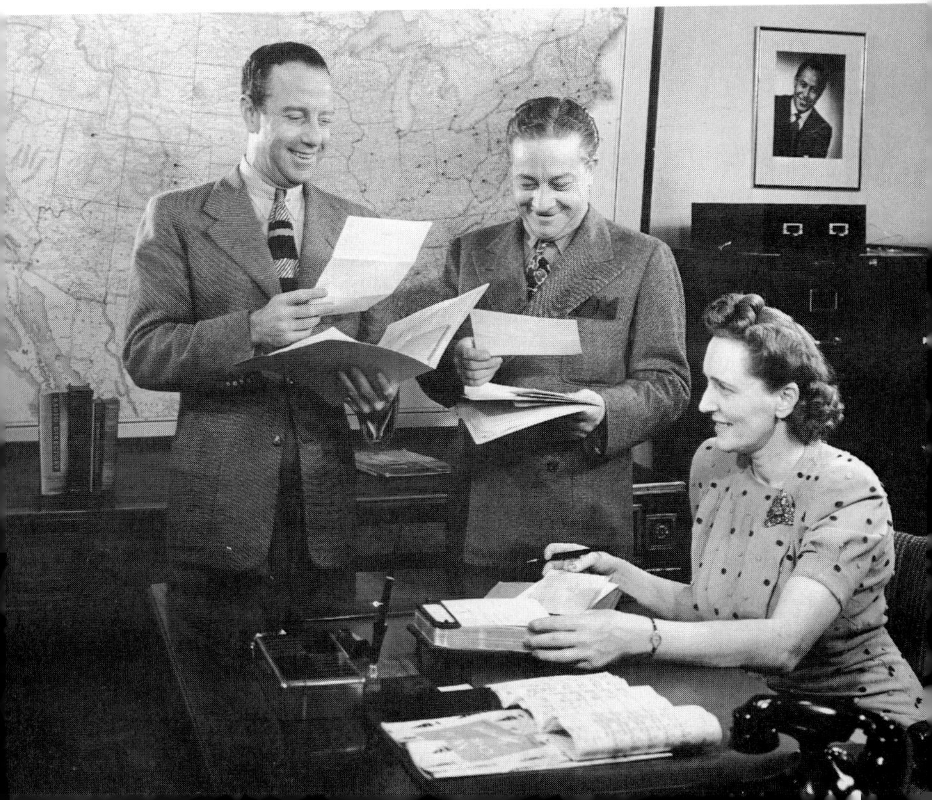

(TOP) Campbell's Soup Company took over the sponsorship of "Amos 'n' Andy" on January 3, 1938. It underwrote the cost of the program for the next five years, while it aired on both NBC and CBS. (*Correll Family Collection*)

(MIDDLE) In early 1939, Gosden and Correll moved "Amos 'n' Andy" to CBS radio, where the shows emanated from Hollywood. (*Correll Family Collection*)

(BOTTOM) To herald their April 3, 1939, premiere on the CBS Radio Network, Correll (left) and Gosden ham it up. (*Correll Family Collection*)

(OPPOSITE) Wearing outfits that RKO Pictures saved for ten years after the making in 1930 of *Check and Double Check*, Gosden and Correll pose for the official CBS publicity photo that the network used to ballyhoo the pair's arrival. (*Correll Family Collection*)

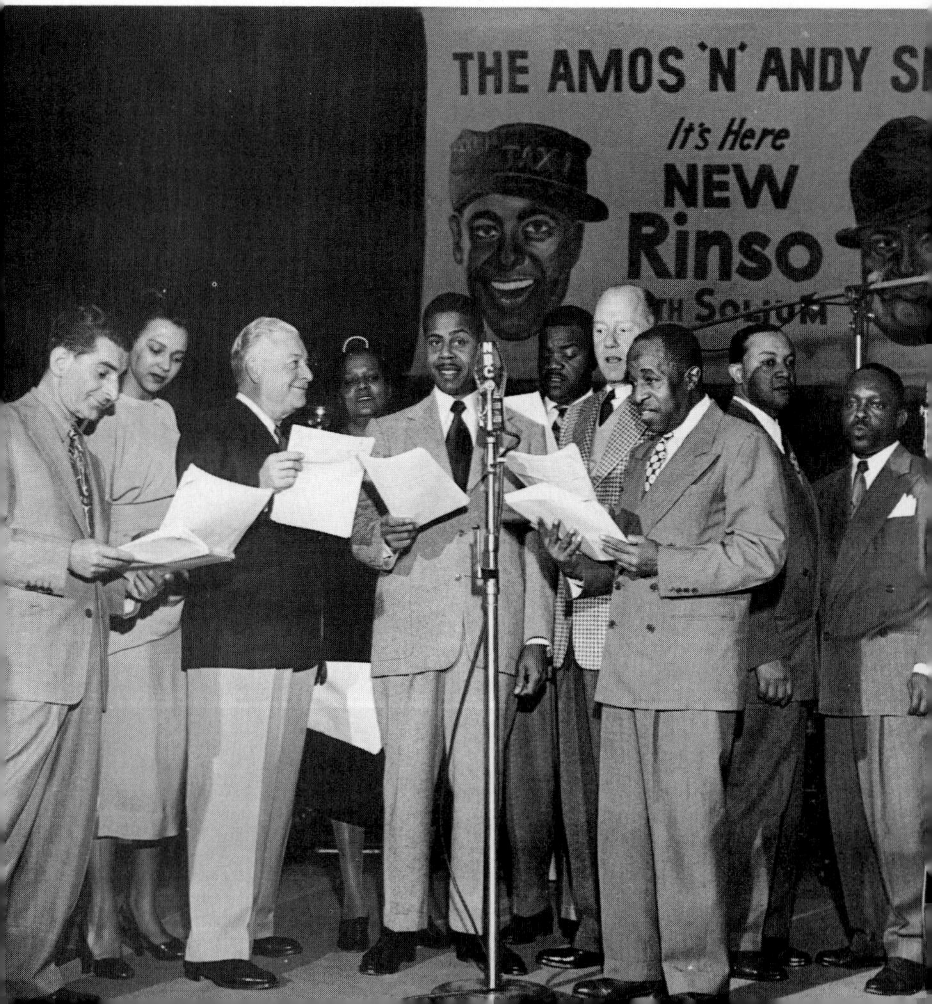

(LEFT) At CBS Columbia Square in Hollywood, Amos (left) and Andy polish the script of the night's broadcast. (*Correll Family Collection*)

(BELOW, LEFT) Announcer: "Rinso, the new Rinso with Solium, brings you 'The Amos 'n' Andy Show.' Yes sir, the soap that contains Solium, the sunlight ingredient, brings you a full half hour of entertainment with the Jubalaires, Jeff Alexander's Orchestra and Chorus, and radio's all-time favorites, Amos and Andy." Left to right: Lou Labin, Dorothy Dandridge, Charles Correll, Ruby Dandridge, Wonderful Smith, Roy Glenn, Freeman Gosden, Eddie Green, and the Jubalaires (George Mac-Fadden, Theodore Brooks, John Jennings, and Caleb Ginyard) on the May 10, 1948, show. (*Correll Family Collection*)

(BELOW, RIGHT) In 1944, the fifty-eight-year-old vaudeville legend Al Jolson appeared on "Amos 'n' Andy," then a half-hour, once weekly program on NBC. (*Correll Family Collection*)

(ABOVE, LEFT) A late 1940s studio portrait of Freeman Gosden and Charles Correll as they were about to translate their wildly successful radio show into an American television institution. (*Correll Family Collection*)

(ABOVE, RIGHT) Gosden and Correll in blackface as Amos and Andy at fictional Harlem Stock Exchange during tax season. This is typical of early scenes that were labeled "parody of black life" by the NAACP. (*Rare Records*)

(BELOW, LEFT) George "Kingfish" Stevens, the scheming head of the Mystic Knights of the Sea. (*Correll Family Collection*)

(BELOW, RIGHT) An autographed photo of Spencer Williams, Jr., as Andrew "Andy" H. Brown. (*Eddie Brandt Collection*)

(OPPOSITE) Outside the Mystic Knights of the Sea lodge hall, Amos (Alvin Childress, left) confirms that Kingfish (Tim Moore, center) has succeeded in tricking Andy (Spencer Williams, Jr.) again. (*Eddie Brandt Collection*)

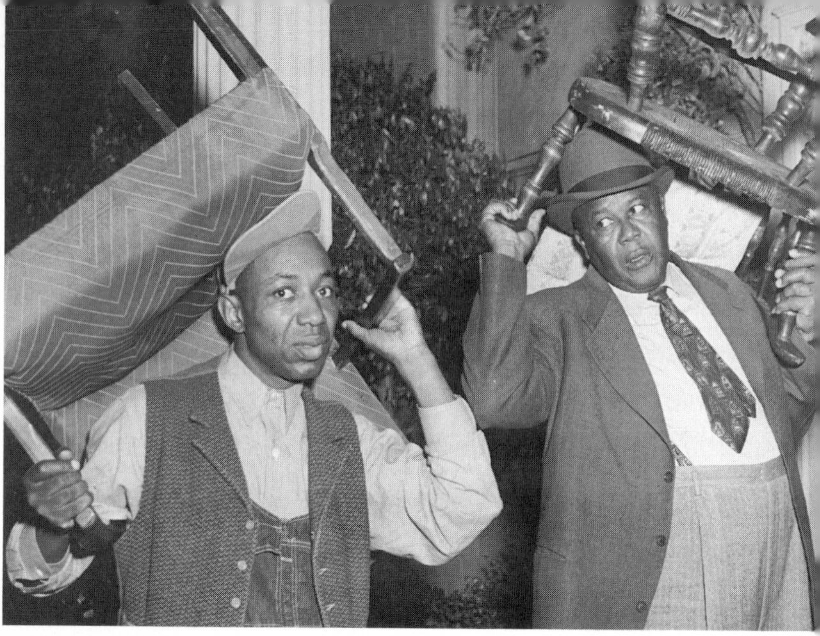
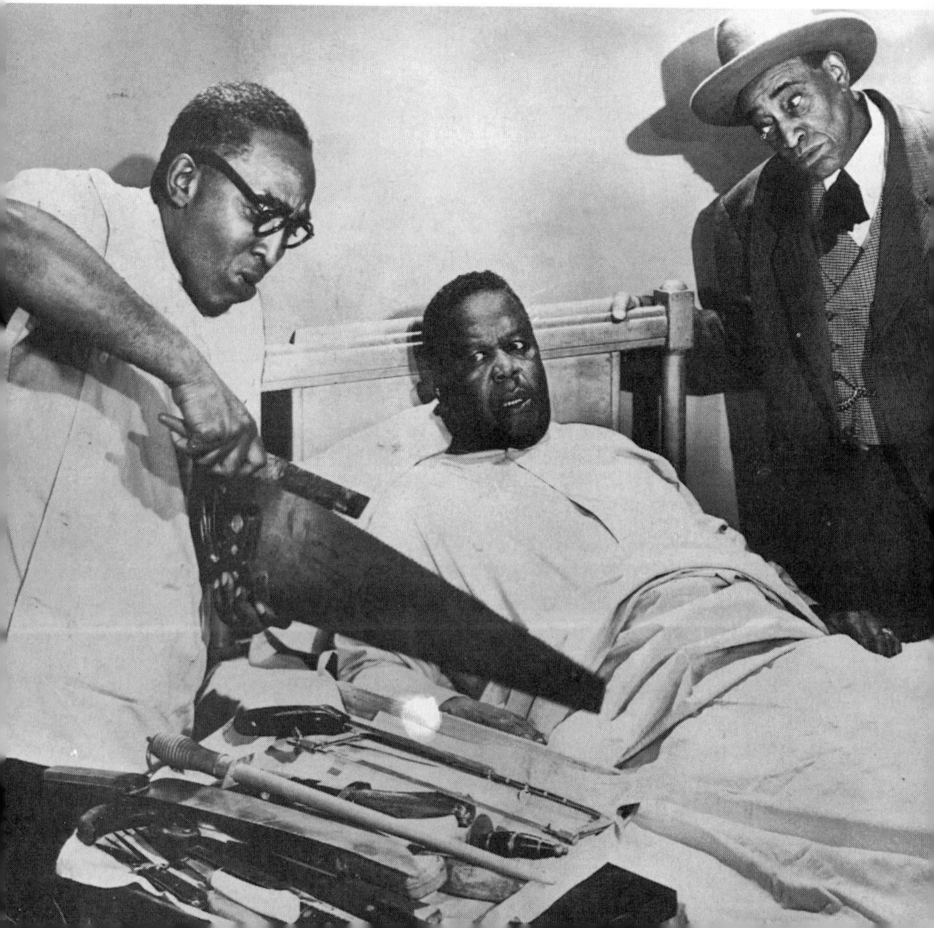

(OPPOSITE) Lightnin' (Nick Stewart, left) and Andy (Spencer Williams, Jr.) have a moving experience without the Kingfish. (*The Bettmann Archive, Inc.*)

(BELOW, LEFT) Algonquin J. Calhoun helps the Kingfish separate more money from Andy. (*Correll Family Collection*)

(BELOW) The classic Christmas show originated on radio with Amos's reading "The Lord's Prayer" to his daughter, Arbadella. This photo of the TV characters in the youngster's bedroom re-creates that scene. Hatty Marie Ellis as Arbadella with her father, Amos. (*AP/Wide World Photos*)

(ABOVE) On the set of the exterior for the lodge hall, creators of the show, Freeman Gosden and Charles Correll, pose for publicity photo behind their television counterparts, Amos and Andy. (*AP/Wide World Photos*)

(BELOW) A 1953 cast and crew shot, taken in front of a Harlem exterior set at Roach Studios. (*Correll Family Collection*)

be on television so some little black kid could see a black face on television that wasn't swinging from a vine. That's important. I know, I grew up without it."

ABC's "The Outcasts" was among the long list of shows featuring blacks that premiered during the 1968–69 season. This hard-riding western introduced the role of a black cowboy to prime-time television. Don Murray played Earl Corey, a Virginia aristocrat-turned-gunman and drifter, who teamed with black actor Otis Young, as a freed slave-turned-bounty hunter.

Young portrayed ex-slave Jemal David with a fierce intensity that bordered on hostility. There would be no mistake: Jemal was a free man. A fine actor, who was later hailed for his co-starring role with Jack Nicholson in *The Last Detail*, Young refused to stoop to the level of subservience or bastardization of the English language. A 1969 article in *TV Guide* discussed Young's refusal to say just any line. One bit of dialogue in particular—"Ain't nothin' like darkies for prayin' "—became a cause célèbre. Defending his position on the matter, Young claimed that "the line is an insult to Negroes. If this line went through, the next thing they'd have up there is Stepin Fetchit. If I compromised myself on this script, it would be a little easier next time, and in three or four years I'd wake up one morning and be a wealthy Negro who forgot who he was. . . . The thing that affected my decision about this line was my responsibility to Negroes in this country. White people think there's nothing like darkies for dancing, there's nothing like darkies for singing, and there's nothing like darkies for praying. Well, that's a lie. The segment of Negroes that is praying instead of doing is dying off. We have a new Negro that hasn't even been to church. One of the things that has hung the Negro up is that he's been too busy praying in the white man's church. This has kept him under the hand of the white Establishment. Any Negro today who is praying instead of doing is a damn fool."

"The Outcasts" lasted one season, the victim of low

ratings opposite TV's number 4 and 5 shows, "Mayberry, R.F.D.," and "Family Affair," both on CBS. "The Outcasts" was an "angry" show, perhaps a few years ahead of its time.

ABC's "Peyton Place," the serial based on the Grace Metalious novel, introduced black characters to its cast in 1968: Percy Rodriguez as Dr. Harry Miles, Ruby Dee as his wife, and Glenn Turman as their teenage son. Oddly, *Variety* criticized the hiring of Rodriguez because he had "definitely un-African features" and "the Negro watchers are going to find it hard to identify with him."

"Mannix," first telecast in 1967, underwent a format change in its second season on CBS, dropping Mike Connors's co-star, Joseph Campanella, and replacing him with a black actress, Gail Fisher, who was chosen from among eighteen women—black and white—who auditioned. The executive producer of "Mannix," Bruce Geller, once said, "The part of Peggy Fair was by no means locked in for a Negro."

Although Peggy was basically Mannix's secretary— like the Jane Foster (Cicely Tyson) role on "East Side/West Side"—she often participated in her boss's private detecting. The series ran eight seasons, a testimonial to the black-and-white combination of Fisher and Connors. Peggy may have been "just a secretary," but she was treated with dignity and respect. Color was not an issue. And Mannix certainly did not exude the cockiness of an Andrew H. Brown, who would pass through the Fresh Air Taxi office spouting, "Buzz me, Miss Blue."

"Rowan and Martin's Laugh-In" was introduced as a midseason replacement for NBC's failing "Man from U.N.C.L.E." series in January 1968. Littered with sight gags, jokes, and topical satire, the hour-long comedy variety series was the nation's most popular show for two consecutive seasons, and was the launching pad for many new stars, including Lily Tomlin and Goldie Hawn. As a purveyor of black talent, the program introduced dancer/ comedienne Chelsea Brown and veteran black comic Dewey "Pigmeat" Markham. Chelsea's animated face and bright-eyed smile had a charismatic appeal, whether she was clad in her signature bikini or in one of the mod outfits of the day.

Pigmeat Markham, most times clad in baggy clothes, brought to "Laugh-In" some of the classic ethnic humor he had become noted for in his nightclub and stage appearances, although it was not nearly as "blue." As one of the first regulars on the show, Markham's catchphrase, "Here come de judge!," quickly became part of the American lexicon. A contemporary of Tim "Kingfish" Moore, Markham used heavy-handed black dialect, which was part of his long-standing trademark, but there were no protests from the black community or from civil rights organizations. Even Sammy Davis, Jr., did not hesitate using the "judge" phrase in his own skits in the late sixties.

The Kingfish on "Amos 'n' Andy" could not have been any more degrading than the characters Markham portrayed. Why was the latter's humor more acceptable? Perhaps it was because there was no mistaking it as old-hat minstrel comedy presented on a comedy show that ridiculed all groups—political, racial, ethnic and religious. The fact remains that millions of viewers—black and white— were grateful to have had the opportunity to enjoy the great comedian Pigmeat Markham.

During "Laugh-In"'s 1969 season, producer George Schlatter added the sparkling Teresa Graves to the cast as a replacement for the departed Chelsea Brown, and hired Byron Gilliam, a young jive-talking black comedian. A year later, chubby comic Johnny Brown became a member of the cast, and finally, black ventriloquist Willie Tyler and his dummy, Lester, joined the weekly madness in 1972.

Michael Dann, who was vice-president in charge of programming for CBS in 1968, commented at that time about the state of the black man in his medium: "The Negro has achieved status and he has attained the highest responsible positions in American life, and if we in television are accurate writers and producers, we will show the Negro in various occupations and endeavors, not for the sake of recognition, but for the sake of accuracy. . . . I think the real problem is creating dramas which really make you care about the Negro as a person. We do not have enough dramas in which the Negro portrays the kind of character with whom you can really identify. I think it is because the Negro is cast all too frequently in the role of a helpful person in solving someone else's problem, a type of person whom you don't really care about as a human being and who functions solely in support of the hero in the play."

One show that premiered in the fall of 1968, and which found a large and loyal audience for the next five seasons, was ABC's "The Mod Squad," a production of the Aaron Spelling–Danny Thomas factory. Based on the true experiences of a former member of the Los Angeles sheriff's department, Bud Ruskin, the original pilot script was written in 1960 and remained unproduced until late 1968. Among the program's stars was a twenty-nine-year-old black actor with Broadway and off Broadway credits, Clarence Williams III, whom producer Spelling cast as Linc Hayes, an undercover "hippie" cop.

Williams was hired on a recommendation by Bill Cosby, who had seen him perform in *Slow Dance on the Killing Ground* on Broadway and called him "the best young black actor." Spelling flew Williams to the West Coast for a test and hired him for the pivotal role in the police series, later claiming "he can explode like charged lightning. Clarence is not a black actor, not a white actor, not a colored actor; he's an actor, the most professional I've worked with in my life. There are things Clarence does like nobody else. He's so good."

Williams, who made no bones about the fact that he

accepted the role because he wanted to work, had definite opinions about the way TV portrayed black characters. In a 1970 *TV Guide* article, the actor said, "When I first turned on television, I wasn't shocked by all the white people in it. Twelve years ago I had no problem watching 'I Love Lucy.' I don't see why everybody's talking about [black actors appearing] overnight. Overnight! A lot of people have died, bled, suffered and gone into poor states of mental health over this damn problem. You see, the cultural acceptance of black people has not happened yet. The black person's culture has not been put on television. Most black parts on TV could be rewritten for whites. . . . It would take the writers about four days to make every character white without harming the story one iota."

During the show's third season, it rose to number 11 on the Nielsen chart, a good showing when you consider that its appeal was generally confined to young people. Like the program, Williams's popularity skyrocketed; viewers obviously related to this "angry young man" from the Watts ghetto who had reformed and was now leading a useful and productive life.

Diahann Carroll spoke about the issue of black images that young people could aspire to, just months before her own NBC program premiered. "It is important that Negro children have symbols with which they can identify," she declared. "They must be taught to have pride in their blackness, and television can help them establish this identity."

Carroll's series, "Julia," was born officially on June 1, 1967, fifteen months before the half-hour sitcom—produced without a laugh track—first aired. It was on that date that writer/producer Hal Kanter completed his thirty-eight-page pilot script (then titled "Mamma's Man"), which was inspired by a moving speech given by NAACP director Roy Wilkins that Kanter had heard only two weeks before. Not until page twelve of the teleplay was the heroine's race revealed, this in a telephone scene between Julia Baker and a doctor evaluating her application for a job. (Julia: "I'm colored. I'm a Negro." Doctor: "Have you always been a Negro, or are you just trying to be fashionable?")

Diahann Carroll—who won the role of Julia over such competition as Leslie Uggams, Ruby Dee, Barbara McNair, Nancy Wilson, Abby Lincoln, and Carol Cole (daughter of the late Nat King Cole)—said about her new series before its debut on September 17, 1968, "It is time to present the black character primarily as a human being. I want to do something that deals with a black person in the everyday situation of ups and downs, good and bad."

The $200,000 pilot, bankrolled by NBC and 20th Century-Fox Television, turned out to be more drama than situation comedy. Mort Werner, the network's vice-president in charge of programs and talent, was disappointed when he viewed the sample film at his Rockefeller Center office in early January 1968, labeling Kanter's effort "too saccharine." The project was all but dead until the following month, when the network was about to "lock up" its fall schedule, but was experiencing difficulty in scheduling a show opposite Red Skelton on CBS (a number 7 Nielsen program for the prior season). Two potential series were being considered, although everybody agreed neither was about to beat Skelton. At that point, the question was which would fail more nobly against the great clown. Paul Klein, who headed NBC's programming department and reported directly to Mort Werner, suggested that if NBC was going to concede that half hour to the CBS competition, it might just as well select a show with value beyond the ratings. "Julia," he contended, might have racial importance at a time when TV was under continued attack by civil rights groups as a "lily white" medium.

"Julia" was scheduled for Tuesday nights at eight-thirty; its lead-in was "The Jerry Lewis Show," a variety show in its second season. Early press releases heralded

"Julia" as "a new experience in television," rather than merely another sitcom. Kanter was hailed as "indisputably one of the most original minds in the television–motion picture–radio fields," a selfless citizen who had created the series from "an idea born of one man's desire to serve humanity."

The series featured Miss Carroll as a widowed nurse with a small son, not unlike the roles then being played on television by Doris Day, Lucille Ball, Fred MacMurray, Ken Berry, Hope Lange, Brian Keith, and Bea Benaderet, all TV widows and widowers. In fact, there was little in the "Julia" scripts that distinguished the series from any other sitcom. The only reason it was labelled a "black show" was because of the color of its star's skin. Julia was everything that Sapphire Stevens was not. Julia, historian J. Fred MacDonald once observed, "was middle-class and beautiful. She spoke English perfectly. She was a liberated woman, a self-supporting professional nurse living in a racially integrated apartment building. As a Los Angeles war widow, she was responsibly raising a wholesome 'little man' son in a homey environment."

As a setting, Harlem seemed to have been obliterated from the map of television in most of the new series. There were no shows during this period that had all-black casts, as was the case with "Amos 'n' Andy." But this would have been unrealistic, given the climate of the times, when integration was the goal.

Three new series were introduced in 1969 that starred or featured blacks: CBS's "The Leslie Uggams Show," ABC's "Room 222," and NBC's "The Bill Cosby Show." All three networks had made much needed bids at top-rated black programming.

"Room 222," the schoolroom drama starring Lloyd Haynes, Denise Nicholas, Michael Constantine, and Karen Valentine, would certainly suggest this was true. As Pete Dixon, Haynes portrayed an easygoing idealist to whom the students gravitated. The program tackled the problems of drugs, prejudice, and school dropouts, issues that were relevant to young people.

Partially filmed on location at Los Angeles High School, "Room 222" was the recipient of numerous awards and commendations. The series was telecast for five years with Haynes and Nicholas (who played a counselor and Dixon's girl friend) personifying black teachers at their finest.

Despite the accolades and relevancy, the series never enjoyed a large audience during its network run.

Bill Cosby's top-quality comedy of 1969, in which he played a high school physical education teacher, Chet Kincaid, was a breakthrough. After "I Spy," Cosby was a hot property who was given virtual carte blanche to create and star in a second series. The warmhearted comedy that he and writer/producer Ed. Weinberger created landed in the number 11 Nielsen position during its first season. Kincaid's relationship with his family and students was the perfect format for Cosby's down-to-earth humor. The show emphasized his special brand of homey philosophy, crossing all color lines.

Leslie Uggams's musical variety show on CBS in 1969 was a groundbreaker for variety television. It was the first hour-long musical series hosted by a black female, and the network gave it a large budget. It would be a year before another black entertainer, Flip Wilson, would headline a variety show and make it a hit. Airing on Sunday evenings, the Uggams cast of regulars included Lillian Hayman, Lincoln Kilpatrick, and Johnny Brown as members of Leslie's family in the continuing comedy skit "Sugar Hill," which focused on the lives of a middle-class black family in a big city. Conscientious writers made an effort to see that this family fit comfortably between the ghetto family of a Linc Hayes and the integrated blandness of "Julia" 's existence. The family represented in this skit was closer economically and culturally to what the George Stevens family was *supposed* to represent in "Amos 'n' Andy."

In the four years since Andy, Sapphire, and the Kingfish were forcibly retired, it had to be admitted that major social changes had occurred. No one expected overnight miracles, so the black community would just have to give the media a fair chance, and see what the next decade would bring.

The fall season of 1970 ushered in the coming era of television with a spate of new shows featuring blacks, starting with a TV series based on Neil Simon's hit play and movie, "Barefoot in the Park," which starred Scoey Mitchlll and Tracy Reed. With Nipsey Russell and Thelma Carpenter in the cast, this all-black treatment of the romantic comedy had a very short run. Comedian Mitchlll was able to inject his own style of comedy into the role; Reed, as his wife, added just the right touch of common sense and class. The Bratters were an upwardly mobile, young couple in Manhattan, about as far removed from Kingfish and Sapphire as possible.

In another ABC newcomer for the season, "The Young Lawyers," Judy Pace played Pat Walters, a well-educated but streetwise black law student. Like "Mod Squad," this show presented a trio of suitably mixed individuals who found themselves fighting, through free legal advice, everything from rip-offs of the poor to drug busts.

Pat Walters was a law apprentice who could debate a case and be as articulate as any of her colleagues, while still being able to relate to the problems of the underprivileged and make them trust her. There would be no sermonizing or posturing for this attractive, young, aspiring attorney. Unlike her infamous forerunner, Algonquin J. Calhoun, she was respectable, and more in keeping with the image most blacks wanted to see in their young professionals.

One of the biggest hits of the season was "The Flip Wilson Show," a comedy-variety outing from NBC. Catapulting Wilson to instant stardom, the one-hour program featured his special brand of outrageous humor, although music and guests were an important part of the format. Geraldine Jones; Reverend Leroy of the Church of What's Happening Now; Herbie, the Good Time Ice Cream Man; and Danny Danger were all part of his collection of stock characters, which endeared themselves to American audiences. The show landed NBC high in the Nielsen ratings, placing second among all programs on television during its first two seasons.

There was no mistaking Geraldine, and her jealous boy friend, "Killer," for anything other than people who are "ghetto blacks." The language and mannerisms were apparently from the lower-income background, but somehow none of this was considered offensive. As with Pigmeat Markham, within the context of comedy-variety, the caricature was palatable.

Reverend Leroy may have received some flak from the black religious community, but not enough to have any bearing on the show's future. Geraldine, Reverend Leroy, and Flip himself flourished, until the show went off the air in 1974 when its popularity waned. Geraldine's famous line, "The devil made me do it!" became a byword of the seventies.

As an enduring sitcom, "The Mary Tyler Moore Show" gets top honors. The long-running, half-hour CBS comedy was one of the most literate and realistic shows to surface during its period on the air. As a torchbearer for the liberated woman, Mary's job at a Minneapolis TV station gave her the ideal career.

Indicative of the positive tone the show took was the casting of black actor John Amos as WJM-TV weatherman Gordy Howard. The show's writers avoided resorting to cheap caricatures, concentrating instead on developing genuinely funny situations. Gordy's color was unimportant.

"The Partners" was a series that was seen only during the 1971 season. The sitcom starred Don Adams, of "Get Smart" fame, and the late Rupert Crosse.

This show is a prime example of how sensitive black performers could be during this period of adjustment—a sharp contrast to the days of "Amos 'n' Andy." On the basis of his 1969 Oscar nomination for his co-starring role in *The Reivers*, Crosse was tapped for a series of his own partnered with Adams.

During the filming of the episodes, Crosse continually complained about script content. A good working relationship with his co-star and sympathetic producers did little to alleviate the misgivings about the image he was presenting. In a comedic sense, most of the scenes were standard shtick, yet Crosse scrutinized the situation for negative undertones.

Opinions of blacks in the community contributed to most black actors' conscientiousness during this period, and some of the dispute may have stemmed from an overzealousness not to be labeled as an Uncle Tom.

Norman Lear and Bud Yorkin's Tandem Productions gained a reputation for shows of a controversial nature when "All in the Family" premiered on CBS in January 1971. The program's concept was adapted from the longrunning British series, "Till Death Us Do Part," written by Ray Galton and Alan Simpson.

What Tandem failed to take into consideration was that Alf Garnett's ignorant bigotry in England bordered on the ridiculous, while the same rhetoric from Archie Bunker often touched a raw nerve in this country. Worse, the Bunker character was actually a validation for many people who felt threatened by civil rights legislation and "affirmative action." It fed the racist thinking of some of the uneducated.

Nevertheless, the half-hour show was one of CBS's

biggest hits, eventually propagating a record number of spinoffs. The first of these shows featured Edith Bunker's liberal cousin, Maude, and it premiered on CBS in 1972, starring Bea Arthur in the title role.

Tandem then entered the 1972 season with another adaptation from the team of Galton and Simpson—with "Sanford and Son," the Americanized version of their "Steptoe and Son." The sitcom, which aired on NBC, starred veteran comedian Redd Foxx as Sanford and Demond Wilson as the son.

The story of a widowed junk dealer who lives with his bachelor offspring was an instant hit, thanks in large part to the comedic talents of Foxx. There were, however, many who contended the show was no more than another exploitive attempt to show the negative side of black life.

For the average Afro-American viewer, it may have been a pleasant surprise to see so many blacks interacting and not trying to emulate whites, but there were others in the community who viewed the humorous antics of Fred Sanford and his abusive cohorts in a poor light.

Most of the black audience was aware of the fact that many of the featured players on "Sanford and Son"— LaWanda Page, Slappy White, and Don Bexley among others—were old show business cronies of Foxx, who did everything in his power to provide them with acting assignments because he knew no one else would.

Ethnic humor among one's own people is always acceptable and usually relished as identifiable foibles, but is seldom considered in good taste outside of that environment. Many of "Sanford and Son" 's regulars portrayed characters developed in burlesque on the so-called chitlin' circuit (black venues). It was difficult to translate their attitudes to the masses without it sometimes seeming they allowed blacks to be the butt of their own jokes. What price funny?

There was no denying the fact that things were beginning to look promising in the world of television. Employment for blacks was reaching an all-time high.

"That's My Mama," "Get Christie Love," "Good Times," and "Barney Miller" all premiered in 1974. Only the latter two series had any endurance.

Teresa Graves starred as the black, sexy super-cop in "Get Christie Love," an ABC drama. As an undercover police officer, Christie broke all the rules, and her role also shattered a few others, as far as the image of black women on television. The attractive Graves could have been anybody's sweetheart, and she was nobody's mama. In comparison to this beauty, Sapphire was an uptight prude.

"That's My Mama" featured suave Clifton Davis, with Theresa Merritt as his authoritative mother. Though the show was steeped in ethnic humor, the Curtis household and neighborhood held little that was objectionable. Davis's barbershop was a positive, realistic private enterprise. Included in the cast was Jester Hairston, who played a neighborhood old-timer. It was Hairston who, twenty years earlier, had played foppish Henry Van Porter and, later, Sapphire's brother, Leroy, on "Amos 'n' Andy."

Many old and new faces were becoming a familiar part of the TV scene, as the effects of the 1960s settled down in the mid-1970s. The civil rights upheaval did promote more opportunities for black actors as well as a large sampling of dignified roles for them to portray. Optimism was obvious—things could only get better. Unfortunately, this was short-lived.

9

THE EIGHTIES ENIGMA

It has been called by more than one media historian "The Age of the New Minstrelsy," and rightfully so. Following the era of the late sixties and early seventies, when television was busy presenting increasing numbers of blacks in more-or-less positive roles, such shows as "What's Happening!!," "Diff'rent Strokes," "The Jeffersons," and "Carter Country" surfaced on the three major networks. In a matter of a few seasons, what important ground the black community had gained in terms of employment and image had been canceled out by this smattering of series that portrayed the old racial clichés, the same clichés that had made programs like "Beulah" and "Amos 'n' Andy" unacceptable two decades earlier.

As recently as the spring of 1985, the National Urban League, discouraged by the bleak outlook for blacks in broadcasting, issued a 230-page report that said, in part, "Self-images of black children are being undermined, and the children are being conditioned for continued deprivation, educationally and culturally, as a result of the media content [that] the large majority of them are wired into.

"Broadcasters may understand entertainment, but they don't understand or they don't have people to interpret for them the concerns of black Americans," the report continued, "particularly when it comes to moving from square A to square B."

While promoting his ground-breaking 1984 sitcom on NBC's "Today" program, Bill Cosby was asked by host Bryant Gumbel if he was doing his show because there was such a paltry number of good black shows on the air. Cosby, ever the quick wit, replied, "I'm doing it because there's a paltry number of good *any kind* of shows on the air today!"

Some people argue that, while there is an abundance of black actors working in front of the television cameras today, their roles, for the most part, reflect anything but positive images. This may have been the partial result of the proliferation of "blaxploitation" films in the seventies, which featured such questionable characters as pimps, prostitutes, and assorted "streetwise" types cavorting on the screen in mostly negative storylines. These low-budget, sexually explicit, and mostly black-directed films professed to show the *authentic* black experience, but, instead, depicted only the lowest elements. The success of these movies prompted a string of television producers—and their customers, the networks—to create TV shows in the same idiom.

These damaging stereotypes began spilling over

into television, ultimately poisoning one sitcom, "Good Times," which had started out in 1974 as a fairly positive portrayal of black family life, despite the fact the program was set in a black housing project in Chicago. A year after its premiere on CBS, network surveys revealed that the most popular character on the show was James Evans, Jr. —better known as J.J.—played by the rising nightclub comic Jimmie Walker. J.J. started out as a positive black image—a hardworking kid, an amateur painter, ambitious, helping out his family, etc. Within four months of the network popularity survey, J.J. had been transformed into a jive-talking (his catch-phrase, "Dy-no-mite," was heard at least once in every episode, to the utter delight of the show's live studio audiences), woman-chasing, questionably honest "ghetto black."

The solid character of the father/husband was pushed into the background, a pitiful situation for actor John Amos, who ultimately decided to leave the hit show rather than have his role undermined. This turn of events left the Evans family fatherless, a situation that in itself was another example of black stereotyping. After another season of J.J.'s buffoonery, series star Esther Rolle, on the pretense of illness, left the series too, informing her Tandem Productions bosses that she would return if the role of J.J. was reverted to its original, respectable self, which it was. (Rolle returned to the show for the 1978–79 season, the series' last.)

Another popular show, also a Tandem production, was "The Jeffersons," a 1975 CBS spinoff of the "mother ship" of bigotry, "All in the Family." The Bunkers' black neighbors, the Jeffersons—long the target of Archie's flagrant racism—had "moved up" to the East Side of Manhattan, thanks to George Jefferson's profitable chain of dry cleaning stores.

As bigoted as his nemesis Archie, George (Sherman Hemsley) flaunted the ritzy life-style of the nouveau riche, as his levelheaded and patient wife, Louise, managed to keep her feet planted firmly on the ground. George's custom-made suits and status-symbol address fooled him into believing he had *real* power. Money, according to George, could buy anything, including happiness. Louise and the family maid, Florence, were constant reminders that, ultimately, George was not the king in his castle. Louise was the boss and she wouldn't tolerate her shallow husband's shenanigans. In many ways, her character was a throwback to Sapphire Stevens, the black matriarchal figure on "Amos 'n' Andy," who would not put up with the Kingfish's behavior.

During its ten-year run, "The Jeffersons" cast included Isabel Sanford as Louise; Mike Evans as the Jeffersons' son, Lionel (Damon Evans replaced Evans briefly in 1975); Roxie Roker as their black neighbor, who was married to a white man, played by Franklin Cover; Belinda Tolbert (as Lionel's wife); Paul Benedict as their proper English neighbor; and Marla Gibbs as Florence.

Despite the stereotypical portrayals, the CBS sitcom had a faithful following of black fans. For many, the Jeffersons were proof that the American Dream could still happen. Writing in *Channels* magazine in 1983, William A. Henry III compared "The Jeffersons" to its 1950s counterpart, "Amos 'n' Andy": " 'The Jeffersons' is not as provocative as the supposed symbol of racial caricature, 'Amos 'n' Andy.' But I have long harbored the suspicion, unverifiable because all episodes have been utterly suppressed, that the flavorsome street life of 'Amos 'n' Andy' would look far less offensive today than when it was measured against the sanitized blandness of 'The Donna Reed Show' and 'Father Knows Best.' Such characters as Lightnin' and the Kingfish may have been inelegant, but they had an enviable vitality."

The Jeffersons might have moved up economically, but had they really changed from the days of the George Stevenses? Doesn't television still cast black actors in stereotypically *black* roles? Why can't minorities play the same roles they have in real life: teachers, mailmen, your average next-door neighbor? To make matters worse, most of the ethnic-cast roles are issue-oriented, the character's race being his foremost trait. Perhaps this will change in the late eighties, but from the mid-seventies to the present, there was yet another pattern being established in television.

A mixed bag of black characters began to emerge that was impossible to categorize, except to say they were "harder" and more streetwise than their video predecessors. ABC's 1975–76 schedule included a heterogeneous group of shows: "Welcome Back, Kotter" introduced talented Lawrence Hilton-Jacobs as a rebellious youth who was one of Kotter's so-called sweathogs, Boom-Boom Washington; with one police comedy ("Barney Miller") already on its schedule, the network premiered a pair of one-hour police dramas, "Starsky and Hutch" and "Baretta."

On the former, veteran black actor Bernie Hamilton was cast as the gruff superior of the two young detectives played by Paul Michael Glaser and David Soul. This was one of the first times that television depicted a black police captain in a continuing role. Unfortunately, this positive role was overshadowed by two black characters who could only be described as flamboyant, criminally inclined, and possessing all the negative traits of informants. "Baretta" 's Rooster, played by Michael D. Roberts, and Huggy Bear of "Starsky and Hutch" (played by Antonio Fargas) could well have been pimps who made a little extra money on the side snitching on their ghetto "brothers." Kingfish posing as a doctor and Calhoun practicing law without a license are rendered harmless in the face of these professional street hustlers. The trickery portrayed on "Amos 'n' Andy" was innocent compared to the antics of two black street predators who betray their friends to save their own skin.

ABC's summer of 1976 submission entitled "What's Happening!!" was based loosely on the popular movie *Cooley High* and centered around a trio of black teenage boys named Roger, Rerun, and Dwayne—the writer, the clown, and the innocent. They were well-behaved kids and meant well, but the show's scriptwriters seemed bent on portraying them in the stupidest of situations, some of them dating back to "Our Gang" comedies of the thirties. Andy and the Kingfish may have been a bit on the ignorant side, but neither was so dumb that he would eat spaghetti before it was defrosted.

Mabel King, as Roger's mother, was a single parent who worked as a maid. Is it possible that when Mabel King was hired, the role had not been completely created? Perhaps the producers cast King as a maid because of her size; someone that large couldn't be a secretary or a supervisor in the cosmetics department of a department store. Shirley Hemphill, another ample-sized actress, played a waitress on "What's Happening!!" She was, perhaps, the funniest of all the actors, due, in part, to her girth. The images of both female leads offered little in the way of role models for black youngsters. By comparison, Sapphire Stevens was the personification of class.

Another sitcom that premiered in the seventies that was a partial throwback to an era (thankfully) gone by was NBC's "Diff'rent Strokes," starring pint-sized Gary Coleman. The comedy find of 1978, Coleman went on to monopolize the screen when the show was on the air, completely dwarfing the series's adult star, Conrad Bain. It was Coleman's innate timing, along with his ability to roll his eyes and make funny faces, that made the show a solid hit. Critics charged that Coleman was playing a seventies version of Buckwheat, with a better wardrobe.

Five years later, the next comic find was pint-sized Emmanuel Lewis, whom ABC spotted in a TV commercial and immediately signed to a network contract. Aware of the commercial success of Gary Coleman's program, ABC fashioned a similar vehicle for Lewis, who would also be adopted by white parents. In both instances the depiction of the characters are not as detrimental as the basic premise that both shows share. Is it more advantageous for a black child to be taken in by a white family—where the surroundings may be totally unfamiliar—than raised in a black environment? Adoption agencies are faced with this dilemma on a daily basis, because black children are among the hardest, along with handicapped youngsters, to find homes for. It would be nice to assume that television creators and programmers have put these shows on because of some feeling of altruism: suggesting, perhaps, to wealthy white people that they should adopt black children and their homes will be filled with laughter.

In defense of the medium, there were several attempts in the mid-seventies to upgrade the image of Afro-Americans on the tube: "The Richard Pryor Show," which aired in the fall of 1977 for only five weeks, presented offbeat humor and a cast of talented regulars. Despite some brilliant moments—such as a parade of beautiful and elegantly dressed women who represented every shade of black skin—the variety show was unable to draw a sizable enough audience against the powerhouse combination of "Happy Days" and "Laverne and Shirley."

Since 1977, Robert Guillaume, a talented actor from the Broadway stage, has portrayed Benson DuBois on two series, "Soap" and "Benson." After playing the butler for two seasons on the former, Guillaume was tapped by ABC to play the same character on his own show, only this time he was butler to a governor. Within two years, Benson was promoted from butler to state budget director, perhaps stretching credibility a bit far—but what's more important is that actor Guillaume was able to make the transition within the context of his character convincingly. One is not likely to watch an episode of "Benson" and say, "He's just the butler, but they promoted him to budget director because he's black."

Another case of positive image is the role of Tootie on the sitcom "The Facts of Life." Played by young black actress Kim Fields, Tootie is the only black student at a private girls' school. Her fellow students were virtually "color blind," never making reference to her race. Like "Benson," this show was a milestone in integrated television. The performances of Debbie Allen and Gene Anthony Ray on the musical drama series, "Fame," are unique depictions of black characters.

Other programs that have cast blacks in positive roles have been "Love Boat," "WKRP in Cincinnati," "The White Shadow," "Paris," "Tenspeed and Brown Shoe," "Sanford" (most notably actress Marguerite Ray as Sanford's sophisticated love interest), "Hill Street Blues," and "The New Odd Couple," the latter featuring an all-black cast.

Do a few good shows constitute a trend? According to television historian J. Fred MacDonald, even "Roots," the highly acclaimed miniseries that ran on ABC in 1977, did not have a long-term impact on the business of incorporating prestigious black roles on TV. To MacDonald, Gary Coleman is merely a thinly veiled modern day pickaninny, but a show like "The White Shadow" had social realism.

Why is it that, so far, the only successful series that have *starred* blacks have been comedies? MacDonald maintains that self-mocking comedy roles "lull whites into complacency by reducing blacks to an inferior position. The uncomfortable alternative for many whites would be to see blacks in less comedic roles, which would make the black person more human. It would be hard for a white to perpetuate his or her prejudicial thinking while saying, 'Hey, they're just like me.' "

Dr. MacDonald concedes that, while whites are often

cast in negative roles, more often than not "whites turn out to be 'good'—doctors, newsmen, basically just well-rounded characters." As for "Amos 'n' Andy," the noted historian claims that "the show portrayed most of the adults as children, filled with pranks and pretensions. Ultimately, just non-threatening."

However, Bill Cosby's "I Spy" and Diahann Carroll's "Julia" have long been regarded as two of the most important television series of the sixties, paving the way for an upgrading of black Americans in the media.

In 1984, Cosby began what looks like a long run on his second situation comedy, "The Cosby Show"—surely one of the most successful and critically acclaimed sitcoms in the history of television. It's not so much a black show as it is a good show. There's a big difference. The program does not tackle the issue of race because it isn't necessary. The Huxtables—Cliff and Claire—are just an upper-middle-class couple with five children. He is an obstetrician and she is an attorney; a working couple, a two-paycheck family. If television producers could find another cast as talented as those on "Cosby"—say, Orientals, or Jews, or Italians, or a mixture thereof—the show still would be a hit. Ethnic background has nothing to do with the success of this show.

Critics point to Cosby as the single reason the show is a hit. That his appeal crosses color lines, that his humor and genuine rapport with children shines through. No one can argue that Bill Cosby isn't a super talent or that he isn't liked by whites and blacks, but one must remember that it takes more than just Cosby's presence to make the show a success.

Equally as charismatic as Cosby is Diahann Carroll, one of the stars of Aaron Spelling's "Dynasty." The show presented a real casting breakthrough when a bona fide "black bitch," Dominique Devereaux, was written into the plot. The vixenish Diahann Carroll plays the part threateningly, showing viewers that Dominique has mapped out her "turf" as Alexis's (Joan Collins) rival. The storyline has gone so far as to establish that the black woman is a blood relative of one of the show's most important characters, the white Blake Carrington (John Forsythe).

Daytime television has long been considered the trailblazer when it comes to depicting whites and blacks in integrated social situations, and just about every other relevant social issue. Agnes Nixon, a pioneer in the daytime drama field, has been responsible for many innovations. Few people realize that one of the shows she created, "One Life to Live," was based on a character who was a beautiful, fair-skinned black. Over the years since its debut, the program has evolved into a totally different story, but back in the early seventies, this twist was revolutionary for television.

Daytime TV has long delved into areas that prime-time producers and networks fear. Stories featuring interracial romances, like one involving two lead characters (Dottie Ferguson and Jesse Hubbard) on "All My Children," result in a ton of fan mail. A few seasons earlier, the same show depicted a romance between a black woman and a white man—a rare situation for TV, daytime or prime time.

The CBS sitcom "The Jeffersons" poked fun constantly at interracial marriages. George and Louise's neighbors and in-laws, the Willises, were composed of a black woman, Helen, and her white husband, Tom. In a case of "reverse racism," it was the character of George Jefferson who was always berating the couple.

The years just ahead of us are crucial to the issue of black-and-white television. Giant strides have been made—witness the success and popularity of "The Cosby Show," among others—but all too often there are major setbacks. Perhaps this "blend"—some good shows, some bad—is all that can be expected for a mass medium like television.

EPILOGUE

When San Diego attorney Michael Avery obtained the rights from CBS to run an episode of "Amos 'n' Andy" within the context of a documentary he was preparing titled " 'Amos 'n' Andy': Anatomy of a Controversy" in 1983, Benjamin L. Hooks, executive director of the National Association for the Advancement of Colored People, told *Variety:* "The record has to be set straight. The passage of time has done little to lessen the devastating effect of [the show's] scurrilous stereotypical treatment of blacks. The revival hardly can be said to contribute to blacks' development of positive self-images. Nor can it be said that 'Amos 'n' Andy' will enhance our white brothers' perception of the reality of black Americans' existence."

When *TV Guide* reported to its more than 50 million readers that the syndicated documentary was in production, calling its subject "a landmark 1950s sitcom," Reverend Robert Willingham, president of the Little Rock chapter of the NAACP, reacted differently from his fellow board member: "Comedy is an art form, and to me, ['Amos 'n' Andy' is] no different from 'The Beverly Hillbillies.' A person has to be fairly naïve to think this comedy depicts the black race as a culture. I get the feeling most of us are more enlightened than that."

Avery's one-hour documentary, which aired in about sixty markets during the spring of 1984, presented both sides of the "Amos 'n' Andy" issue. "It was an objective study of the controversy surrounding the show," said Avery, who specializes in real-estate law. The effort took no less than three years, during which time he encountered resistance from nearly every faction, beginning in 1981 when he sought production financing from cable companies (such as HBO) and the commercial TV networks. "I had a lot of people interested, but everyone was afraid of it."

Avery eventually sank $150,000 of his own money into the project, just to get it done. Then, when it was finished and edited, he found that most major advertisers wouldn't touch it. "They were afraid that they would come out with a bad image if they lent their name to it. But they all loved it. Even black advertising agencies were recommending that their clients buy time on the show," he revealed.

Avery's interest in the subject was sparked a year or so before he became actively involved with his plans to produce the documentary with writer/producer Bob Greenberg, when he happened upon a videocassette tape of four "Amos 'n' Andy" episodes—"The Rare Coin" (the series pilot), "The Kingfish Gets Drafted," "The Broken Clock," and "Invisible Glass." For $39.95, the California attorney was able to relive part of his youth watching these reruns. "It's a legitimate part of black history. It was the first time there's ever been an all-black television sitcom, and I think blacks are entitled to have their past—good, bad, or indifferent—be a part of their heritage. Young blacks should be allowed to see it and enjoy it and understand it—it could help them understand some of the changes they've gone through."

George H. Hill, who calls himself "the only black communications historian in the country," teaches a course called Blacks in Television at Southwest College in Los Angeles. A serious student of the subject, Hill says, "Over the years, many blacks have felt that 'Amos 'n' Andy,' through its stereotyping of blacks, set the cause back by reinforcing a negative image, but I think blacks are seeing that in the thirty-five-year history of television, there never has been a balance."

Today, "Amos 'n' Andy" cannot be seen on commercial television, the result of the 1965 CBS decision. However, at least twenty-five episodes exist on cassette tapes that can be purchased or rented at video outlets, or viewed at such media archives as the Museum of Broadcasting in midtown Manhattan, where they are among the most popular shows requested. Technology has made it possible for anyone—no matter what his view of "Amos 'n' Andy" —to reevaluate his feelings about a show that was among television's earliest pioneers. The contributions made by actors Tim Moore, Alvin Childress, Spencer Williams, Jr., Johnny Lee, and Ernestine Wade cannot be left forgotten.

Before her death a few years ago, Ernestine Wade answered the charges by black organizations—once again —that the show on which she played Sapphire Stevens contained "deplorable racial stereotyping": "I don't think people tune in a comedy show for an education. If ['Amos 'n'

Andy'] had been a documentary, it would have been a different thing. All people will scream about things they don't enjoy. You take *The Grapes of Wrath* and *Tobacco Road.* There was a lot of static about those. But people like that really exist; their names might not be the same, but their prototypes exist. There is no need to deny the existence of something just because you don't like it. ['Amos 'n' Andy'] was strictly for entertainment."

At the time that "entertainment" was under fire by the NAACP in the mid-sixties, Henry Lee Moon was the organization's director of public affairs, as he had been since 1947. Now retired, Moon recalled the controversy: "We were very much concerned about the image being projected of our people. We felt it was a false image, something that didn't represent us, as a people."

When Flip Wilson was headlining a popular variety show in the early seventies, his outrageous characterizations also came under fire by blacks and many critics. Les Brown, the astute television analyst for *The New York Times,* recalled: "He had performed his act before black audiences in segregated clubs and theaters for many years before his first television exposure and, within the group, the satire was appreciated for healthy reasons. Irish can satirize the Irish, Jews the Jews, and Italians the Italians. Within the respective ethnic circles the stereotypical truths, although embarrassingly amusing, have a way of strengthening an individual's identification with the group and heightening his pride in belonging to it. But on television, with its vast and heterogeneous audience, the honest kidding of ethnic types becomes something else, tending to validate the stereotype as a true representative of a whole people and in that way contributing to prejudice."

This was the very problem with "Amos 'n' Andy." The NAACP knew full well that the show was being watched mainly by white people who could afford the few sets that existed in those days (20 million). The show's negative Negro portrayals could only help heighten racial bigotry. Whites could be depicted in comedies as stupid and bumbling, and no one would conclude that all whites are stupid and bumbling; but when the only show starring black actors portrays the characters in precisely the way bigots imagine black people to be, the NAACP found it disgraceful.

Like so many elements of this issue, even the cast members differ on the subject. Like Ernestine Wade, Alvin Childress, who played the mild-mannered Amos Jones, defends the program: "What its detractors fail to mention is that it was the first time we saw a few blacks playing professionals—judges, lawyers, doctors." But Nick Stewart, the only other surviving cast member (along with Childress), looks back in anger today. "I thank God for the 'Amos 'n' Andy' show. In those days, it was a survival ticket. It was like slavery, but it was a means of survival."

Asked what he meant by the word "slavery," Stewart replied, "It was like surviving the slavery mentality. And thank God for that life preserver. Thank God for the character of Lightnin', but I wouldn't want my kids to go through that. I wouldn't want them to have to do that."

Marla Gibbs, who played the sharp-tongued maid on "The Jeffersons" for nearly ten years before starring in her own NBC series, was not a member of the "Amos 'n' Andy" cast, but like countless other blacks she watched the show before 1966 and enjoyed it. "I especially liked the Kingfish," Gibbs said in 1983. "He represented a lot of people we knew. Of course, it was a little exaggerated because of the writing, but I thought he was very natural and hilarious. As a matter of fact, most of the people on the show were funny; it was a well-orchestrated, believable group of performers.

"Personally, I don't think it reflected the *wrong* image of black people; I think that it was the fact that it was the *only* image of black people. In that context, the only image of *any* people—no television show can represent that —would come up short. If you take a program to task, saying it represents the Italian community or the black community, or the Oriental community—no, you can't do that.

"And because 'Amos 'n' Andy' was all we had, then I think the NAACP was really trying to say we needed a balance. Instead, they said this show reflects our people in a negative image, that when other people see us, they think this is the only way we are," Gibbs concluded.

Television was in its infancy when "Amos 'n' Andy" arrived, and it can be argued that *some* show starring blacks had to be first. "Whatever they were doing," says comedian Redd Foxx about the cast of the trailblazing program, "they were doing for an era. And they made it possible for me to do something so that after me, some other youngsters could do something, and after them others."

Reverend Jesse Jackson echoes Foxx's contention: "I think the record must show that they paid the dues that made it possible for those who now play roles with much more dignity. First of all, they proved that blacks could act. They proved that blacks could entertain. They showed the dynamism of the black mind."

"Amos 'n' Andy" has been a thorn in the side of the NAACP ever since the show went on the air in Chicago back in 1928. Right or wrong, the organization condemned the show from the start and now, nearly sixty years later, the seventy-eight television episodes continue to strike a dissonant chord. When Michael Avery's controversial documentary aired in Los Angeles on March 29, 1984, Willis Edwards, president of the local chapter of the NAACP, issued this statement: "We are appalled at the apparent insensitivity of the television station [KABC] to reopen old wounds inflicted years ago by a television series fraught with flagrant stereotypes and demeaning black characterizations.

"Whether it is under the guise of a documentary or a public affairs format, the NAACP does not feel that dredging up this parody of black life has any positive purpose. . . . We can only hope that the next time programming decisions are made, the station shows some semblance of common sense and decency for the American public at large by not airing a show of this nature."

This argument has long been opposed by many of the viewing public. The show still has its champions, both black and white.

Richard Correll, son of one of the creators of "Amos 'n' Andy," sums up his feelings about a family "member": "The show's creation and longevity were not built on the basis of racism and making fun of blacks. It existed to entertain. . . . Perhaps if CBS would allow the TV show to surface in reruns, then a new generation of young blacks could decide for themselves whether 'Amos 'n' Andy' was racist, or just out-and-out good comedy."

If we can someday look back at ethnic humor with some objectivity—and with a large measure of nostalgia—from a happy point in our future when black people will take their share of both heroic and villainous roles on television and in films, perhaps the innocence of "Amos 'n' Andy" might return to the small screen.

THE "AMOS 'N' ANDY" LOG

From Thursday, June 28, 1951, to Thursday, June 11, 1953, the CBS Television Network broadcast seventy-eight episodes of "The Amos 'n' Andy Show." Here are synopses of each half-hour segment.

ANDY GOES INTO BUSINESS

Andy's new doughnut shop is prospering when Kingfish learns that Mr. Daniels, his mother-in-law's suitor, intends to set a wedding date if he can find a business that costs only $500. Without success, Kingfish attempts to persuade Andy to sell, but then hits upon the idea of inserting a nail in one of the doughnuts and later "accidentally" buying it, hoping that the fuss will hurt Andy's business. Unfortunately, Kingfish can't find the "spiked" doughnut soon enough, and Sapphire's future stepfather withdraws his marriage proposal.

KINGFISH BUYS A CHAIR

An auctioneer mistakes the Kingfish's sneeze for a bid and the lodge brothers become the proud owners of a beat-up old chair, then discover it is crammed with cash. Andy and Kingfish divide the spoils and soon acquire fancy clothes and cars. The duped pair mistake the two ex-cons who hid the money for investment counselors and hand back the money. The crooks are arrested, and the boys have to return their ill-gotten gains.

NEW NEIGHBORS

To get rid of his new neighbors, the Fosters, the Kingfish uses the nocturnal wailings of a young baby left in his care for a few days. The Fosters, who have borrowed everything, including some of the Kingfish's clothes, are driven to distraction. When the baby is finally returned to its parents, Kingfish has Andy play a sound-effects record, which includes the howling of wolves and barnyard sounds. The landlord serves an eviction notice—but not to the Fosters.

THE LODGE BROTHERS COMPLAIN

The members of the Mystic Knights of the Sea hire a secretary for the Kingfish because they are dissatisfied with his management of their affairs. Sapphire's jealousy prompts her to take a job as a secretary to writer John Bentley, who is marrying his ex-secretary. When Kingfish reads that Bentley is romancing his secretary and later overhears him discussing wedding plans, he assumes he will marry Sapphire. He attempts to stop the wedding by carrying the bride away.

VIVE LA FRANCE

On a visit to the United Nations building with Amos, romantic Andy becomes enamored with a pert French girl, Colette Duval, who doesn't understand English. Not understanding French, Andy assumes from Colette's pantomime that she returns his feelings. Andy gets a primer in international etiquette from Kingfish, and asks Madame Duval for her daughter's hand in marriage. The mother misunderstands and accepts Andy's proposal for herself. Calhoun tries to extricate Andy from his predicament, only to read later that it is he who is now engaged to Madame Duval.

INCOME TAX

Amos aids Andy and the Kingfish with their income tax returns. En route to a mailbox to deposit the forms, Andy is distracted by a former sweetheart. They do not know the forms are lost until they receive a letter from the Internal Revenue Bureau, which puts them in a state of panic. Amos, again, comes to the rescue; and released with a warning, Andy and the Kingfish fill out new forms. This time the Kingfish ensures the delivery of the tax returns.

VACATION TIME

The Kingfish doesn't have the money he is supposed to have banked for his family's vacation, so he sells his car, only to learn that Sapphire has bought a trailer to hitch to the car for their trip. In order to buy back the car, he hits upon a scheme to promise to take Andy on a trailer trip around the United States. Taking consultant Calhoun into his confidence, the trip is actually made through Central Park. All goes well until Sapphire decides to take a walk through the park.

THE LIGHT BLUE CAR

While Kingfish is napping, his maroon and white car is borrowed for a hold-up. The Kingfish knows the police have a description of the car, but he hesitates to admit ownership, fearing his accumulation of debts might make him a prime suspect. Unsuccessful in his attempt to give the car away, he and Andy are caught by a policeman while they're trying to paint the car light blue. Hauled into court, lawyer Calhoun and the Kingfish's friends create more problems with their character references.

THE CLASSIFIED AD

Andy receives an avalanche of mail in response to his wife-seeking ad, and he selects attractive Suzanne Wilson. The lodge brothers throw a bachelor dinner for Andy, which ends abruptly when he learns from Brother Thompson that

Suzanne needs hundreds of dollars worth of dental work. He regroups but goes on with his wedding plans, which warrants another bachelor dinner. This time he is interrupted with the announcement of Suzanne's engagement to a childhood sweetheart. Selecting another sweetheart, his third bachelor dinner is interrupted with a call from his new fiancée informing him of *her* dental problems.

THE SOCIETY PARTY

In order to buy Sapphire a new dress for the swanky Van Pelt party, Kingfish sells her fur coat to Andy. Then he learns that his wife plans on wearing the coat to the party, too. Andy has already given the coat to his girl friend, Rosemary; the two friends resolve to steal it back. The robbery fails, and matters are complicated when Kingfish learns Rosemary plans to wear the coat to the party.

THE CONVENTION

Arriving in Chicago to attend the annual convention of the Mystic Knights of the Sea, Sapphire is persuaded to turn over their expense money to Kingfish. He has convinced her that the hotel is crawling with confidence men. Posing as chairman of the Protective Committee, Honest Huey Higgins gets Kingfish to give him the money for safekeeping. When Higgins vanishes, Kingfish, Andy, and Calhoun must pay the hotel bill with their watches and jewelry.

THE GIRL UPSTAIRS

The Kingfish has a diary written in shorthand translated by a public stenographer. Because he found it in Sapphire's closet, he is convinced his wife is in love with another man. The diary actually belongs to a teenage neighbor whose father disapproves of her romance. Learning that his "rival" is a gangly high school boy, he is disheartened and bewildered. Even after news of an elopement, Kingfish tries to look more youthful, just in case.

KINGFISH GOES TO WORK

Sapphire's threats to leave prompt Kingfish to take a job as a handyman at a university. After the first day, the Kingfish has had enough and convinces Andy to take the job and turn his salary over to him. In exchange, the Kingfish offers him a home-study college course. Sapphire is satisfied that her husband is finally employed after more than twenty years, until Andy mentions the home-study course.

ENGAGEMENT RING

The Kingfish is mistaken for a matrimonial agent by Juliet Williams, a plain-looking woman in her forties. He devises a scheme to collect a fee by convincing Andy that the best bride is a mature one. Andy can't afford an engagement ring, so Kingfish "borrows" his wife's while she is asleep, to finalize the deal. Learning of Andy's engagement, Sapphire invites Juliet to a party, and that's when the complications set in.

THE EYEGLASS

Because he needs eyeglasses to correct his vision, Andy's license is suspended by a traffic court judge. The Kingfish uses this opportunity to try to dupe Andy for his car. Telling his best friend that he has completed a correspondence course in optometry, he offers to fit Andy for the required glasses. After Kingfish fits him with glasses that further distort his vision, Andy fails the driving test, and he finally agrees to sell the car at a quarter of its value.

HOSPITALIZATION

Kingfish goes into the business of selling hospital insurance to healthy people, convinced this is the way to make a fortune. Andy, his first customer, turns him down. But Kingfish is relentless and Andy takes a policy. However, the sales pitch is so effective that Andy soon feels ill and checks into the hospital. Unable to pay the hospital bills, Kingfish forces Andy out of bed with horror stories about the doctor in charge.

SAPPHIRE'S MYSTERIOUS ADMIRER

The Kingfish fears that Sapphire is in love with another man, and that the two are trying to get rid of him. He goes to great lengths to surround his bed with an elaborate alarm system, and borrows a guinea pig as a food taster. His lodge brothers also fear for his life and hire a bodyguard for him. His precautions eventually backfire, when he finds Sapphire preparing a surprise birthday party for him.

THE ADOPTION

The Kingfish is convinced by Sapphire that they should adopt a baby. To prepare him for the pleasures of parenthood, she leaves her nephew, Horace, in his care. Kingfish loses interest in the plan after one afternoon with horrible

Horace, but at Sapphire's insistence he goes to an adoption agency and falls in love with an adorable child. To prove his financial stability, he sets himself up as president of a successful firm, until the premature return of the real company president.

THE BROKEN CLOCK

Andy and the Kingfish go to a clock factory to demand a replacement for a clock that doesn't work, and a plant executive mistakes them for the mechanics who are supposed to test a super-secret electronic altimeter clock at sub-zero temperature. After aiding in the testing, they depart with the clock, believing it to be their replacement clock. The FBI is called in, and only Amos's quick thinking prevents their arrest.

THE BALLET TICKETS

The Kingfish finds a wallet that also contains two ballet tickets, which he presents to Sapphire as a purchased gift. He does not know that Thorndyke, a con man, has dropped the wallet with the tickets and $245 in cash, and then reports it to the police. Sapphire is in a happy mood when she takes her mother to the ballet, until they are arrested and thrown into jail on suspicion of robbery.

THE BOARDER

Kingfish and Sapphire rent a room to Mr. Benson, a singer who practices constantly. She is elated with the cultural addition to their household, while Kingfish is disgusted at the boarder's voracious appetite. He tries to find a loophole in Benson's lease, which seems unbreakable. Kingfish turns to consultant Calhoun, who points out that the lease does not stipulate the number of people who can occupy the room. When Kingfish's friends move in, too, Benson moves out.

ARABIA

The Kingfish is in desperate need of money when he learns that an oil company is offering $200 to employment agencies that deliver personnel for work in Arabia. Determined to maintain his no-work policy, he devises a scheme to get Andy on the trip—a fake raffle; the first prize is a pleasure cruise to Arabia. When Andy discovers the trick, Kingfish's ruse backfires, and he is shipped off instead.

THE RACE HORSE

Sapphire's cousin Louie has a broken-down race horse that the Kingfish volunteers to sell. Andy becomes the new owner, but as soon as he sees the animal stumble around the track during a workout, he realizes the Kingfish has conned him again. With Amos's help, Andy convinces Kingfish that the horse is valuable and reluctantly lets Kingfish get the horse—and the horse laugh.

ANDY GETS MARRIED

Andy gets engaged to a woman named Loretta and rushes to Amos's house to tell him the good news. When he arrives, he is attracted to Amos's guest, Mary Thompson, and decides to withhold the announcement. Soon Andy is engaged to Mary and tries to break his engagement to

Loretta. When Loretta learns of his new fiancée, she stirs up trouble. In desperation, Andy tries to marry Mary secretly, but there is a mix-up and he leaves both girls at the altar.

THE PIGGY BANK

The Kingfish has been filching money from Sapphire's piggy bank, and replacing the money with lead tokens to keep the bank heavy. He relates his tale of woe to his lodge brothers a few days before his twenty-fifth wedding anniversary. Sapphire has been saving the money for years, for a second honeymoon in Niagara Falls. Fearing Sapphire will leave him when she discovers the bank empty, Kingfish tries to raise money, finally winning the jackpot on a quiz program.

SUPERFINE BRUSH

Sapphire takes a job as a secretary at the Superfine Brush Company, to earn money for new home furnishings. She persuades her boss to hire the Kingfish as a door-to-door salesman. After one day on the job, he persuades Andy to sell for him as an apprentice, with no pay for two months. When Sapphire finds out about it, she becomes irate and goes home, kicks the Kingfish out of bed, and forces him to sell the brushes.

MR. JACKSON COMES TO TOWN

Sapphire's former boy friend, Bill Jackson, comes to town, and the Kingfish goes on a self-improvement campaign. Despite his buying flowers for her, getting himself fitted for a corset, and ordering a heavily padded suit, Sapphire still seems much more interested in Jackson, a former Marine. The Kingfish devises a plot, and with the help of his lodge brothers, Amos and Calhoun, forges Marine Corps orders for Jackson's return to active duty.

COUSIN EFFIE'S WILL

Because the Kingfish and Sapphire have no children, they are ineligible for a $2,000 bequest under the terms of Cousin Effie's will. So they can receive the inheritance, the Kingfish decides to adopt his forty-year-old friend Andy Brown. Sapphire is against the idea, but as soon as she goes away for a visit, the Kingfish disobeys her. Even though Sapphire tells the lawyer the truth, he tells them the papers are in order and does not withhold the bequest.

RESTITUTION

Inspired by a sermon, the Kingfish tries to do a good deed. He decides to repay Simpson the jeweler for the expense incurred when he attached a line to Simpson's store and obtained free electricity. With a key the jeweler once gave him, he lets himself and Andy into the store. An alarm goes off, and the two flee, not knowing that an attached camera took their picture. They are soon fugitives from the law.

KINGFISH FINDS HIS FUTURE

After Kingfish says he feels useless, Andy advises him to take an aptitude test. He learns he has a hidden talent for painting. The Kingfish gets to work immediately on several paintings, but is told his work is on the level of a three-year-old. The examiner mixed his test results up with someone else's. He suggests a solution that would keep Kingfish painting—but not on canvas.

THE ANTIQUE SHOP

The Kingfish wants to get his hands on his cousin Leo's investment cash. He enlists lawyer Calhoun to help him persuade Leo to buy an antique shop, from which the Kingfish will get a sales commission. The overzealous Kingfish sends all his lodge brothers into the store, providing proof of its prosperity. Leo is impressed, but so is the owner, who decides against selling after all.

KINGFISH SELLS A LOT

Andy purchases a piece of property that Kingfish has had for twenty-odd years. A movie company once used the site as a location, and left the front of a mansion on the lot. At first Andy is delighted, but soon realizes he has been victimized by the Kingfish once more. Once he is confronted, the Kingfish tries to avoid a legal suit by Andy with another phony scheme. This time Andy has the last laugh.

THE BIRTHDAY CARD

During his birthday celebration, the Kingfish receives a greeting signed "Sweetheart." Sapphire is suspicious, even though Kingfish, who is puzzled himself, swears he doesn't have a girl friend on the side. When Kingfish learns that Gloria Farnsworth, a former flame, is in town, he assumes she sent the card. He arranges a meeting, but before he can ask about the card, an enraged Sapphire discovers them.

ANDY FALLS IN LOVE WITH AN ACTRESS

Andy is upset at the thought of Bosworth Carruthers kissing his fiancée, even though they are only rehearsing a love scene in a play. Kingfish advises Andy to hire an acting coach and take the leading role in the production. Carruthers is persuaded to leave the play by the Kingfish, and Andy becomes the star. Andy's acting debut causes a riot onstage because of his mishaps with scenery, costumes, and the Kingfish's prompting. Finally, he loses the role and his fiancée.

KINGFISH AT THE BALL GAME

Rich Mrs. Wentworth gets excited during the ball game and drops a valuable ring into the Kingfish's Cracker Jack box. Thinking the ring is a prize that is a good imitation of an expensive ring, he sells it to Andy. Soon the Kingfish hears about the reward and learns the ring's true value, and plots to get the ring back. When he retrieves the ring and collects the reward, an enthusiastic fan slaps him on the back, scattering the cash in the throng of spectators.

KINGFISH'S LAST FRIEND

Kingfish's conscience visits him in a dream, and warns him that he is running out of friends because of his swindling. An informal survey confirms this nagging thought. He decides to go away, only to be sorely missed by his lodge brothers. They offer a reward for information leading to his whereabouts and receive a letter from a detective agency. He returns to a royal welcome, and in the final scene he collects the reward money at a post-office box.

SAPPHIRE'S SISTER

Kingfish determines to get rid of his sister-in-law, Hortense, when he finds himself sleeping on the sofa and entangled in thirty pairs of stockings every time he has to shave. Sapphire and her "Mama" insist that Hortense stay, despite the crowded conditions. Things become so difficult for the Kingfish that he determines to marry her off to Andy. But then he learns she has $10,000 in a savings bank.

SEEING IS BELIEVING

Sapphire becomes suspicious when the Kingfish comes home at three in the morning for several days running. In fact he has taken a job as a waiter in a nightclub, and wants to withhold this information from his wife. But she is convinced he has a girl friend, so she decides to make him jealous by having dinner with another man—Andy Brown. Because she made sure the neighbors could see all, they quickly tell the Kingfish, whose reaction is predictable.

LEROY'S SUITS

The Kingfish is supposed to sell some of his brother-in-law's suits. He takes Andy with him to pick them up, but they enter the wrong apartment and take suits belonging to a police lieutenant. The policeman tracks the theft to the boys at the lodge hall, where they are conducting a clothing sale. He arrests them, but their testimony is corroborated by Sapphire, Lightnin', and Amos. Upon their release, the boys promptly get into trouble again.

RARE COIN

The Kingfish discovers that Andy possesses a nickel worth $250, and tricks him into giving it to him. In his excitement he uses it to call a coin dealer. He then tricks Andy into helping him pry open the coin box, but they are caught by a policeman and taken to court. Luckily, Amos recovers the coin and explains the situation to the judge, who lets them off with a warning. Kingfish still insists on profit-sharing, but Andy manages to trick him.

COUNTERFEITERS RENT BASEMENT

Andy and Kingfish inadvertently rent the lodge hall basement to a gang of counterfeiters. They discover the truth when Andy gives his girl friend a box of candy he accidentally switched with another box in the cellar. They call the police, who phone back, but one of the gang answers and assures the police that it is a mistake. When the two lodge brothers return, the gang holds them at gunpoint, but Andy's quick thinking saves the day.

KINGFISH HAS A BABY

Sapphire leaves the Kingfish when she gets fed up with his idleness. When he learns she has been seen in the office of an obstetrician, he assumes he is going to be a father. His suspicions are confirmed when he sees her leave a hospital wheeling a baby carriage. In fact, his wife has become nursemaid to the obstetrician's child. But, until he learns the truth, the Kingfish becomes a reformed man.

KINGFISH'S SECRETARY

The Kingfish's first effort to improve the lodge hall with the money willed by a departed brother is hiring a beautiful secretary, Daphne Jackson. He then dictates a letter to an employment agency for a scrubwoman. However, Andy has also dictated a letter to a mail-order bride. It is this letter that the Kingfish signs, without reading it. When the woman arrives, and the truth is revealed, he keeps it from Sapphire—for a while.

KINGFISH GETS DRAFTED

When the Kingfish receives a draft notice for George Stevens (his legal name), he becomes a hero in the eyes of his wife and lodge brothers. But the notice is intended for a younger George Stevens. When he learns of the mistake, he tries to enlist with all the services, and they turn him down. Unwilling to lose his hero status, Kingfish pretends to go to camp, then has to fake a furlough. The truth turns his home into a battle zone with Sapphire and her Mama.

THE GUN

The Kingfish, accompanied by Andy, shops for an anniversary gift for Sapphire. He accidentally selects a bag containing a gun, dropped by a runaway thief. When Kingfish tries to pawn the gun, the manageress of the shop faints, thinking it is a hold-up. When she recovers, she calls the police and gives his description. Then Sapphire discovers the gun and believes he is guilty. She turns him in for his own good.

THE YOUNG GIRL'S MOTHER

In spite of his friends' advice, Andy plans to marry a girl much younger than himself. Unknown to Andy, his fiancée is the daughter of Madame Queen, whom he jilted many years ago. When the wedding is announced, Madame Queen comes to town to meet her future son-in-law. Andy, learning the truth, takes the advice of the Kingfish and plays dead, and ends up returning unexpectedly. He swears he'll never look at another woman—a pledge quickly broken.

FUR COAT

The Kingfish becomes a delivery boy for a department store. He writes to Sapphire, who is away, that he will have a surprise for her when she returns. He brings one of his packages home the night Sapphire arrives, and she is ecstatic when she finds a fur coat in the box and assumes it is her surprise. His explanation falls on deaf ears, and he decides to figure out a way to keep the coat. Then a family friend visits with her new fiancé—the store manager.

SAPPHIRE DISAPPEARS

Sapphire leaves the Kingfish "for good." As he sits in his lonely apartment he resolves to win her back. He and Andy go to his mother-in-law's, but can find no trace of the two women, and the house is occupied by a strange man. With his imagination working overtime, the Kingfish suspects foul play. He decides to play detective, and find her murderer if it "kills" him.

JEWELRY STORE ROBBERY

Andy wants photos to distribute to his girl friends. Kingfish snaps the pictures outside of a jewelry store. Andy wants the last snapshot to be of Kingfish. Just as he takes the shot, a man runs in front of the camera, so they think the photo is ruined. The next day they learn that the man had just robbed the jewelry store. They believe they can develop the picture and collect the reward, but the hold-up man learns about their film.

THE WINSLOW WOMAN

Sapphire tells the Kingfish that an unattractive but wealthy widow has just moved to town, and he devises a scheme to share the wealth—he wants Andy to marry her. Mr. Winslow, missing and presumed dead for fifteen years, reappears once the wedding date is set. He threatens to see—and win back—his wife, unless Kingfish and Andy give him $1000. When they do, they are faced with a stunning blow.

CALL LEHIGH 4-9900

Going through an old suit of clothes, the Kingfish finds part of an advertisement that reads "Best in Town—Free." He is intrigued and calls the phone number included in the ad. The receptionist promises to have her boss call back. The Kingfish does not realize that he has called a Lonely Hearts Club. Sapphire answers when the call is returned and assumes he is out to two-time her. When an attractive girl is sent to the lodge from the club, Andy is infatuated and poses as the Kingfish.

LEROY LENDS A HAND

Andy starts off his first morning as co-owner (with the Kingfish) of a parking lot by denting a couple of fenders. When Leroy, the Kingfish's brother-in-law, drops by later and offers to watch the place while Andy and the Kingfish have lunch, he assumes it is a used car lot. He sells one of the cars for $600, and when the owner returns and finds his car missing, he threatens them with jail. The car is returned to its owner but now another vehicle is missing.

AMOS HELPS OUT

Sapphire and the Kingfish have a fight, and she tells him she wishes she had never married him. To make her regret the remark, he fakes a letter from the license bureau stating that their marriage is not recorded. He is amazed to see that she doesn't beg him to remarry her and moves back with her mother. In reality she is teaching him a lesson, because she knows the letter is fake. To make her jealous he goes out with another woman, and bumps into Sapphire with another man.

ANDY BUYS A HOUSE

The Kingfish takes a job with a real-estate agent, and in order to keep the job must sell one of a group of houses standing on condemned property. He sells the house to Andy, who is enraged when he learns the house does not have a lot. Trying to pacify Andy, the Kingfish finds a lot, but it's too small. In the end Amos helps Andy outfox the conniving Kingfish.

THE CHRISTMAS STORY

While Andy is window shopping before Christmas with his godchild, Arbadella (Amos's firstborn), she is especially thrilled with a large and costly doll. The present he has picked for the child is very small, so he decides to earn enough money to buy the doll by taking a job as Santa's helper. In the end he takes the doll in lieu of pay. Also included is Amos's famous interpretation of the Lord's Prayer.

ANDY GETS A TELEGRAM

When the Kingfish learns that Andy has received a telegram from a rich uncle offering him a high-paying job in South America, he promises to help his old friend. Planning to keep some of the passage money for himself, the Kingfish makes a reservation for Andy on a cattle boat. By helping Andy, he breaks his promise to Sapphire to avoid his worthless friends. Duping Andy out of the ticket, Kingfish is on the high seas before it is revealed that Sapphire sent the phony wire.

THE DINER

The Kingfish talks Andy into going into business with him. They raise the capital to buy a prosperous diner. After reopening the diner, their first setback is the rerouting of a bus line the diner had served. Raising more money, they relocate, but Lady Luck does not smile on them: the diner is moved back to its original location. Soon they have to face their angry sponsors, Amos and Sapphire's Mama.

GETTING MAMA MARRIED—PART I

The Kingfish wants his mother-in-law out of his home, so he decides to marry her off to a wealthy old man who has just come to town, Hubert J. Smithers. Enlisting Andy's help, he sends a series of letters to both Mama and Mr. Smithers. Both are very interested by the time a personal meeting is arranged. Amos sees Smithers's photo in a detective magazine, describing him as a con man who fleeces widows. The boys try to stop the elopement.

GETTING MAMA MARRIED—PART II

The Kingfish has unwittingly introduced his mother-in-law to a nationally known con man, who fleeces middle-aged widows. Mama tries to elope with him, but just before the ceremony she breaks her leg. The Kingfish cannot bear to face her with the truth, so he tells Hubert Smithers, the con, to leave town. Meanwhile, the announcement of the wedding in the newspaper brings letters, calls, and visits from women who have been jilted by Smithers. But, even knowing the truth, Mama does not want to give him up.

THE HAPPY STEVENSES

The Kingfish and Sapphire want to change the pattern of their stormy marriage, so they decide to emulate her favorite radio show, which features Happy and Harriet Harrington. The Kingfish tries by giving Sapphire a bouquet of flowers, but they irritate her hay fever; a piece of candy breaks a tooth; and a sparkling evening out on the town becomes quite gloomy. An early morning appointment with the Harringtons gives an intimate glimpse into the stormy life of radio's sunniest couple.

READY-MADE FAMILY

The Kingfish has received $500 from his Uncle Clarence by telling him he has a child, and now Clarence is coming to visit. Because Sapphire is out of town, Kingfish uses Andy's girl friend as his "wife," and a neighbor's child for a "son." The ruse works, until Sapphire's early return. When Uncle Clarence finds him kissing her, he storms out, thinking his nephew is a philanderer. Kingfish knows he will be written out of the will, and claims "that once a year kiss" to Sapphire cost him $20,000.

RELATIVES

The Kingfish gets a judge in a domestic relations court to issue an injunction against his mother-in-law and his brother-in-law, Leroy, which forces them to move out. But, shortly thereafter his cousin Sidney and his wife, their parrot, and dog arrive and are worse than his in-laws. Unable to cope, he has Mama and Leroy move back, figuring that is the only way to rid himself of cousin Sidney and family.

TRAFFIC VIOLATION

The Kingfish and Andy become co-owners of a car, agreeing to use it on alternate weeks. They put both licenses in the glove compartment for safekeeping. Kingfish has the car the second week and within days gets four tickets and a warning that the fifth will warrant a stiff penalty. Nervous about the warning, the Kingfish smashes into a hydrant. Fearing a jail term, he gives the police Andy's license and learns, to his dismay, that Andy has been convicted of seven traffic violations during his turn with the car.

THE TURKEY DINNER

Sapphire's club is having their annual dinner, and the Kingfish talks her into letting him get the turkeys, which he figures can net him a profit on the purchase and resale. He buys them from a homespun farmer in the country and stores them in the lodge hall basement, only to learn from a newspaper account that they are stolen. Not wanting to be arrested for theft, he disposes of the birds. When he returns there are more turkeys, and he is confused, not knowing that Sapphire has bought the birds herself.

QUO VADIS

The Kingfish's hometown believes he is a big success, because he has been writing and telling tall tales throughout the years. The biggest is that he married a millionaire's daughter. His old hometown friend Sam Jackson comes to town and wants to give a party in the Kingfish's honor. Knowing he won't be able to pass his wife off as an heiress, he goes alone. The Kingfish does not know that Jackson has hired Sapphire to serve at the party.

THE CHINCHILLA BUSINESS

The Kingfish needs ready cash, and Andy needs a fur coat, so the Kingfish sells Andy a couple of cheap rabbits and tells him they are chinchillas that will multiply enough for a fur coat. The Kingfish gives his ill-gotten $50 to his mother-in-law so she can move out as promised. But she refuses to leave until she finds a business to invest in. It turns out to be Andy's rare chinchilla company.

THE URANIUM MINE

Andy gives the Kingfish $200 for a lot in New Jersey, sight unseen. When Andy sees the property, he discovers it's swampland, and demands his money back. Later, the Kingfish overhears Andy say he wants to invest in uranium, so he craftily shows up with all the mining gear where Andy cannot miss seeing him. Gullible Andy decides he wants to keep the lot, and gives Kingfish another $300 for equipment.

MADAME QUEEN'S VOICE

After seeing Madame Queen win a television talent contest, Andy and the Kingfish decide to turn personal manager. In order to achieve this, Andy must propose marriage to his old flame, which, according to the Kingfish, will ensure the contract. Madame Queen is all for the marriage, but wants her vocal teacher, Mr. Mason, to manage her career. The Kingfish is undeterred by opposition and even puts up half the money for an engagement ring.

ANDY THE GODFATHER

Andy's goddaughter, Arbadella, is so lovesick over a twelve-year-old boy that she won't eat. Being cavalier, he promises to take care of the matter. Then he learns the name of the boy and regrets his promise. Andy has consistently been made the butt of all the boy's practical jokes. He decides not to back out of his promise, and lives up to his commitment.

THE INSURANCE POLICY

Sapphire gets the Kingfish a job with a construction company after she puts her foot down and insists he become the breadwinner in the family. She also makes him take out an insurance policy, but before the policy is approved the doctor makes him go on a three-week diet. Andy misunderstands, and believes his friend has only three weeks to live. For the Kingfish this is a heaven-sent opportunity to pass on the misconception to Sapphire.

KINGFISH GETS AMNESIA

Kingfish must buy Sapphire a new dress, so he sells his friend Andy a broken down Model-T roadster. When Amos hears what has happened, he steps into the picture, and the Kingfish says he has turned over a new leaf. Hearing that the Kingfish has gone straight, his office fills with people trying to collect old debts. The only way out is for the Kingfish to be hit on the head and develop amnesia.

THE GIRL AT THE STATION

The Kingfish volunteers to help his hostess serve coffee at a party. Sapphire walks into the kitchen just as he is trying to retrieve a necklace that has fallen down the back of the lady's dress. He tries to explain, but Sapphire leaves in a huff. Trying to buy a present to appease his wife, he finds he lacks the cash, as usual. Andy and the Kingfish decide to collect a $10 debt from a train steward, when the Kingfish is mistaken for a debutante's uncle. A photo of her kissing him appears in the afternoon paper.

KINGFISH TEACHES ANDY TO FLY

The Kingfish suggests that Andy become an airplane pilot, when Andy's girl friend Charmaine stands him up for a guy with a motorboat. For a fee he arranges to have Andy take lessons from a freelance flyer, Ace Judson, whose past is questionable. When the Kingfish and Andy arrive at the airport, Ace's plane is impounded and he has absconded with the money. To keep his part of the contract, the Kingfish starts teaching Andy to fly—on the ground—by reading instructions from a manual. Unfortunately, Andy decides to take to the air.

KINGFISH BECOMES A PRESS AGENT

To make a go of his job in public relations at a posh hotel, the Kingfish must attract foreign celebrities with big news value. He hits upon the idea of using Andy as the Punjab of Javapore, and attires him in an Oriental costume. He registers him, with an impressive entourage that includes a baby elephant, and everything works out fine. That is until the management of the hotel insists the Punjab give them a portion of the enormous tab he has managed to run up in just a few days.

THE MEAL TICKET

When told by the Kingfish to select her own birthday present, Sapphire buys an elegant new dining-room set. She anticipates entertaining her intellectual friends. The Kingfish sells, without telling Sapphire, a supper meal-ticket for a month to five bachelors, to help ward off the cost of her extravagance. When the guests, including Andy Brown, come to dinner, she expects "experts" in their field, who will contribute "high-brow" conversation. But when her guests behave as if they are in a restaurant, she becomes incensed.

SECOND HONEYMOON

Planning a return visit to Niagara Falls on their twenty-fifth wedding anniversary, Kingfish and Sapphire coo like two lovebirds. Happiness prevails until the two disagree on how they met, and the argument becomes so violent that the Kingfish storms out of the house. When he finds lawyer Calhoun, he asks him to prepare separation papers.

FATHER BY PROXY

Andy volunteers to take over Amos's cab and has to rush a pretty young woman to the hospital. The nurse mistakes Andy for the husband, who is away in the Army. Though Andy tries to explain, the domineering nurse is convinced that Andy is the father, Calhoun the uncle, and the Kingfish the grandfather. The more they protest, the more complicated the matter becomes.

THE INVISIBLE GLASS

The Kingfish learns that the glass-company stock he sold Andy has suddenly become worth $100 a share, and he schemes to get it back. Andy does not buy his story, for a change, even though the Kingfish swears that all the stockholders are about to be indicted for defrauding the government.

INDEX

Abbott and Costello, 41, 57
ABC, 44, 53, 61, 66, 100, 104, 105,
    110–11, 125, 126, 128, 131,
    133, 137, 142, 143–44
"Abie's Irish Rose," 79
"Adventures of Robin Hood, The,"
    105
Agee, James, 13
"Alan Young Show, The," 52, 58
"Alcoa Hour," 104
All About "Amos 'n' Andy" (Gosden
    and Correll), 16
"All in the Family," 135–36, 140
"All My Children," 147
Allen, Andrew, 9
Allen, Debbie, 145

Allen, Fred, 41
Allen, Gracie, 41, 44, 52, 61
Allen, Steve, 60, 63
"Amanda Show, The," 79
American Civil Liberties Union,
    112
American Negro Theatre, 47, 76
Amos, John, 81, 134–35, 140
"Amos 'n' Andy" (radio program),
    47, 50, 52, 53, 67, 69–70, 76,
    77, 100–101, 118
  characters on, 29–31, 37, 46, 53,
    54, 69, 78
  controversy over, xviii, 20, 23,
    24, 25, 33, 38–40
  creation of, 15–16

the Depression and, 21–23,
32–34
moves to CBS, 37, 43
NBC signs, 19–20
popularity of, xv–xvi, xix, 16, 18,
20, 25–26, 28–29, 31, 33
returns to NBC, 40–41
"Sam 'n' Henry" precedes, 5,
10–14, 15–16
syndication of, 18
two broadcasts nightly of, 21
"Amos 'n' Andy" (television
program), xv, xvi–xvii, 35, 37,
43–44, 45–59, 69–70, 85–103,
104, 114–15, 116, 121–22, 126,
131, 133, 139, 142, 143,
148–54
casting of, 46–52, 53–54, 55,
57–58, 59, 72, 74–75, 79, 81
characters on, 69–84, 89–90, 124,
137, 141
controversy over, xvi–xix, 1,
61–63, 66–68, 85–86, 101–103,
107–108, 118, 127, 148–49,
151–54
documentary about, 148–50,
153–54
pilot for, 52, 54–55, 57, 58–59,
86–87, 149–50
plot synopses, 87–98, 155–81
popularity of, 62, 98
premiere of, 57, 59, 61, 66
syndication of, 101–102,
107–108, 113, 118
theme song, 55
"Amos 'n' Andy Music Hall,"
101
Anderson, Eddie "Rochester," 36,
39, 80, 103
Andriot, Lucien, 55
Anna Lucasta, 47, 48, 76
Arden, Eve, 41
Arnaz, Desi, 110
Armstrong, Louis, 36, 104
Arthur, Bea, 132
"Arthur Godfrey and His Friends,"
104
Ashby, A. L., 31
"Aunt Jemima," 79
Avery, Michael, 148, 149–50,
153
Aylesworth, Merlin H., 18–19

Bailey, Pearl, 106, 116
"Barefoot in the Park," 133
"Baretta," 142
Barnett, Charlie, 72
Barton, Charles, 57
Basie, Count, 106
Belafonte, Harry, 65, 104, 106,
112, 116
Benedict, Paula, 141
Benny, Jack, xv, 36, 39, 40, 42, 44,
62, 103, 112
"Benson," 144–45
Benton, William, 19
Bergen, Edgar, 40, 41, 44
Berle, Milton, 43, 65
Berlin, Abby, 53, 57
Best, Willie, 104
"Betty and Bob," 35
"Beulah" (radio program), 58, 66
"Beulah" (television program), 39,
53, 61, 66, 103, 108, 116,
139
Bexley, Don, 136
"Bill Cosby Show, The," 131
"Billie Burke Show, The," 37
Birth of a Nation, The, 12–13, 55
Black, Harry, 54
Black American Reference Book, The,
9–10
Blacks and White TV (MacDonald),
63
Blatz Brewing Company, xvi, 56,
59, 61, 99–100, 101, 102,
107
"Bob Burns Show," 37
"Bob Howard Show, The," 64, 65
"Bold Journey," 105
Boneil, Bob, 4
Brando, Marlon, 112
Bren Producing Company, Joe, 2,
3, 4, 6
"Brother Jonathan" character, 7–8
Brown, Chelsea, 127
Brown, Garrett, 5–6
Brown, Johnny, 127, 132
Brown, Les, 151
Brown, Wildon, 25
Bryant, Willie, 65
Burke, Georgia, 35
Burns and Allen, 41, 44, 52, 61
"Burns and Allen" (radio
program), 52

"Burns and Allen Show, The"
(television program), 61
Butle, Picayune, 9

"Cain's 100," 118
"Californian, The," 106
Calloway, Cab, 35, 51, 80, 106
Cambridge, Godfrey, 117
"Camel News Caravan," 100
"Candid Mike," 44
Cantor, Eddie, 6, 19, 36, 41
Capps, McClure, 54
Carpenter, Thelma, 130
Carroll, Diahann, 112, 118, 129–31,
146–47
"Carter Country," 138
CBS, xvi, 37, 41–44, 60–61, 64–65,
74, 100, 114–15, 127–28, 130,
131, 132, 136, 140, 141, 147
"Amos 'n' Andy" television show
and, xvi, 1, 45–59, 61–63, 66,
67, 72, 74–75, 98, 99, 100,
101–103, 107, 113, 118, 150,
154
CBS Films, Inc., 102, 107
Check and Double Check, 29, 44, 46
Childress, Alvin, 48, 49, 50, 52, 55,
75–76, 83, 91, 150, 152
Cole, Nat King, 104, 105, 130
Coleman, Gary, 143, 144, 145
Connelly, Bob, 41, 52
Contrast, The, 7
Corley, Bob, 34
Correll, Alice Janes (wife), 14
Correll, Charles, and Freeman
Gosden 2, 3–5, 10–12, 13–31,
103
"Amos 'n' Andy" radio program
and, xv, xvii, 15–31, 33, 37,
40–41, 42, 43, 47, 54, 56, 63,
69–70, 78, 79, 101
"Amos 'n' Andy" television
program and, 43–44, 45–56,
58, 61, 79, 81, 103
backgrounds of, 2–3, 5–6
"Sam 'n' Henry," 5, 10–14
syndication idea, 14, 18
Correll, Richard (son), 26–27,
45–46, 154
Cosby, Bill, 85, 120–22, 128, 131,
132, 139, 146, 147
"Cosby Show, The," 139, 146, 147

Cover, Franklin, 141
Crosby, Bing, 42, 78
Crosby, John, 62
Crosse, Rupert, 132
Culp, Robert, 120, 121

"Daktari," 122, 123–24
Dandridge, Dorothy, 118
Dann, Michael, 114–15, 127–28
"Danny Kaye Show, The," 37
Davis, Clifton, 137
Davis, Ossie, 104
Davis, Sammy, Jr., 64, 104, 105,
112, 115–16, 127
Davy Crockett, 7, 8
Dee, Ruby, 126, 130
DeGrasse, Robert, 55
Desilu productions, 110, 122
"Diff'rent Strokes," 138, 143
Don't Touch That Dial! (MacDonald),
24, 34–35
"Dragnet," 100, 124
DuMont, 46, 61, 65, 66
"Duffy's Tavern," 58
"Dynasty," 146–47

"East Side/West Side," 112, 123,
126
Ebony Showcase Theatre, 81, 82
Eckstine, Billy, 106
"Ed Wynn Show, The," 52
"Eddie Cantor Show, The," 36
Edwards, James, 68, 118
Edwards, Willis, 153–54
Ellington, Duke, 34, 35, 65, 80
Emmett, Dan, 9
Evans, Damon, 141
Evans, Mike, 141

"Facts of Life, The," 145
"Fame," 145
Fargas, Antonio, 142
Federal Communications
Commission, 103
Federal Radio Commission, 33
Federal Theatre Project, 76
Ferguson, Dottie, 147
"Fibber McGee and Molly," 41
Fields, Kim, 155
"Fireside Theatre," 104
Fisher, Bob, 41
Fisher, Eddie, 105

Fisher, Gail, 126
Fitzgerald, Ella, 64
"Flip Wilson Show, The," 134, 151
Fonda, James, 47–48, 49, 50, 51, 53, 56
"Four Star Playhouse," 100, 101
Foxx, Redd, 85, 136, 153
Freeman, Al, Jr., 81
Funt, Allen, 44

"Garry Moore Show, The," 104
"General Electric Theater," 104
"Get Christie Love," 137
Gibbs, Marla, 141, 152–53
Gilbert, Mercedes, 36
Gilliam, Byron, 127
Godfrey, Arthur, 43–44
"Goldbergs, The," 44, 52
"Good Times," 81, 137, 140
"Goodyear Television Playhouse," 104
Gosden, Freeman, see Correll, Charles, and Freeman Gosden
Gosden, Leta Marie Schreiber (wife), 14
Gosden, Walter (father), 2, 6
Graves, Teresa, 127, 137
"Great Gildersleeve, The," 37, 41
Gregory, Dick, 109
Gribble, Henry Wagstaff, 48
Griffith, D. W., 12, 13
Gross, Ben, 18
Guillaume, Robert, 144–45
Gumps, The (comic strip), 5

Hairston, Jester, 54, 137
Hal Roach Studio, 52–53, 54, 100
Haley, Jack, 41
Hall Johnson Choir, 69
Hamilton, Bernie, 142
Harris, Vivian, 72
Hawkins, Erskine, 72
Hay, Bill, 16, 41
Hayman, Lillian, 132
Haynes, Lloyd, 131–32
"Hazel," 114
Helm, Harvey, 41, 52
Hemphill, Shirley, 143
Hemsley, Sherman, 140–41
Henry, William A., III, 141
Here They Are—Amos 'n' Andy, 29
Hernandez, Juano, 118

Hill, George, 150
Hill, Herbert, 111–12, 114
Hilton-Jacobs, Lawrence, 142
Hooks, Benjamin, 148–49
"Hopalong Cassidy," 44
Hope, Bob, 40, 41
Horne, Lena, 104
Howard, Bob, 36, 64, 65
Hubbard, Jesse, 147
Hurt, Martin, 23

"I Love Lucy," 86, 98, 99
"I Spy," 120–22, 124, 132, 146
Illo, Shirley, 41, 52
Ingram, Rex, 118
"Ironside," 124
Italian Antidefamation League, 110

"Jack Benny Show, The," 36, 39, 62, 103, 112
"Jackie Gleason Show, The," 104, 105
Jackson, Reverend Jesse, 113–14, 153
Jackson, Mahalia, 104, 106
Jeff Alexander Orchestra, 41
"Jeffersons, The," 138, 140–41, 147, 152
"Jim 'n' Charlie," 14, 16
Jolson, Al, 6, 62
Jones, Ginger, 66
"Judy Canova Show, The," 37
"Julia," 129–31, 132, 146

Kanter, Hal, 129, 130, 131
Kier, William, 74
Kilpatrick, Lincoln, 132
King, Mabel, 143
King, Dr. Martin Luther, Jr., 112, 119
Kline, Benjamin, 55

Lasker, Albert, 19
"Law and Mr. Jones, The," 118
"Laytons, The," 79
Lear, Norman, 135
Lee, Canada, 38
Lee, Johnny, 35, 53–54, 76–78, 83, 150
Lee and Perry, 77
Leonard, Sheldon, 120–21

"Leslie Uggams Show, The," 131,
132–33
Lewis, Emmanuel, 143
"Life of Riley, The," 57, 86
Lincoln, Abby, 81
"Lineup, The," 124
"Lone Ranger," 44
Lunceford, Jimmy, 72
"Lux Radio Theatre," 41

McCanna, Ben, 5
McDaniel, Hattie, 23, 35
MacDonald, J. Fred, 24, 34–35, 63,
65, 131, 145–46
Mack and Moran, 19
McQueen, Butterfly, 37
"Make Room for Daddy," 104, 112
"Man from U.N.C.L.E., The," 121,
124
"Mannix," 126
Mariners, The, 104
Markham, Dewey "Pigmeat," 127,
134
Marx, Groucho, 100
"Mary Tyler Moore Show, The,"
134
"Maude," 136
Meighan, Howard, 42
Merrill, Theresa, 137
Miller, Flournoy, 34, 49
Mills Blue Ribbon Band, 80
Mills Brothers, 34, 36, 42, 106
Minstrel shows, 6–10, 12, 24, 94
"Mission: Impossible," 81, 122,
123
"Mr. District Attorney," 41
"Mr. Five by Five," 51
Mitchell, Don, 124–25
"Mod Squad," 128–29, 133
Moon, Henry Lee, 151
Moore, Tim, 49, 51–52, 70, 71–72,
83, 85, 113, 127, 150
Morris, Greg, 81, 123
"Mose the B'Howery B'Hoy," 7
Mosher, Bob, 41, 52
Music Corporation of America
(MCA), 43
"My Little Margie," 86, 103–104

NAACP, xvi, 12, 13, 25, 33, 39, 40,
61–62, 64, 66–67, 68, 98, 101,
102–103, 107, 108–109, 111,

113, 114, 120, 129, 148, 149,
151–52, 153–54
"Naked City," 118, 124
"Nat King Cole Show, The,"
104–107
Nathan, Daniel A., 55
National Urban League, 113, 139
NBC, 23, 31
radio, 18, 19–21, 27, 29, 35, 36,
37, 40–41, 42, 43, 46
television, 46, 61, 65, 66–67,
100, 102, 104–107, 120, 121,
129–31, 134, 136, 143
New York State Division of Human
Rights, 110, 114, 117
Nicholas, Denise, 131, 132
Nichols, Nichelle, 123
Nixon, Agnes, 147
Noel, Hattie, 36
Norford, George, 117

"One Life to Live," 147
"Original Amateur Hour," 44
"Outcasts, The," 125–26

Pace, Judy, 133
Page, LaWanda, 136
Paley, William S., 1, 41–42, 43, 44,
50, 63
"Partners, The," 135
Pepsodent toothpaste, xvi, 19, 20,
21, 28, 29
"Peter Gunn," 118
"Peyton Place," 126
Post, William, Jr., 66
Prima, Louis, 72
Pryor, Richard, 85, 144

Radio Comedy (Wertheim), 12
Randolph, Amanda, 37–39, 78–79,
83, 104
Randolph, Lillian, 35, 36–37,
38–39, 78
Ray, Gene Anthony, 145
Rhodes, Hari, 123–24
Rice, Thomas D. ("Jim Crow"), 8–9
"Richard Pryor Show, The," 144
Roberts, Harlow P., 21
Roberts, Michael D., 142
Robertson, Stanley, 121
Robinson, Bill "Bojangles," 65, 78,
82

Robinson, Jackie, 65
Roddenberry, Gene, 122–23
Rodriquez, Percy, 126
Rogers, Will, 33
Roker, Roxie, 141
Rolle, Esther, 140
"Room 222," 131–32
Ross, Bob, 41, 52
"Rowan and Martin's Laugh-In,"
    126–27
Royal, John F., 27–28
Russell, Nipsey, 133

Sales, Clifford, 66
"Sam 'n' Henry," 5, 10–14, 15–16,
    40
Sanford, Isabel, 81, 141
"Sanford and Son," 136
Schlatter, George, 127
Schreiber, Taft, 43
Scott, George C., 112, 123
Scott, Hazel, 65–66
Screen Actors Guild (SAG), 108,
    110–11
"Screen Guild Players," 41
Seid, Art, 55
Selinger, Henry, 4–5
Shore, Dinah, 100, 105
"Show Boat," 35
Sissle, Noble, 34, 78, 79
"$64,000 Question," 105, 106
Skelton, Red, 35, 41, 44,
    130
Slater, Jack, 23
"Slick and Slim," 35
Smith, Bessie, 78
Smith, Kate, 42
Smith, "Wonderful," 35
Smythe, Mabel M., 9–10
"Soap," 144
Spelling, Aaron, 128, 146
Stander, Arthur, 41, 52
"Starsky and Hutch," 142
"Star Trek," 122–23
Stewart, Nick ("Nick-O-Demus"),
    37, 57–58, 80–82, 83, 84, 86,
    152
Storey, Moorfield, 13
"Stu Erwin Show, The," 104
"Studio One," 104
Sugar Hill, 48–49, 54, 80
"Sugar Hill Times," 64–65

Sullivan, Ed, 43, 63, 72
Swan, Bootsie, 78

Tandem Productions, 135–36, 140
"Tarzan," 124
"Texaco Star Theatre," 64–65, 104
"That's My Mama," 137
Thomas, Danny, 104, 128
Thurston, Howard, 2
Tinker, Grant, 121
"Toast of the Town," 43, 64, 65,
    72, 104, 105
Tolbert, Belinda, 141
Tolbert, James, 111
"Tonight Show, The," 124
Trammel, Niles, 19
"Treasury Men in Action," 61, 100
"Trouble with Father, The," 86
Turman, Glenn, 126
TV Guide, 101, 112, 116, 120, 125,
    129, 149
20th Century-Fox, 39, 79, 130
Tyler, Willie, 127
Tyson, Cicely, 112, 118, 123, 126

Uggams, Leslie, 130, 132
"Untouchables, The," 110

Vallee, Rudy, 37
Vanda, Charles, 47
Van Keuren, S. S., 53
Van Volkenburg, J. L., 56
Variety, 25–26, 39–40, 65, 66, 102,
    107–108, 109, 110, 111, 113,
    126, 148–49
Vaughn, Sarah, 64
Verbert, Frank, 56
Victor Talking Machine Company,
    29

Wade, Ernestine, 37, 38, 53, 68–69,
    83, 150–51, 152
Walker, Jimmy, 140
Walker, William, 108
Warren, Edward, 109
Wasserman, Lew, 42–43
Waters, Ethel, 34, 66
Webb, Jack, 100
Weinberger, Ed., 132
Weintraub & Co., Inc., William, 56
"Welcome Back, Kotter," 142
Wertheim, Arthur Frank, 12, 32–33

West, Mae, 58, 80–81
"What's Happening!!," 138, 143
White, Slappy, 136
White, Walter, 39–40, 102
Whiteman, Paul, 34, 42
Wilcox, Harlow, 41
Wilkins, Roy, 107, 129
Williams, Bert, 10
Williams, Clarence, III, 128–29
Williams, Spencer, Jr., 49, 50, 52, 58, 73–75, 83, 150
Willingham, Robert, 149
Willkie, Wendell, 39
Will Mastin Trio, 64

Wilson, Cal, 122
Wilson, Flip, 85, 132, 134, 151
Winchell, Walter, 41
Winters, Jonathan, 105
Wolcott, James, xvii–xviii

Yorkin, Bud, 135
"You Bet Your Life," 100
Young, Otis, 125
"Young Lawyers, The," 133
"Your Show of Shows," 62

Zanuck, Darryl, 39